Jeane
There Was No Choice

Jeane

There Was No Choice

JANICE BROWN GRIMES

American Literary Press, Inc.
Five Star Special Edition
Baltimore, Maryland

Jeane: There Was No Choice

Copyright © 2003 Janice Brown Grimes

All rights reserved under International and
Pan-American copyright conventions.
No part of this book may be reproduced, stored in a retrieval system, or transmitted in any form, electronic, mechanical, or other means, now known or hereafter invented, without written permission of the publisher. Address all inquiries to the publisher. This is a work of fiction.
All names and characters are either invented or used fictitiously.
Any resemblance to persons living or dead is unintentional.

Library of Congress
Cataloging-in-Publication Data
ISBN 1-56167-805-8

Library of Congress Card Catalog Number:
2003091162

Published by

American Literary Press, Inc.
Five Star Special Edition
8019 Belair Road, Suite 10
Baltimore, Maryland 21236

Manufactured in the United States of America

Preface

For many years, I dreamed of writing a trilogy about life in Kansas from the dust storms and drought years of the 1930s through World War II and the fifties. The subject of the third book took the McLyrres away from Kansas when Curt was called to active duty. Their first three years were in California, the second four were in Ohio, and the last three were in Japan.

In the 1950s, there were problems growing in the United States with fears of Communism spreading and Russians coming to preach the wonders of their ideology. According to them, everyone would be equal and no one would want for anything. Most people ignored these utopian promises.

Jeane, the main character in the novel, was happy in Norton, Kansas with her husband and living in their big Victorian house, but she was a good wife, and when he is called to serve his country, she had to follow him and make a home wherever he was stationed.

I can't take all the credit for my three books. My husband, Walter Grimes, had experience in editing, and he was always ready to take the time to listen to what I had written. He had never been in a small town in Kansas until after we met. I feel I should say my books had two authors instead of only one.

Janice and Walter Grimes

It takes more than one person to write a book, and with Walter's help all the way, it has been done!

There is no way the book would have been completed if I had worked alone.

Contents

West to California
- Where's April? 9
- The Courtesy Call 22
- Faith Marko 31
- Home in Kansas 42
- 1953 Happy New Year 55
- Alone on Route 66 65
- Shock 74
- 1954-We had no choice 80

East to Ohio
- The Little Gray House 93
- Call Me Flo! 96
- Monday Morning Calls 100
- Christmas in Kansas 111
- Peace 117
- 1957 Orders—There was no choice 128
- Days of Dread 137
- Time to Go 143

Welcome to Japan
- The Little House in the Woods 160
- Home in Asugi Heights A-17 165
- Fear! 179
- Oberin Gauken 185
- Mr. Ashii 190
- Robbed!! 194
- Communism and Japan 198
- The Scooter and the Tank 205
- Tunnels and Typhoons 212
- Iris 216
- Happy Day! 225

Book One
West to California

1951-1954

West to California

Jeane McLyrre had not slept well. She was torn between wanting to move to California and needing to be close to her family. She had expected to live in Kansas all her life, but now everything had changed.

When Curt was discharged after WW II, in 1945 he stayed in the Naval Reserve. He was tired of being broke, so they moved to Norton and he worked for Jeane's father. He drove to Denver for the Navy Reserve training each month. In September 1945 he enrolled at Colorado University to complete his engineering degree. It helped to stay in the Naval Reserve and earn thirty dollars a month. In his senior year at the University he applied for a commission in the U.S. Navy and after he graduated he was commissioned an Ensign.

In January 1951 he had received orders to report for active duty in San Diego, California, March first. The situation in Korea was not good and Curt had expected to be sent overseas, but the Navy needed engineers and he was assigned to Miramar Naval Air Station.

Now he was in Norton to help move his family and their household to San Diego.

Jeane was awakened by the bright sunlight that filled the room. She opened one eye and turned over. Suddenly she remembered this was the day they were moving to California and Curt was still sleeping soundly. She sat up and rubbed her eyes, then she walked over to the window. It was June and all the elm trees had brilliant green leaves.

The McLyrres had bought this house with the help of Jeane's parents, the Browns. They had lived there for just a year. Curt didn't tell anyone how delighted he was to be called for active duty

Jeane

in the U.S. Navy. Now he was in charge of the radar shop for a reconnaissance squadron at Miramar. He had taken leave to come back to Kansas, help finish the packing, and drive his family to California.

Jeane turned around and saw Curt standing in the middle of the floor. He shook his head. "Jeane, I've been watching you look out that window for ten minutes. What are you looking for?"

"I don't know, I'm all mixed up. I want to go to California with you, but my parents need me." With that she slipped on her tennis shoes, shorts, and shirt. She was ready to go. She glanced at the crate that held her old-fashioned standing mirror waiting to be carried down the stairs and put on the moving van.

She smiled as she ran down the stairs. The McLyrres had two children, April, who was six and Danny, four, and they had followed her in their pajamas. Jeane turned around. "Do you two intend to wear your pajamas all the way to California?"

April glared at her mother. "I don't care! I want my Granny! Where is she? She told me she would be here early!"

"Be patient," Jeane answered. "She will be here as soon as she finishes her breakfast."

Jeane was the Browns' only child; April and Danny were their only grandchildren. The Browns had helped Jeane and Curt during their college years after World War II by letting him work when college was not in session.

Curt graduated from Colorado University in 1948 with a degree in electrical engineering. He dreamed of working for the Bell Telephone Research Laboratory in New York. When he filled out his application he was sure he would be hired by Bell Telephone Research Laboratory. They offered him two hundred dollars a month as a starting salary. When he talked to his friends, he found no one had been offered more.

Curt was disappointed. He knew he could not support his family on that salary. Jeane had her teaching degree and she wanted to help, but Curt refused. He said no wife of his would ever have to work. Early in his senior year at CU, the Browns offered him a partnership in Browns' Plumbing and Cabinet Shop. He rejected the offer from Bell Telephone and accepted the Browns' offer. He never complained and he worked hard to learn the business, but he

Jeane

told himself they wouldn't always live in Norton, Kansas.

    Down the street and around the corner Jeane's parents had finished their breakfast. Her mother, Ethel, was worried about her family and their move to California. She knew she would see them at least once a year, but her grandchildren would have changed in that time.
    Ethel knew Maurice wasn't well. His doctor said he had a tired heart. The doctor told him if he would have one of the new pacemakers put in he could live a long time. Maurice refused and never mentioned it again.
    "Ethel, don't be cross with Curt. He did what he was ordered to do. I know he would never have left me except for the U.S. Navy orders. *He had no choice.*
    Ethel glared at Maurice, "The Navy didn't know how much we needed him here." She tried not to think about it. Curt was no longer with them and in less than an hour Jeane, April, and Danny would be gone, too. Until Curt received his orders to active duty, the Browns had begun to think he would take over their shop some day.
    "Maurice, I worry about Jeane and her family in California. To us it is like they are in a foreign country. I remember how hot it was in California when we visited your friend twenty-five years ago. We stayed only one night and started home." Maurice didn't answer.
    Now they were anxious to get to the McLyrres' house. Ethel opened the garage door and Maurice backed the car out. In less than five minutes he parked their car behind the Lyon Moving Van. The driver and his helper had just loaded Jeane's crated mirror and the driver had closed and locked the back doors.
    Jeane was running toward Ethel. "Mother, I'm so glad you're here. Curt has been pacing up and down this sidewalk since seven o'clock this morning. He says we have to start west right away. Mother, all of a sudden I'm frightened. I don't know what to expect. Curt keeps telling me everything out there is wonderful."
    "Jeane, you lived in Corpus Christi, Texas where you knew no one and in Boulder, Colorado, in a trailer house. You will be fine." She turned and picked up both her grandchildren. April and Danny threw their arms around her neck and kissed her. Then they wiggled

Jeane

out of her arms, and ran to their grandfather for another hug.

The Lyon Moving Van pulled away and was soon out of sight.

Curt was glaring at Jeane. "Come on, Jeane, we have to go. It is eight o'clock now. You know we are already an hour behind our schedule. We can't waste time or Lyons will be in San Diego first. Come on, kids, it's time to go." The children kissed their grandparents once more and hopped in the car.

Tears ran down Ethel's cheeks, but she managed a weak smile as she kissed Jeane and Curt before they got in their 1948 Dodge.

The Browns watched the McLyrres' car follow the moving van out of sight. Even though their car was gone, the Browns kept watching as though watching would bring them back.

Maurice looked at Ethel and saw she was crying. He pulled her to him and with his thumb he lifted her chin and kissed her. She looked up and smiled. He seldom showed affection in public.

"Ethel, are you daydreaming? I told you it was time for us to get to the shop."

"I didn't hear you. Do you think our children will ever come back here to live?"

"I don't know. Forever is a long time. We know Curt was ordered to active duty. He would not have left me otherwise."

"Maurice, we are alone. April and little Danny will change before we see them again."

"Come on, Ethel, don't worry! We knew when they came back here in 1948 they wouldn't stay forever. You know Curt has always wanted to work as an engineer and now he is managing a radar shop for the Navy. We will see them next winter in California, but now we will be lonely. We knew Norton would not be their permanent home. We had them for three years more than we expected. You know they have to lead their own life."

Ethel looked up at him. "You're right, we will be fine. You remember what I always say:

'Live for today! Yesterday is gone and tomorrow may never come.'

Ethel was a very private person who didn't make friends easily.

Jeane

She knew she would be busy in the shop and in Almena every few days to help with her father. In Norton she was a business woman who worked every day. She ran the shop when the men were installing a new kitchen or something else and she answered the phone and sold the plumbing supplies.

Curt was annoyed as he drove out of town; he turned and glared at Jeane. "We should have been in Colorado by now. Don't you understand? We have to get to San Diego and our new home before the moving van gets there."

"Curt, what's wrong? You have been tense and short with all of us since you got back here. What's the matter?"

"Nothing is wrong with me, Jeane, but you don't seem to understand how long it takes to get to San Diego."

Curt was right. It had been four, long, hard, days on the road between Norton and San Diego, the McLyrres were exhausted.

"You were right, Curt; it was a long way from Kansas to California."

"Curt, look! That sign says San Diego. Are we there?"

"We will be in thirty minutes. San Diego is a big city like Denver and it is growing every day. Soon we will leave this highway and drive west on University Boulevard. Watch for the sign to turn right. Then we drive a few more blocks until we turn right on Clifford Street. Our house is less than a block from that grocery store we just passed.

I want you to know I was never angry with any of you, but I needed to get back to my work as soon as I could. My work here is important."

The McLyrres were all exhausted; Jeane hadn't realized how hard the trip would be. She hated the narrow winding mountain roads and the deep canyons through Colorado and Utah. When their car began to overheat after they left Las Vegas. They quickly learned to carry a ten gallon jug of water at all times.

"Jeane, it's almost over. I'm glad we had those two days when we slept in the daytime and drove all night. I have heard it's always miserable in the desert. Now we are less than a half hour from our new home. Jeane, do you understand why I'm eager to get back to my radar shop? I want my shop to be the best radar shop in the

Jeane

United States. I'm sure Chief Brock will have everything under control, but I want to be there every day, it is my responsibility.

"Just before I came back to Norton, I almost had a serious problem. You know I have had no experience running a shop or handling men. I made a serious mistake with my sailors. All I knew was when I was an enlisted man in World War II, I wanted to be treated as an equal where I was working. When I took over this radar shop I wanted to handle my enlisted men like that. I thought all of us should be the same.

"I thought everything was going fine. But one day after I had been there two weeks, Chief Brock came to me and asked if he could speak to me after work and I agreed. When we were alone, he explained there would be trouble in the shop if I didn't stop acting like a sailor and become an officer. He told me the men didn't respect a leader who was not in command. First I was angry, and I stood up and thanked him for his time. After I thought about what he had said, I knew he had done it to help me. Suddenly, I realized that very day one of my sailors had called me Curt. Now I knew Chief Brock was right."

When the McLyrres stopped in front of their house on Clifford Street it was four o'clock. A notice was stuck in the door, and it said the moving van would be back in the morning at nine with their household shipment.

Curt exploded. "I told you in Norton we would never get here before the moving van. We could have said good-bye to your parents the night before we left. I knew how long this trip was going to be." Jeane was in tears, she was exhausted after the long days in the car entertaining two tired children. She didn't say a word, but she was disappointed when Curt blamed her for missing the moving van.

Curt was tired, too, but he was anxious to tell Jeane how hard he had worked to find this house. It was Spanish style and near Balboa Park and Zoo. The house was also close to the San Diego Mission. They would hear the mission bells ring every morning and evening. The mission had been founded in 1769 by a Mexican priest, Junipero Serra. It was the oldest building in San Diego, now it was a museum, but it still looked like a mission to the people passing through San Diego.

Jeane

Curt had told Jeane their new home was on a quiet street thirty minutes from Miramar Naval Air Station. He told her the house had three bedrooms, a living room with fireplace, separate dining room, and a kitchen big enough for a table.

Jeff and Mae Simpson had bought the house with Jeff's GI eligibility from World War II. Jeff was a San Diego policeman and his wife, Mae, stayed home with their son. They bought the property with very little money down, but they soon learned Jeff's salary as a policeman would not permit them to live in it since Mae couldn't work. They remodeled their garage on the alley, and moved in there with their two children and rented the house on Clifford Street. Curt knew the Simpsons had two children, a boy, twelve, and a girl, seven. He thought his children would have playmates.

When Curt unlocked the door, it was after five in the afternoon. Jeane was excited, "Curt, this house is perfect!" The children ran ahead into every room.

Curt turned to Jeane. "I didn't tell you before, but some of my new friends from our squadron planned a "Welcome to the Navy" party for you. We will meet them at Papa's Pizza Pantry on University Boulevard near here. They knew we would be tired when we got here, so they suggested we meet early and get back here by eight and I accepted. Every week some of us get together there for pizza. Papa is Tony's uncle, and Tony is in our squadron."

"Curt, who is Tony? What is Pizza? What about the children? We can't leave them alone!"

For a moment Curt was furious. "Did you think I would leave my children alone? Our children are invited, too. Come on, I know we're all tired, but being in a squadron is like being part of a family. It is important for them to meet all of you. Before long you will know all of the officers and their families. Come on, I brought some towels from the base. Let's all take a bath and go to Papa's!"

At that moment Mae Simpson knocked on the McLyrres' door. She had heard the car stop on the driveway. She hoped the new people would be happy in their house. The Simpsons needed the rent checks to make the house payments. When Curt opened the door, Mrs. Simpson smiled.

"Welcome to San Diego, I brought a few cookies for the children." Just then a little girl came around the house and Mrs.

Jeane

Simpson looked startled, she grabbed the little girl and pulled her out of sight.

Jeane stood inside the door. "Curt, did that woman act strange? Did you think she seemed frightened? Was she like that before I came?"

"It was nothing. I think she just wanted to be friendly. Are you ready to go?"

Jeane was surprised and pleased the party was just for her. Everyone at the party was friendly like the people in Kansas and she forgot she was tired. She was amazed how the children entered into the party mood. Everyone wanted to know if she liked Tony's Pizza. She explained she had never heard of Pizza in her little midwest town, nor even at Colorado or Kansas University.

She was surprised it was dark and smoky in the Pizza Pantry. All the tables were covered with red checked tablecloths, and in the middle of each table there was an empty wine bottle with a candle in its neck, and as the candles burned, the wax dripped down on the bottles, and some of the bottles had layer upon layer of different colors of wax. A nickelodeon in one corner was playing popular tunes. Curt looked at Jeane and smiled when *"Smoke Gets in Your Eyes"* was played. It had been their song always.

Even that first night, Jeane liked the strangers who would become her friends. She felt good to know they belonged. It was like one big family. The women told the children about the swimming pool at Miramar and the sandy beaches where they could play in the surf.

By nine-thirty the McLyrres were back in their new home lying on the floor with the pillows and blankets they had brought from Kansas. They slept soundly after the four long days in the car.

Before breakfast the car was unpacked and everybody was sitting on the front steps while they ate their breakfast rolls and drank their orange juice while they waited for their moving van.

Curt felt he was needed at the base and he was sure Jeane could handle the moving people. He left for Miramar before the moving van arrived. Jeane gulped when she saw the huge van stop in front of their house. The driver unlocked the back doors and four men began to unload the boxes and furniture. She watched

Jeane

closely until she saw the men unpacking her tall standing mirror. She inspected it carefully and found no damage. Now she had her old friend with her again. She told the men to put the mirror in the front bedroom. She relaxed a little as she stood on the porch and continued to check off the number on each item as it was taken in the house.

Where's April?

So much was happening so fast she suddenly realized she had no idea where her children were. She called Danny and he ran around the house with a bouquet of flowers for her, he was disappointed when she ignored them.

"Danny, where's April?"

"I'll go find her," he answered.

"Wait a minute. Where did you see her?" He shrugged his shoulders and walked away.

The men had unloaded most of the truck and were anxious to finish. Jeane was frantic. Finally the driver offered to take over her check list. Jeane walked around the house calling April. She knocked on doors of every house near them, but no one answered. She was frightened and she didn't know what to do first.

About that time Mrs. Simpson came around the corner and stopped. Jeane looked up. "Mrs. Simpson, have you seen my daughter? She is only six. I am afraid she is lost."

"I saw her earlier playing with your little boy and the neighbor's cat. Perhaps they followed the cat home." Mrs. Simpson turned pale and she wouldn't look at Jeane.

"Is something wrong?" Jeane continued, "Why won't you look at me?"

"Mrs. McLyrre, I haven't seen your daughter, but I will look around here. Would your little boy like to come with me?"

"No! I want him with me. May I use your telephone to call my husband? Don't you understand, our daughter is missing. She is gone!" There were tears in Jeane's eyes and Mrs. Simpson looked frightened.

Curt was home in less than twenty minutes. The moving men

Jeane

had finished unloading and were eager to have their papers signed so they could be on their way. Curt and Jeane were frantic. They insisted on looking through what remained in the moving van.

Mrs. Simpson came around the house and stopped. "I called Jeff. He will be here soon to help us search. He's worried, too." Mrs. Simpson looked down at her feet, she was clenching her fists. "Mrs. McLyrre, yesterday I didn't mention that our son is a good boy, but he is different. He is twelve years old and he can't go to school. He doesn't understand anyone but us. When my husband gets home, I'm sure he can find our son. Perhaps he will know where your daughter has gone."

Jeane's eyes shot fire. She wanted to grab the woman and shake her. "Mrs. Simpson, what is happening? Tell me! I feel you have not told me everything."

"Mrs. McLyrre, my son is a good boy."

"Stop! Stop now. You know where he is. Do you think he took our daughter with him? Stop! Take me to where they might be. Take me now!"

Mrs. Simpson quickly walked away and Jeane followed. Curt stayed at the house with Danny. Jeane called April's name as she followed Mrs. Simpson, but April never answered.

"Can't we go faster, Mrs. Simpson? Do you know where my daughter is?"

Mrs. Simpson didn't look back as she crossed a vacant lot and passed the deserted house. Jeane shuddered as she prayed April was not in there. Mrs. Simpson climbed over a stone wall and Jeane followed. As they ran through the weeds and over the rocks, Jeane saw a dead tree on the edge of the cliff, and she had a glimpse of April as she screamed and clung to the dead tree. A big boy was yanking her by the hair, but she didn't let go of the tree. When he looked up he saw Jeane and his mother. He let loose of April and darted down the cliff. Jeane ran and picked up April who was sobbing. Her arms were scratched and her hair was tangled and full of weeds. Her arms and legs were muddy. She was shaking like a leaf.

"See, Mrs. McLyrre, your daughter wasn't hurt. I told you my son was a good boy."

Jeane

Jeane didn't say a word. She held April close as she hurried back through the rocks and weeds to their house. Mrs. Simpson followed behind trying to reassure Jeane that her son had taken care of April. She vowed her son had never harmed anyone. She repeated he was a good boy.

April's face was muddy, and tears were still streaming down her cheeks. She sobbed as she clung to her mother. Curt ran to them and took April in his arms. He glared at Mrs. Simpson, then turned away. Danny caught up with his family and held out his arms to be picked up.

Jeane swept him up and hugged him as they walked back into the house. Curt followed while April was clinging to him and still sobbing. Curt locked the door and rubbed April's back while Jeane washed her arms and legs with warm water.

She had tears in her eyes. "Curt, believe me, I am sure April was not safe. I cannot live here. My children are not safe! I would have to watch them every minute."

"I know you're right. They did not tell me about their 'different' boy. We will not stay here. Thank God, April is safe."

Curt told the Simpsons his family could not live there. They agreed to refund the rent and security deposit. The Simpsons allowed them a week to move out.

Jeane got in the car with the children while Curt locked the house. He didn't know where to go. He hadn't gotten any help from the Miramar housing office, but he didn't know where else to go. One woman in the office suggested they look at Clarimont, a new subdivision near Miramar. The McLyrres went there and found only one house for rent. Jeane knew about construction sites. She felt it was too dangerous for her children to live with trucks, cement mixers, and heavy road building-equipment. There was no place for a child to play.

Curt was worried. He knew there were very few decent rentals in the San Diego area, and the Navy was bringing more people in every day. Curt had looked long and hard before he rented the Simpson house. Now he was angry with Jeane and her misgivings about living in Clarimont. They filled out an application and put down a deposit on the house, but Jeane told the clerk she knew it

Jeane

was not safe for her four-year-old son, who had always lived in old established neighborhoods. The clerk was sympathetic and gave them forty-eight hours to decide about the house.

Curt drove around in Pacific Beach and finally found an old motel where they rented a room for the night. Jeane knew they couldn't stay there long and she refused to let him take the children back to the Clifford Street house. He agreed it was better for him to go back there alone. Their bags were still packed, and he put them in the car. Then he picked up the blankets and some of the children's toys and put them on the back seat.

When Curt came back to the motel, he brought a copy of the *San Diego Union* and searched it for rental houses. There were none. Curt and Jeane took the children to the office and asked the owner of the motel for help. He suggested they might want to look at a new apartment complex that accepted children. He said it was between Pacific Beach and La Jolla. Curt asked Jeane if she would consider an apartment.

"I will consider anything that is clean and safe." She was frightened and for a moment she wished they were all back in Norton.

The next morning Jeane told Curt she wanted to see the place the motel owner called Clarimar Garden Apartments. When the McLyrres saw the apartment complex, Jeane gasped. It was beautiful. The apartment buildings were arranged so each building faced a cul-de-sac where cars parked. Each building was surrounded by green grass, shrubs, and flowers.

"Curt, I can't believe we might be able to live in this beautiful place. It looks like something out of *House and Garden*. Look at all those playgrounds for the children! There are even lighted tennis courts. Let's go in the office to see if anything is available."

The clerk told her they had both two and three bedroom apartments available now, but they might not have any tomorrow. She handed Jeane a brochure that told about the room sizes, laundry facilities, playgrounds, and lighted tennis courts. The rent for a three bedroom unit was $122.50 and tenants paid their own utilities. That was more than they could afford, but it didn't matter. Jeane wanted to live there, and Curt agreed. When she stood in the living room, she could look out in two directions and see flowers, grass, and

Jeane

trees. From the dining room, she could see the playground.

"If you like it, we will take it," Curt replied. He was impressed with the location in La Jolla and he remembered that several of his friends already lived there. He liked the fact there were apartments on ground level so the children could go and come easily. Each building had four apartments, with two units down stairs and two up. Each main floor apartment had a private back door and a front door that opened into a common foyer. They hurried to the office and signed the lease, paid the security deposit, and one month's rent in advance.

When Curt's friends at Miramar heard about their experience on Clifford Street, they all volunteered to help him move his possessions to La Jolla on Saturday. Curt rented a truck and with his friends they loaded everything in the truck and drove from Mission Hills to their new apartment, 610 Sonny Way. Now, Jeane felt secure.

By noon the truck had arrived. The men were tired. Jeane had prepared lunch for everybody when Curt ran in and told her the men wanted a cold beer before lunch. She was shocked, but she hurried to the car and soon came back with a case of cold beer.

After lunch the first thing they took off the truck was Jeane's mirror. They were careful after Curt told them how important it was to her. There was room for it in the master bedroom. She looked at it in place and told herself this was going to be a different life. Jeane felt secure now.

All the children in the neighborhood watched the truck unload. Danny and April were there with the neighborhood children. Jeane was delighted there were so many small children living there. She decided this would be Utopia for her. By evening the beds were made and everyone was ready for the night. Finally the chaos was over.

The next day was Sunday, but Jeane didn't think of church. After breakfast the children were out in the play yard and Curt was asleep. Jeane decided the most important thing she could do was write her parents a long letter, but she would never tell them what had happened to April. Instead, she told them about their nice new home.

In Norton, Ethel was at home and she was worried about her family in California. She decided to call them before she realized

Jeane

she had no telephone number. It had been more than a week since they had left Norton. She was sure there were problems. All her life she had felt she had ESP. Her family had been gone five days when her ESP told her something was wrong. She didn't tell anyone, even Maurice; he would have laughed at her. Now she must wait. Every morning she watched for the mailman, asking herself, "Why didn't I tell Jeane to call collect when they reached their new house. I guess I thought long distance calls were too expensive."

On Wednesday morning she was washing dishes when she heard the mail drop through the slot in the wall and fall on the floor. She dried her hands and hurried into the living room where she scooped up the mail and found a letter from Jeane. Quickly she finished washing her dishes before she sat down to read the letter.

June 15, 1951
Dear Mother and Dad,
We are settled now and I have time to write. Our trip out here was interesting, except for those mountain roads that were so narrow! We didn't do much sightseeing and Curt was anxious to get back to San Diego. We saw Hopi Indians beside the road selling moccasins, feathered head bands, dolls, and blankets. April was afraid of them with their painted faces so we didn't stop. When we got to Las Vegas, the car was so hot we had to sleep during the day and drive at night.

There was a mix-up about the house Curt had rented in San Diego, so we had to find somewhere else to live. Nice houses for rent don't exist, but we did find a very nice big apartment with three bedrooms. I can look out our dining room window and see the children in the playground. This is just like a house, it is new and spotlessly clean. We have a front and back door and a porch, too. You will see our new address on the envelope. La Jolla is much closer to Miramar than the house in San Diego.

Finding a decent house near the base was impossible. More service people are coming here every day. We found one small house for rent in a new subdivision that wasn't even half finished and I was afraid for the children to live there. There were no surfaced streets and no sidewalks. The subdivision was full of workmen with huge trucks. Finally we heard about

Jeane

the new Clarimar Garden Apartments in La Jolla. Curt says several of the men in the squadron live here and he can join their car pool.

I never dreamed we would live in a apartment, but this one is as big as a house. Most of the people I see walking around are about our age with lots of young children. We have three bedrooms, a large living room, and dining area like yours. The apartment has lots of big windows and good storage. We can park our car in the cul-de-sac in front of our apartment.

We are only a few blocks from the beach, and the children are anxious to go. Curt promised to take them this afternoon. The children have made friends already. April met a little girl she likes whose name is Martha; she lives in the next building to ours. Danny has lots of boys his age to play with.

Curt says he knows four families where the men are in the same squadron. When he joins the car pool no one will have to drive more than once a week. Next week I will buy material and make curtains for the bedrooms. Our floors are oak and easy to clean and I am glad they are not carpeted. I will put the pink rug we had in Norton in half our living area. There is a porch off our living room and because it has a low wall on two sides Danny can jump off and not get hurt.

I forgot to mention there is a playground near our back door.

Curt says we will have no problem getting a baby-sitter since all the squadron families who live here have a list of girls who want to earn extra money.

Our rent is high, $122.50, and we pay our own utilities, but it is worth it since this place is nice and safe with lots of children. The girl in the office told me an elementary school is being built behind these apartments.

Did you know we have free medical care now? There is a huge Naval Hospital thirty minutes from where we live. That is where we go if we need a doctor.

There is a store for all the military people to use at Miramar where Curt works. The clothes are cheaper and nicer than we could buy at Penneys. On Coronado Island there is a big grocery store just for the military families, but it is an hour drive from

Jeane

here; they call it a commissary. That will save us a lot of money when I learn how to get there.

The Miramar Officers' Club has special parties every week for the officers and their wives and sometimes for the children too. Behind the club is a swimming pool with a snack bar that sells hamburgers for a dime. Miramar is sort of a country club for the officers and their families. I plan to take the children to the swimming pool almost every day. I am sure they will learn to swim this summer.

We went to the Naval Officers' Club Dining Room for dinner last night. I was surprised when most of the people, both men and women, were drinking wine, beer, or cocktails. I ordered a Coke.

My mirror came through in perfect condition. When I stand in front of it, I feel like I am back in Norton, Kansas.

Love,
Jeane

Ethel folded the letter and put it back in the envelope for Maurice to read. She was glad to have the long letter, but she felt Jeane was not telling her everything. Ethel felt her ESP had warned her, but now everything seemed fine. Maurice made fun of her, so she never told him when she sensed trouble. She felt Jeane would have written sooner if something hadn't happened that frightened her. She knew Jeane would never tell her, so she decided to forget it. The letter sounded like she was happy now. Ethel picked up her purse and Jeane's letter. She locked the back door and headed for the shop less than a five minutes walk from the house. She hoped Maurice had not gone to Friendly's for his ten o'clock coffee.

As she walked into the office she held out their letter from Jeane.

"Ethel, I was just ready to go for coffee; I'll read the letter at noon. You worry about our children too much. Their life is different now. I hated to see them go, but now I feel it was right. Curt will grow with his new job." Maurice walked out the door.

After he had read the letter, he looked at Ethel. "I'm surprised they rented an apartment after living in the Grant Street house, but it does sound like it is a good place for children. Why don't you

Jeane

write her this afternoon and tell her we are glad they are settled.

Everything in Ethel's world had changed. Maurice refused to talk about his heart problem and he refused to follow Dr. Kennedy's orders. He had cut back on work when the McLyrres moved back to Norton in 1948. Now, he worked only in the shop where he designed and built custom cabinets and other furniture. He kept employees who handled small plumbing, electrical, and carpenter jobs.

Ethel wrote Jeane while she sat at her desk in the Brown's Plumbing and Cabinet Shop. The machines were making more noise than usual. She hoped the telephone wouldn't ring. On most days she could hardly hear it. She liked being in the shop and she liked meeting the public, but the noise from the machinery often gave her a headache. A glass wall was between the work room and the office but it didn't stop the noise. Ethel was part of the business; she did all the book work, she ordered all of their supplies. She paid all the expenses, wrote the payroll, and took messages. She was the manager and often she sold plumbing supplies too. Sometimes she wondered if she was losing her hearing when she couldn't hear someone on the telephone, but she ignored it.

She sat back and continued with the letter to her family in California. She told them she was anxious to see their new home when they came to visit in January. In the letter she reminded Jeane how all the Brown men had drinking problems. It was a subtle warning to not start taking alcohol.

From their first day in their California apartment, the McLyrres were amazed how the people in their squadron wanted them to be comfortable and happy. It was like the McLyrres were old friends. The first day they brought so much food Jeane didn't have to cook for days. Curt explained when you were a dependent of the U.S. Navy everything happened quickly. Friends were made quickly and in less than two weeks Jeane knew he was right; she felt she had known them for years.

She was learning to be the wife of a U.S. Naval Officer. She knew she must always look nice, and she was glad she had her standing mirror. Now she would take a hand mirror and see how she looked from the back. She had to be sure the seams in her stockings were always straight. She often smiled at the mirror and

Jeane

told it she was happy in her new home.

Jeane had majored in Home Economics and Literature at the University of Kansas. She had learned to make patterns for clothes she liked in a magazine. No one could believe she made them herself. She started sewing when she was about twelve years old and now she made most of what she and April wore. Danny wouldn't wear anything his mother made for him; he wanted to be a cowboy and he wore Levis, plaid shirts, boots, and a cowboy hat.

Jeane thought California was wonderful. She enjoyed her lazy days at home as she watched April and Danny, but soon she wanted to do more. In Norton there was always things to be done, like painting a closet or working in her garden. Now she finished her house work before ten o'clock in the morning and all there was left to do was look for the children, read a book, or look through Vogue magazine again. She wanted to sew, and finally she started reading the yellow pages in the telephone book to find a store that sold good fabrics cheap.

April had never been a friendly child, but during the first day when all the McLyrre's household was being unloaded April was standing alone when a little girl about her age walked up beside her.

She said, "My name is Martha Holder. What's your name?"

April smiled. "My name is April McLyrre. How old are you? I'm six!"

Martha answered, "April, I like that name. Do you want to be my friend?"

"Yes, let's be friends, Martha. I have never had a friend named Martha."

Jeane met Martha's mother in the first few days they lived in Clarimar and she told her how the girls found each other.

Mrs. Holder had been looking for Martha and Jeane was looking for April. Jeane wished she looked like Mrs. Holder who was tall and thin with high cheek bones and dark blue eyes. That day she was wearing white linen slacks with a pale pink silk shirt and pink sandals. What Jeane remembered most was her heavy black hair that was coiled at the nape of her neck. Her fingernails had been manicured pale pink that matched her shirt. Jeane had never seen heavy gold jewelry like Mrs. Holder wore.

After they found their girls, Jeane excused herself and went

Jeane

back in their apartment. She stood in front of her mirror and scolded herself. She asked her mirror why she couldn't look like Mrs. Holder. She knew why: she was short and chubby. Both of them had thick black hair. Jeane knew her eyes were hazel and she had a nice smile. She wanted to be skinny, but she couldn't keep her hands out of the cookie jar. She made beautiful clothes, but when she looked in the mirror she hated herself.

Two weeks after the McLyrres moved into Clarimar, Martha and April brought Jeane a note. They couldn't wait to tell her it was an invitation to a tea party. She read the note, and she saw the girls were so excited she sat down and answered it so the girls could deliver it to Martha's mother.

After the girls left Jeane slipped across the hall to see her new friend, Connie Fellows. When Jeane and Connie met it was like they had known each other forever. Connie was from Chicago and she was lonely. Her husband, Jim, was a doctor in Korea. Both of the young women were eager for friends. Connie was medium height with short curly red hair and fair skin. She was always eager for company. Both young mothers were from the Midwest so they felt they had many things in common.

Connie lived with her two children, across the hall from the McLyrres. Her little girl was four and her little boy was just a year old. Connie had to stay close to her apartment.

"Connie, have you ever known anyone from Spain? April and I have been invited to tea with Martha's mother. What should I wear? She seems so sophisticated I won't know what to talk about."

"Jeane relax. She is probably nervous, too. Let her lead the conversation, I'll bet it will be about your daughters. I'll keep an eye out for Danny while you're there."

April asked her mother if she had to drink tea and she felt better when Jeane assured her the tea would be pretend tea.

When they reached the Holders' apartment, Mrs. Holder smiled as she opened the door and invited them in. "Mrs. McLyrre, I'm so glad you could come today. Martha wanted us to all have a special tea. The girls enjoy being together and I want to know you better. Please call me Catherine. I expect we will see each other often. Excuse me, and I will finish our young ladies' tea."

Jeane sat by the window and looked all around the living room

Jeane

and dining area. The Holders had heavy hand-carved chairs in front of a tall mahogany paneled screen. Each panel had a different design with trees and flowers. Jeane saw sitting at a small table with two chairs that matched the screen. Sheer silk curtains with matching swags over the tops of all the windows. In the living room area there was a large oriental rug with a cream color background. In the center of the rug were flowers and vines and the border repeated the same design.

Mrs. Holder had set a small tea service in the dining area for the girls, and Jeane sat and admired the beauty that radiated around her. A large oil painting in a gold frame hung on the long wall in the living room. The painting was of a man and a woman admiring a baby in a bassinet. Jeane smiled when Mrs. Holder sat down at the table.

"I saw you admiring my painting. Yes, it is me with my parents soon after I was born. Did you notice that our rug is the same as the one in the picture? My parents were nervous about the political situation in Spain even then, and they knew a well-known painter who painted this picture before they emigrated from Spain to the United States. I grew up in Palm Beach, Florida, surrounded by our friends who came there. As the problems in Germany increased they were glad they had left Spain."

Jeane said, "We are very new here. My husband, Curt, was a Naval Reserve Officer who was called to active duty. He expected to be sent to Korea, but with his degree in electrical engineering he was kept in San Diego where he was needed more.

"Catherine, please call me Jeane. You are the first person I have ever known who had to leave their home country. I was born in a small town in Kansas. I am proud of my ancestors who were forced to leave Scotland during the Highland Clearances of the nineteenth century. First they came to Canada and in the 1860s they came to Illinois. In the late 1870s they sold their farm in Illinois and came to Kansas with their big family of adults to homestead land and they are sill there. My ancestors had the money from their farm, but most of the people who came west were poor; all they wanted was to own land."

"Jeane, many people came to the United States from Europe at about that time for the same reasons. I admit I didn't understand.

Jeane

The people we knew who came from Spain were wealthy and wanted to live much as they did in Spain.

"My husband has many responsibilities here and across the country. We feel we want Martha to go to school and learn about California and the United States. We chose to live here where there were lots of children, but it is hard for me.

"I hope we will see each other often." Catherine added. "I take Martha many places and now she wants April to be included. We go to the beach, the zoo, and the children's theater in Balboa Park. There are other places, but now she doesn't want to go without April. I hope you will allow her to go with us often.

"I understand you are busy, since you are the wife of a U.S. Naval Officer. Martha and I are so glad you are here. Most of the children here are younger than our girls. Martha's birthday is next week and we both want April to go with us to the theater. My life is wrapped up in Martha. I am often alone as my husband's work keeps him away most of the time. He has his own plane so he can keep in touch with all his projects across the country."

"Catherine, everyone here is friendly and uses first names just like we do in Kansas. I'm happy April has found Martha. She never made friends easily before."

Jeane wasn't comfortable in the beauty of the Holders' home and she thought her first visit should be less than an hour." Catherine, this has been a wonderful treat for April and for me, but we must go find Danny."

As April and Jeane walked home, April looked up. "Mama, did you like Mrs. Holder?"

"Yes, April, I liked her very much." Jeane had been overwhelmed by the Holders' home. Jeane knew she had little in common with Catherine, yet she was anxious to be her friend. Jeane knew she had to be home most of the time with Danny.

Every month Jeane studied Vogue magazine. She enjoyed following the new fashions. By the time she graduated from Kansas University, she was married and the mother of two children. She made the patterns for the clothes she saw in Vogue. She knew she could never have made the clothes she wore without her standing mirror.

She knew she had to stay at home and take care of her two

Jeane

children just like the other Naval Officers Wives. She continued to make the newest fashions since she had found a good discount fabric store. The new suits had short jackets and straight skirts. She decided the new look would make her look taller.

She knew Dior had introduced a new princess line in the Paris shows. Jeane was happy with her discount fabric store that had advertised in the *San Diego Union*. The advertisement said "We sell quality for less!"

The store was in Hillcrest Heights near Papa's Pizza Pantry. After she had found the store she was anxious to start sewing. Her mirror stood alone near her sewing machine and now she needed it. Jeane knew she couldn't fit her clothes without the mirror. Every morning she looked at herself. She smiled in the mirror and saw her eyes sparkle.

The Courtesy Call

Curt insisted they must make their Courtesy Call on the squadron skipper. After two weeks Curt called Cdr. Conway and arranged for their call. He didn't tell Jeane what he had done until the day before they were to make the call. Jeane was furious. She had known since they arrived in California the call had to be made, but she thought Curt should have asked her first. The call was for Sunday afternoon at three o'clock, always the time for the officer in charge and his wife to meet and look over the new officers and their wives.

Jeane had studied her *Navy Wife* book and she knew what to wear. The book said to dress like she did for church. She decided on her pale yellow linen dress and natural straw hat with a yellow ribbon around the crown. She liked what she saw in the mirror. She pulled on pale nylon hose, white pumps, and white gloves. Curt looked at her and smiled. He was proud of her.

When they reached the Conways, Carol Conway opened the door. She was wearing beautiful black silk pants with wide legs and a white silk shirt. Her black hair was cut short and close to her head. Jeane noticed she had long, tapered, bright red fingernails. She put her hands on either side of Curt's face and kissed him. "So

Jeane

this is your bride! I thought she might not come. Now I will have competition for a dance partner."

She waved Curt and Jeane to chairs as she left the living room. Curt's face was red, and Jeane could hear her laughing in the kitchen. Soon she came back carrying a silver tray with four small glasses of sherry and a small crystal plate filled with small hard balls that she called wine biscuits.

Carol sat down opposite Curt. "It is so nice to meet your lovely wife. Please tell her everyone calls me Carol, don't forget. You must save at least half your dances for me. We always look wonderful together on the dance floor."

Jeane was shocked and at a loss for words. She was angry and she didn't know what to say or do. She sat and worried, she didn't know which was proper to eat with her gloves on or off so she finally slipped them off. She picked up her glass and took a sip, and she tried to smile. She had never tasted wine, and to her it tasted terrible. She smiled as she sat her glass on the table.

Conversation was difficult because the McLyrres were new to the Navy. Carol asked Jeane where they lived when Curt was called to active duty. Jeane answered Kansas.

Now Carol was at a loss for words. She turned to Jeane, "Oh, my dear! I'm so sorry for you. I hope you didn't have to live there long. We drove through Kansas last summer when the temperature was over a hundred and dust was blowing everywhere. We could hardly see the road. Oh, you poor thing! I can't think of anything worse than having to live in Kansas."

Jeane was angry, but she smiled. "I have lived in Kansas all my life, except for two years when Curt and I finished college and earned our degrees at the University of Colorado. I was born in Kansas. Yes, it is hot in July but the temperature changes often. When you drove across Kansas, did you see any of our famous sunsets? I love Kansas and now I want to learn about California."

The conversation moved from the weather to the beach to Happy Hour on Friday night, and the good food at the Miramar Officers' Club. It seemed the Conways knew Curt well, because they were all at Happy Hour every Friday night. Jeane knew nothing about Happy Hour so she smiled when someone mentioned that the team from their squadron was back and had been at Happy

Jeane

Hour Friday night.

Jeane tried to talk, but she didn't know what to say. She looked around and smiled. "I guess there will be other planes going to Alaska next week. I always wanted to visit there some day." There was dead silence in the room, Mrs. Conway asked to refill their glasses but everyone refused. Cdr. Conway looked at Curt when he stood up. He thanked the McLyrres for their visit, and he held out his hand to Jeane who looked confused; she thought they were having a nice time.

Curt pulled Jeane up by the arm, then he hurried her to the car and opened the door. He didn't say a word as she slid into her seat. When he opened his door, she saw his jaw was set as he glared at her. He slammed the door and started the car without a word.

"What's wrong, Curt? I thought we were having a nice visit when you stood and pulled me up." Curt didn't answer; he drove home in silence. When they reached home, Jeane went into their bedroom to put away her hat and gloves before she changed her clothes.

Curt stood and glared at her. "I was shocked by what you said this afternoon." He stopped and his eyes shot sparks. "Don't you know what you have done? You may have ruined my Navy career." He took a deep breath,

"Where did you hear that a team from our squadron was going to Alaska next week? Don't you know that is privileged information? Have you ever heard the phrase, *"the need to know?"* Jeane, that means unless you have *"a need to know"* you will not be told by me or anyone else. Some officers do not believe in the need to know phrase, but it will be honored in this household as long as I am in the United States Navy."

Jeane was crying as Curt studied her face. His eyes had a cold hard look. He watched her and he never blinked. Finally he said, "Now, who told you about the deployment to Alaska?"

"I don't know, but several of our squadron wives were talking about it in the laundry room the other day."

"Jeane, we both have a lot to learn. This is a different world with different rules, and I like them. Forget Kansas, forget Colorado and Texas. No matter where we live the rules are going to be the same from now on. Listen carefully, I will never tell you where I

Jeane

will be assigned even temporarily. You will hear it first from other wives. In an emergency you can call the skipper's office.

Curt walked out of the bedroom still glaring. "Jeane, go wash your face."

She had never seen Curt like this. She wondered what had changed him so quickly, yet she remembered he had ordered her around the night they met at the USO in 1943. Even then she knew he was different from any fellow she had dated, and she was impressed. That night he had told her his idol was Mark Twain who always said, "The truth is an oddity and should be used sparingly." At that time she didn't know how it would change her life.

Already she knew their life would be different since he had been called to active duty. Jeane felt she didn't know him anymore. He stood with his shoulders back like he was important. After they were married he had always been gentle and considerate until now. She didn't know what had happened, but it frightened her. Jeane knew she must not ask him. It seemed he didn't live by her standard, *"Truth is next to godliness."* She hated things that were hidden.

Curt never forgot what happened when they paid their courtesy call on the Conways. One Sunday late in July, he brought the children home from the beach. He showered, packed his bag, kissed his family good-bye, and left by taxi. Jeane wondered when he would be back. By noon Monday she knew he would be gone four weeks. He was one of two officers who had been ordered to the U.S. Navy Intelligence School for a month in San Francisco. The other wives could not imagine a husband like Curt. Jeane couldn't understand him either.

August was pleasant, and Jeane and the children made new friends. The children in Clarimar Apartments explored every corner of the grounds every day. Jeane wrote long newsy letters to her parents and grandparents. She told them she felt she and the children were in the Navy too. She realized their squadron was like a family. Everyone looked out for the others. Clarimar was like a small town and Jeane felt like she was living in Almena, Kansas once more. Jeane wrote her parents that everyone who lived in Clarimar knew each other. Her parents smiled when they got that letter.

Jeane was friendly and worked to make a place for herself in

Jeane

the squadron family. She offered to keep her new friends children when they went to the commissary or on errands. The other wives were concerned because Jeane was alone so soon. If they were going to the commissary they would call her and offer to do her shopping. Another day they would suggest they all go to the Miramar Officers' Club swimming pool for the day and Jeane appreciated being included.

Before Curt was called away, every evening they had listened to the radio for the nine o'clock news. Jeane had not planned to do that alone, but it had become a habit. She realized now she was the head of the family when Curt was gone and she needed to know what was happening in the world.

She tried to understand more about Korea, but all of the strange-sounding names made it impossible. She heard how many men had been killed and she always said a prayer that Curt wouldn't ever have to go there. She heard forty-nine countries would sign the Japanese Peace Treaty allowing the United States to continue to maintain military forces in Japan after September 8th. She knew she needed to learn more about her own country and what was happening. She read more and kept the family happy.

None of the wives she met seemed interested in the news. When she asked Catherine Holder what was happening in Korea, she looked puzzled. She would rather tell Jeane about the Civil War in Spain and how many of her relatives were killed during those years after her parents brought her to the United States.

When Curt was away, Jeane had never felt lonely until now. He had never been away for over one night since he was discharged after World War II. She didn't know that being alone with the children was part of the Navy life. Her new friends assured her she would get used to it and maybe learn to like it.

One evening when she was listening to the nine o'clock news she heard Senator Joseph McCarthy read his long list of well known people he had accused of being Communists. She had never heard of Senator McCarthy and she wondered why he was so determined to call attention to himself.

Jeane walked across the hall and knocked. Connie urged her to come in. "Jeane, you look worried. What's the matter?"

"I was listening to the nine o'clock news and I heard about all

Jeane

those people Senator McCarthy, said were Communists. Do you think that is true?"

"I don't think so. My mother has a friend who knows Senator McCarthy and she says he has a bad drinking problem and he will do anything to call attention to himself. They say he accuses without facts. More than one newscaster says he would do anything to stay in Congress. I've read in the newspaper how he rants and raves when he talks about Communism. He is a fanatic about many things he can't prove. I read that some of the other senators were trying to make him resign from the Senate.

"Jeane, I don't keep up with the news and I don't understand Communism, but I read an article in *Time* magazine that said he threatened many fine people to protect himself."

"Connie, I want to know more about Communism because now I live in a city, and I want to understand what is going on."

"Good luck," Connie smiled, "I'll let you study, then you can explain it to me."

Jeane went home and to bed. She wished she were back in Kansas where her Grandfather Graham would help her understand. The next day she went to the public library and checked out a book on Communism. After she read it, she still couldn't understand why the Russians wanted the world to become Communists. All she read was that the Russians thought if they took over the world it would be a better place to live. The news seemed to say Russia would force countries to join, even if it meant war.

Senator McCarthy claimed he had studied Communism and now he wanted to fight anyone who had joined the Communists. He claimed many college professors, entertainers, and people in government had been taken in, and the public would be shocked at how many officers in the military had joined the Communists. He said the numbers were growing every day. Jeane read the lists of people from California who were called to Washington to testify in front of the un-American Affairs Committee. Many of them were in the entertainment field. What was worse, there were many famous people in the field of science under suspicion including some of the people who helped develop the atom bomb and were still creating more secret defense weapons.

While Curt was away Jeane read the *San Diego Union* every

Jeane

day. There was very little news about unpleasant things. Most of the news was about what was happening in San Diego. She read about two koala bears from Australia that had been given to the Balboa Zoo. She read about the San Diego Baseball Team and the Padres, who were winning most of their games this year.

What interested Jeane most was about La Jolla and especially the La Jolla Playhouse where some of the Hollywood stars performed in person every season. She noticed that the fall season would open the last week of September. The item said Dr. and Mrs. Basil Marko would open their lovely home on Cliffside Drive to the cast and sponsors of the La Jolla Playhouse. Jeane wondered what it would be like to have enough money to entertain movie stars.

Later that afternoon she was bored. She asked the children if they would like to go for a ride and get a hamburger for supper. She looked up the Marko's name in the telephone book and wrote down their address. She found the street on her map and realized she lived near them. When she found Cliffside Drive, all of the houses were huge. The Markos' home sat back toward the edge of the cliff. It was brick and stone, it looked like the Tudor houses in England. There was a long, low, stone wall in front of the house with short stone pillars where the circular drive left the street. Jeane drove past the house three times and noticed something different each time.

April was disgusted. "Mama, you promised us hamburgers. I'm tired of driving past that old house." Jeane agreed and they stopped at Hamburger Heaven in the neighborhood and then returned home for the children's baths. After their bath the children were both sleepy, but they wanted to hear another chapter of *Alice in Wonderland*. After she read the chapter and told them good night, she sat down and wrote her parents a letter. By the time she finished, the children were sound asleep.

She folded her letter and slipped it into an envelope, then she walked across the foyer and knocked on Connie's door.

"Jeane, come in. Sundays seem to be the longest day in the week since Jim is in Korea. It will be so good when he gets to come home. When he was called to active duty we lived in Chicago, and Jim was continuing his medical studies. When he was ordered to

Jeane

San Diego, we decided I would come with the children. He had been ordered to the San Diego Naval Hospital, then later he had to go to Korea."

"Connie, I read the paper this morning and I saw something crazy. I was restless and bored, so when I read that Mr. and Mrs. Basil Marko of La Jolla planned to entertain the cast after the first production in La Jolla Playhouse on opening night. Just think, movie stars in your own home.

"Jeane, the lady who lives there might be just like us, but probably older. When I was little we lived in a big house like that in Chicago, but during the depression my family lost a lot of money and the house. Now things are good for them, but they don't want that kind of house anymore." The young wives talked for hours, and soon the time for bed had passed.

In Norton, Ethel received Jeane's letter from California, and she knew Jeane was trying hard to be happy while Curt was gone. She wrote her mother how different things were in the Navy. She told her mother about the Navy policy, *"we have no choice."* That means a Naval Officer or sailor has no choice in what he had to do. All the men knew nothing could change their orders. Ethel decided being in the Navy was hard.

Jeane mentioned Senator McCarthy and the people he accused of being Communists. When Jeane received the next letter from her mother, it was clear that no one in Norton seemed concerned about Communism. The letter said that most people in and around Norton were not interested in what happened in Washington, D.C. They were only interested in the weather and the sale price of farm products.

Farmers listened to their radio for the farm news every day. Most farmers had heard Senator McCarthy and his threats and accusations, but they knew he wouldn't put a farmer on his list. He wanted only famous people. Little was printed about Senator McCarthy in the *Sunflower Times*. Jeane remembered how her dad listened to WNT from Topeka every night. He knew that Senator McCarthy continued to accuse famous people of being Communists. Newsmen said McCarthy had a serious drinking problem.

Jeane

Curt came home the last day of August. Jeane knew where he had been, but they never discussed it. The other wives couldn't understand why Curt wouldn't tell Jeane anything, but Jeane knew he thought she talked too much.

April was excited about going to her first day in Bird Rock School. Jeane walked with her since it was her first day. Jeane saw Catherine, and they waved good-bye to their daughters and walked back home.
"Jeane, I dreaded this day; I wondered how I would fill my days, but now I know I will give more time to my church, That is important to me." Catherine always had an aura of peace; she never seemed restless or bored. She suggested Jeane might want to come with her to a Bible study program. Jeane explained she had Danny at home and she had to be available for the squadron wives' activities.
Jeane never missed a squadron wives' activity. She wanted to be the best Naval Officer's wife in the squadron. When she asked questions of the senior wives they laughed. Their best advice was keep quiet and keep smiling.
She wanted to learn the history of San Diego so she volunteered to be a hostess at a historic sight, but after her interview she was told to come back when her children were in school. She wondered how she could meet people who had always lived in San Diego.
She remembered then when she was in college, Sigma Kappa had a chapter at San Diego State College. She found their telephone number in the telephone book and she inquired if there was a Sigma Kappa alumnae chapter in San Diego. The girl on telephone duty gave Jeane the name of the president of the alumnae chapter and her telephone number. Jeane telephoned the president and was urged to come to the first fall meeting. When she went to the meeting, she volunteered to help with pledge training at San Diego State. The pledges met Monday evenings and the college was a thirty minutes drive from La Jolla. She dreaded telling Curt what she had done, but to her surprise he didn't object.
Curt was restless when he came home in late August. He said there was nothing to do at home. He told Jeane he watched television every evening in the BOQ {Bachelor Officers Quarters}. He said

Jeane

there were great news programs about important people around the world. One of the other officers told him the children's programs were educational and entertaining. He told Jeane they should buy a television. They agreed they should know the news from everywhere and they were sure the children would learn from their programs. Finally they convinced themselves a television was necessary, even if they had to pay for it by the month.

On Saturday morning Curt got up smiling. "Hey gang, let's go shopping."

"Not me." April answered. "I want to go to the beach with Martha and her mother."

"All right, you go with your friend. Danny, will you come with us?" Danny cocked his head and looked up at his daddy with a smile. "OK, let's go."

Curt saw an advertisement in the *San Diego Union* from Hamilton's Appliance Store that claimed their televisions were the best buys in San Diego. The McLyrres found the store and were overwhelmed by the crowd. They looked at new sets, but the least expensive was over five hundred dollars. They could not afford that, but their salesman asked them if they would consider a second hand set. Curt was delighted, he told the man he was an electrical engineer and he knew he could keep an old set running. The salesman showed them a television in a limed oak cabinet that Jeane liked. The picture tube was eight inches round. They arranged to pay twenty dollars down and twenty dollars a month for a year. The salesman and Curt loaded the set on the back seat of the car. Jeane and the children had never seen a television program and she was anxious to see it now.

Faith Marko

In October Jeane looked forward to the second Sigma Kappa alumnae meeting. She liked the people she had met in September and she wanted to tell them how much she enjoyed doing the pledge training at San Diego College and she wanted to share her experiences. When she got to the meeting fifteen women were already there. Jeane was one of the youngest alumnae and all of

Jeane

the women were glad to see her again. She sat down next to a lady who introduced herself as Faith Marko. Jeane was stunned.

Mrs. Marko turned toward Jeane, "Have I met you? I don't always get to these meetings, but it seems they are all lovely ladies." She asked Jeane where she had been a Sigma Kappa and Jeane told her Kansas University.

"Jeane, we are both from the Midwest" Mrs. Marko replied, "I graduated from the University of Illinois. Where do you live here?"

"I live in La Jolla, the U.S. Navy ordered my husband, Curt, to active duty last March. He had been commissioned a Ensign in the Navy when he graduated from college and he continued in the Naval Reserve until this spring. I was teaching school when he reported for duty. We thought he would be sent to Korea, but when the Navy needed electrical engineers they sent him to Miramar Naval Air Station. We joined him when school was out. Now we are living in the Clarimar Garden Apartments.

Mrs. Marko smiled. "I watched those apartments being built." She liked the friendly young woman beside her. "Those apartments are very attractive since they are finished. We live very near there. Perhaps we could get together one day."

She smiled as she told Jeane she had grown up in Illinois and Jeane was anxious to tell her about Kansas. Faith seemed shy among strangers, but when she met Jeane it was different. At the end of the evening she asked Jeane for her telephone number and said she would call her soon. When the meeting was over Jeane gave her the telephone number.

It was a week before Faith called Jeane and invited her to come for coffee. Jeane accepted immediately. When the call ended, she ran across the hall to ask Connie what she should wear for coffee with Mrs. Marko.

"Jeane, what does she look like? What did she wear to the alumnae meeting?"

"She is beautiful. She is tall and thin and she wore a rather simple old fashioned pale blue silk shirtwaist dress which was perfect with her pale blonde hair. Connie, did I tell you she wears her hair in a page boy, shoulder length, and this time she had fastened it back with a long silver barrette. She is very quiet. Sometimes she seems sad. She doesn't realize how tears fill her eyes, but none fall."

Jeane

Jeane was nervous when she dressed the next morning. She tried on several dresses before she decided she would wear her pink skirt with a white cotton blouse and white sandals. She wanted to look her best when she visited Mrs. Marko. Connie offered to watch Danny. She was still nervous when she parked on Cliffside Drive and walked up the Markos' driveway and rang the doorbell. Mrs. Marko answered so quickly Jeane was sure she had been waiting inside.

She stepped back so Jeane could come in. "I'm so pleased you could come, I have looked forward to getting to know you better. Since it is such a beautiful day, I thought you might enjoy sitting on the balcony. We can have our coffee there."

She led Jeane through the house to the breakfast room where the French doors were open on to the balcony. "Jeane, isn't this a wonderful view? On a pretty morning you can watch the surf break against the rocks below us. I'm so glad we met; I couldn't believe there was another Sigma Kappa from the Midwest is my neighborhood. You said you were from Kansas, didn't you?"

"Yes, I'm from a small town in northwest Kansas just south of the Nebraska line. All my relatives live or have lived in Norton County, Kansas. I have always been proud to be a Kansan, even though some people can't understand why."

Faith replied, "I grew up on our family farm in Illinois and then I went to the University in Urbana where I pledged Sigma Kappa. My family had been hurt by the depression of the 1930s, but maybe not as much as you were in Kansas. Did you say you have two children?"

"Yes, we have a little girl, April, who is six and a little boy, Danny, who is three."

"You are a very lucky lady, Jeane."

Faith turned and put her handkerchief over her mouth and near her nose. She sat down and turned away from Jeane as she started to pour the coffee. "Jeane, it must be wonderful to watch your children grow up. If we had children I would never let them out on this balcony."

The surf hitting the rocks almost made a melody that repeated itself time and time again. They sipped their coffee and talked of their sorority days in college and growing up in a rural community.

Jeane

Jeane looked at her watch. She couldn't believe she had been there more than an hour.

"Mrs. Marko, I feel like I have known you a long time. I would like to stay longer, but my neighbor is watching Danny so I should go home."

"Jeane, please call me Faith. I feel like I have known you for a long time, too. You don't know how much I have enjoyed this short visit and I do look forward to seeing you again soon. When you come next time, please bring Danny, if you want to." As Jeane left the Markos. Faith called after her. "Please come see me soon. I will call you next week."

When Jeane got home, the first thing Connie asked her what Mrs. Marko was wearing. Jeane answered. "She had on a pale green shirtwaist dress with matching canvas shoes."

"Connie, her kitchen and breakfast room look like they should be in *House Beautiful*. The house is huge. The cabinets in the kitchen on one wall reach from floor to ceiling. The counter tops are marble, and the cabinets above the counter also reach the ceiling. The floors are ceramic tile. In the breakfast room there is a round oak table and chairs on a round oriental rug. On one wall there is a large oil painting. It looks like a European street scene."

"Jeane, what about the back of the house so near the cliff?"

"Faith suggested we have our coffee there. It was beautiful and I just stared over the railing, but when I looked down, it was frightening. I could hardly breathe. The balcony is thirty feet above huge boulders where the surf crashes as each wave hits the rocks below. She came out on the balcony as I was looking down on the rocks. She stood beside me for several seconds, then she looked down and quickly away. I thought that if anyone fell off that balcony they would be killed."

"It sounds eerie. Jeane, do you think Mrs. Marko is unhappy?"

"I wondered the same thing, Connie. She was delighted when she saw me; I wondered why she seemed so anxious for me to visit her. The house is big and she seemed to be alone. I felt she was eager for a friend. I saw a tear when I told her about April and Danny."

During the day Jeane thought about little but her visit with Faith Marko. She was delighted when Curt came home as she was

Jeane

anxious to tell him about it. She looked at him and smiled.

Curt frowned in returned. "Jeane, why didn't you tell me you were going to visit the Markos? Where did you meet that woman anyway? Don't you understand that you can hurt my career by associating with a Russian who might be a Communist? Do you realize that the number of Communists in this country is increasing every day, and Russia is under the control of the Communists? I'll bet those people are Communists! I forbid you to go there again! My God, Jeane, first you get friendly with that Spanish woman, and now it's a Russian. What's the matter with you? Why are you determined to make friends with Communists."

Jeane glared at Curt, her eyes looked icy cold. She was furious. "Listen here, Curt McLyrre, I am not your slave, and you can't order me around. Faith Marko is my sorority sister and she will be my friend. She is from Illinois where she grew up on a farm. She seems lonely and she likes me, I know. We can talk about college, our sorority, and the Midwest. Not many people want to talk about growing up in the Midwest. Don't try to forbid me. It won't work."

As Christmas came closer Jeane dreaded it more. The McLyrres had been with the Browns every Christmas except 1944 just after they were married. She hated to think of Christmas without her parents. She had written and urged them to come because the children missed them so much. The Browns hated to disappoint their grandchildren, but they had not planned to come until after the new year.

When Curt put the Christmas tree in the stand early in December, Jeane brushed a tear away and tried to smile. Her parents had given her their Christmas ornaments when they moved back to Norton in 1948, her mother said she would never put up another tree.

Jeane realized she was being selfish, but she still hoped her parents would get there before Christmas. The children were excited because they were putting the ornaments on the tree just like their parents. This year the tree looked the same as always after Jeane put the three little celluloid birds on a high branch of the tree. These birds had been on every Christmas tree but one, since Jeane's first Christmas when she was three weeks old.

Jeane

Jeane's mother always had their income tax ready to mail before the new year. She finished the report on Christmas Day. Maurice called Jeane and told her they were ready to come, but they would not leave Norton until she called them collect and told them she had an apartment for them to rent for two weeks. They wanted to be alone.

Jeane was disappointed they were not on their way, but the next day she began her search for an apartment. She was glad they wanted their own space. Her dad needed to go to bed early and not get too tired. She knew he took nitroglycerin tablets for his heart. In three days Jeane found a one bedroom apartment on ground level just off the beach, and less than a mile from the McLyrres. The rent was seventy dollars for two weeks. It included a fully equipped kitchen so they could cook for themselves. She called home collect that afternoon and told them about the apartment and how nice and warm it was in San Diego. She said the children were outdoors playing with their new Christmas toys.

As the new year drew near Jeane reminded Curt that they had celebrated 1951 New Year's Eve in the Norton Country Club. She remembered most of the people who went to the Country Club were drunk and loud. The young crowd that included the McLyrres just sat and watched.

This year several people in their squadron had planned New Year's Eve parties and the McLyrres were invited. Jeane hoped no one would get drunk. The night was warm, and no one was more than a half block from home so they checked on their children often.

On the fourth of January, the Browns arrived in La Jolla. When they came up the sidewalk, Ethel was carrying a small basket with a lid she held down. When everyone was in the apartment and the door was closed, Ethel sat the basket on the floor and the lid popped open and a tiny Siamese kitten hopped out. Jeane couldn't believe her eyes. "Mother, did you buy this kitten?"

"No, I didn't. You remember Mrs. Saylor from the sanitarium raises Siamese cats and when she heard we were coming to see you, she called and asked me if we would bring you a kitten from the last litter."

Jeane

Jeane was excited about having a Siamese kitten once again. She named it Tinky after the first Tinky she had in 1935. When the Browns moved to Norton and Jeane went to college, Tinky became Ethel's pet. Curt ignored the kitten, but he was happy to see how much it delighted Jeane. That evening Jeane ignored everybody but the tiny kitten. Curt had never had a kitten when he was growing up so he didn't understand what it meant to Jeane. The Browns just smiled.

Ethel admitted their Christmas had been miserable. They packed the car and started their trip on the day after Christmas. They realized there might be snow, so they drove straight south from Norton on U.S. 383 through Oklahoma and on to Abilene, Texas where they got on U.S. 66 west into California. The weather remained good all the way to California.

The Browns told Jeane their apartment was perfect. They had planned that April would spend nights with them and Danny would be with them in the daytime. The children thought it was a great idea. Maurice knew he and Danny would have a wonderful time. He walked with Danny along the shore and let him stop often to dig in the damp sand and hunt seashells. Maurice went to bed early; April and her grandmother played games in the evening. At bedtime April always wanted a story before she went to sleep. She remembered all the stories her grandmother had told them before they moved to California. Everyone was happy and by evening, Danny was tired and ready to get in his own bed.

The two weeks the Browns were there went quickly. Jeane was lost after they started home. She had been busy every minute, but now she didn't have enough to do. She watched some of the other squadron wives as they sat in the sun and continued to darken their tan, paint their fingernails, and nap in the sun. Jeane had never liked to sit in the sun. Some of the other wives spent their time on the tennis court or shopping. Jeane would have liked to play tennis, but her game was not good enough and she couldn't afford tennis lessons.

She realized it was a new year as she turned the pages of Vogue magazine again and again. She wanted to know exactly what color nylons she should buy and how many inches the skirts should

Jeane

be from the floor. As she turned the pages she realized most of the models had their hair cut short and close to their head. Jeane had not had her hair short since she was fourteen years old. Curt loved her long black hair; he said it was her best feature and he refused to let her have it cut only enough to keep the page boy. She had worn her long dark hair in a pageboy since she met Curt.

She decided to have her hair cut short without telling him. When he came home that evening and saw it he was furious. "Jeane, what have you done? You know how I like your hair."

"Yes, I know, but I wanted to try something new. I don't want to look like a high school senior. I am a mother. I have the right to have my hair cut to please myself."

In January at the Sigma Kappa alumnae meeting Jeane was asked to prepare her pledge class for initiation. Faith had gone with her to the meeting and on their way home she hesitated, then she offered to help Jeane with the pledges. Jeane was delighted. "That's great. I do need help and I hate to drive to the college alone."

Jeane wanted to do something that didn't cost money and that she could do at home. First she discovered the library. In Norton she had read books written by James Michener, Herman Wouk, Frances Parkington Keyes, and others. She didn't like Wouk's *The Caine Mutiny* even though it remained on the best seller list for months. She started reading the book section in the *San Diego Union* and learned there were secondhand bookstores. She had never heard about buying used books cheap. She could hardly wait to visit one. She was surprised when they had many of her favorites and she could buy one often. She decided this was the time to start a library of her own and be home with Danny too.

Some of the squadron wives played bridge while their children were in school. Others spent time at the Miramar Officers' Club bar. Jeane enjoyed bridge, but not every day. She never took a drink unless everyone else did. She felt drinking was evil. She missed her flower garden in Norton. Now the garden she saw wasn't hers. Since 1948 when Curt graduated and they moved back to Norton, she had always had a flower garden. So now she bought flowering plants in pots for their terrace.

The squadron wives' luncheons were once a month. Connie

Jeane

watched Danny those days; Jeane didn't enjoy them, but she felt insecure even though everyone was nice to her. Curt insisted she go. She heard everyone talk about their new fall clothes and the coming parties at the Miramar Officers' Club. Jeane was glad she had her standing mirror so she could be sure her clothes fit perfectly. Her clothes pleased her, but there was no money for accessories. One day when she went to the fabric store a clerk told her about a discount shoe store in the next block and she couldn't wait to go there. Jeane was only five feet tall and she wore sample size shoes. She found the shoe store and bought two pair for the price of one. She hid one pair for several months.

When Curt was away, Jeane turned on the television for the nine o'clock news. She heard Senator Benton of Connecticut attempt to discredit Senator McCarthy's anti-Communists campaign. Jeane recognized the tactics Senator McCarthy used were the same Lenin used to stress the importance of Communism in Russia, and the Russians believed him. She sat looking at the black eye of the television after the news was over. What was happening frightened her.

She decided she wasn't ready to be an educated women if she had to get her news from that little black box. She was shocked when King George VI died and his daughter became Queen Elizabeth II. She could hardly believe someone that young reigned over all of Britain. When she heard Senator McCarthy read his lists she was angry. Now he insisted most college professors had become Communists. She thought about it and decided she didn't believe him.

Curt insisted it was time for them to have a party for their friends. They were careful how they spent Curt's pay, but he insisted they had to have a well-stocked bar. She thought that was not necessary. He ignored her and brought home scotch, bourbon, gin, wine, and beer.

Jeane was angry. Curt never helped her with anything, but he demanded the house be perfect before he got home in the evening. Before the party she washed their windows and bought more flowering house plants. She haunted antique shops and found an oil painting of mountains they could afford and Curt approved. She

Jeane

dusted the living and dining room every morning and she smiled as she remembered she had to dust when she was eight years old. She hated it then, now she spent thirty minutes polishing the brass card tray that sat on top of the television set.

Jeane and Curt were learning to live in a city and finding it inviting. They learned to enjoy Mexican food in Old Town of San Diego. The food was not expensive. Their favorite restaurant there was Ramona's Wedding House where they ate in the back garden under the biggest tree Jeane had ever seen. For Jeane's birthday Curt took her to a new restaurant in La Jolla, called the Talk of The Town. Their specialty was teriyaki. It was thin sliced beef that had been marinated in soy sauce, fresh ginger, a little bourbon and brown sugar. The beef had to be marinated for several hours before it was grilled and served over rice. Jeane tried to make it at home, but it wasn't the same. Both Curt and Jeane watched the *San Diego Union* for other ethnic restaurants including Chinese, Japanese, and Greek.

Jeane wanted to go to church and take the children to Suncay School.. She looked in the telephone book for a Methodist Church in La Jolla but the only phone number was for a Methodist Retirement Home. She knew that wouldn't do. She had admired St. James-by-the-Sea Episcopal Church near La Jolla Cove every time she passed by. Since KU days she wanted to learn more about the Episcopal Church. In 1922 her dad built Trinity Church in Norton. It was beautiful. It was his first big contract, and he didn't know how to figure his costs. He always claimed he was the biggest contributor to the church; and he was almost forced to declare bankruptcy.

Jeane remembered when she was at KU she went to the Episcopal Church nearest her sorority house. In 1940 when the Browns moved to Norton where her dad had built a new modern motel and her mother ran it and her dad continued his contracting. She decided she would continue to be a Methodist. After Curt and Jeane moved back to Norton in 1948 they continued attending the Methodist Church. Now that wasn't possible. The children liked the St. James Sunday School, and it kept them out of the apartment

Jeane

on Sunday morning. Curt promised them an afternoon on the beach if the house was quiet until noon on Sunday.

The pastor at St. James, Father Glasson, made Jeane feel welcome. The children went to Sunday School and Jeane went to the nine o'clock service. She sat in the back of the church because she didn't know anyone but Faith, and she sat in the front of the church. One Sunday Jeane saw Faith had taken out her handkerchief and twice she had wiped away a tear. She wondered why Faith was crying but she never asked.

On Sunday afternoons Curt took the children down the cliffs to the tide pools along the shore of the Pacific Ocean. Below the steep path the beach was rocky. The children liked to look in the tide pools without getting their feet wet. Then they wanted to run all over the dirt mounds where tunnels and caves riddled the cliff. Much of this was there from the days of World War II. Curt knew it was a dangerous game and he watched them every minute. He forbid the children to go inside any of the dirt forts. At four o'clock he brought home two dirty children.

"Jeane, you look happy. What did you do all afternoon?"

"Faith called and invited me for tea."

"Did you go? Did you see Basil Marko?"

"No, Curt I saw only Faith. Why do you ask?"

"You know why. There are many rumors he is a Communist. I told you he is on Senator McCarthy's list of alleged Communists. I'm sure he will be called again and again by the Un-American Affairs Committee. Today the *San Diego Union* reported fourteen California Communists had been convicted under the Smith Act. Now do you know why I don't want you there."

"Curt, Faith is my friend. Maybe your information is false. She told me they lived in Las Alamos, New Mexico, for several years after they were married in 1940. She didn't know anything about his work, and she knows no more now. She said Basil never shared anything about his work with her. She assumed he had worked on the Atom Bomb, but she never asked. Later he told her he intended to continue research.

"Faith told me he didn't believe in the H-bomb. He thought it was too dangerous and could destroy the world if it was used. She

Jeane

said everything at Los Alamos was secret. Every person who worked there was sworn to secrecy. She told me that whole area was fenced and the gates were guarded day and night with men and dogs. The guards all carried guns and walked around the area inside the fence all the time. Does that sound like a Communist would have been chosen to work there?"

Jeane had said enough. She knew she had better not mention it again.

Curt stood up, he was glaring at Jeane. "You just wait and see. Remember what has been said this afternoon." Curt left the apartment without saying a word and returning before dark. Jeane had gone to bed and pretended to be asleep. Curt was angry; he believed his wife should obey him. His mother had always obeyed his father and smiled. Curt adored his mother but not his father. He knew Jeane would rebel if he tried to give her orders. He knew his father was demanding but Curt could see that it might be necessary for him to get control of his own family.

In March Curt came home with orders for the month of June. All he told Jeane was that he would be at Ohio University in Columbus, Ohio. He suggested they all go together to Denver in late May and he would fly from Denver to Columbus. Jeane and the children could visit her family and friends in Norton and Almena. On their way back to California they could visit their friends in Denver and spend a few days with his parents in Hugo, Colorado.

Jeane was delighted that they could all drive east together. She made some summer clothes for the children and asked Connie if she would take care of Tinky while they were away.

Home in Kansas

On May 28th at 9:30 in the evening the McLyrre family left La Jolla to drive straight across the desert through Grand Junction, and on to Denver. Their trip to Denver was easier than last year. Curt drove from La Jolla to Grand Junction and Jeane drove on to the Denver Airport where Curt would wait for his flight. Jeane still felt fresh and she was anxious to be home. She wondered what it would be like to see Norton again. Their year in La Jolla had been what

Jeane

Jeane dreamed about. She had met some interesting people and some she avoided. She had made friends with most of the squadron families. Some of the squadron families had already been ordered to a new assignment. Curt told Jeane she might see some of those people again. Every officer knew he would have orders by the end of the three years. Orders were usually cut in the spring.

Jeane still felt fresh after they left Curt at the airport. She was in charge now as she drove east toward Norton. She thought about her new friends in California. She knew Connie Fellows was a friend who was always ready to help. Faith Marko was a mystery; Jeane felt she was sad even though she lived in a mansion. She didn't know Catherine Holder very well, she felt their friendship was based only on their daughters. Jeane thought Catherine led a lonely life.

Jeane had always been busy. She couldn't understand the squadron wives who wasted most of their days around the swimming pool at Miramar or around the bridge table. They worked hard to make themselves beautiful. Jeane didn't have the money for all that foolishness. She knew most of the squadron wives would forget her as soon as they were apart.

Curt had changed during the past year. Jeane knew that he had gone to the U.S. Navy Intelligence School from what other squadron wives told her. He didn't tell her anything. She knew Communism was rapidly spreading in California, but she didn't talk about it. Frequently she saw notices of parades and lectures to learn more about Communism at San Diego State College. The Communists met every ship that docked and passed out information on the importance of Communism in America. The pictures in the *San Diego Union* saw sailors throwing away the propaganda, yet she had no idea where or what was happening in Curt's private world.

Jeane thought how tense and angry Curt was most of the time and she wondered why. This assignment was one he dreamed of and he had learned a lot during the past year. He insisted Jeane would not see Faith. She ignored him and continued their friendship. Curt was angry when she didn't take part in the squadron wives' activities. He insisted she must smile and be nice to all the senior officer's wives, so she avoided them.

She watched Carol Conway at the squadron wives' morning

Jeane

coffees. Jeane was surprised to see her order Scotch before she had her coffee at eleven in the morning. She usually had a second Scotch before lunch and Jeane stayed away from her because she might do or say something that would offend her. She wondered if Curt knew about Carol's drinking problem. Jeane had never forgotten the tantrum he had after their courtesy call on the Conways, but she didn't mention those things. She wondered if Carol had been sober when they made that call.

The children were excited when they saw yellow sunflowers on a sign. Jeane told them it said Kansas, but it was still a long way to Norton. Jeane and the children reached Norton in time for supper. She pulled in on the driveway and opened the car door so the children could run to the house. She stood and admired her mother's flowers. For a moment she wished they still lived here, but she knew it would never happen.

The next morning as she drove east to Almena she smiled. She wondered if Cora Crabtree still looked out her front window as she did long ago. It didn't seem right to stop at an old house just off Main Street to see her Grandmother Brown. No one had told her why her grandmother had moved after so many years in her other house.

Her grandmother was sweeping the sidewalk when Jeane stopped. Fanny, her little dog never left her side, but now she ran to the car barking, then she ran around the house out of sight. Fanny never trusted small children. Jeane got out and the children followed her. She urged them to run and hug their Great-Grandmother Brown.

Jeane led them into the house where it was dark even though it was morning, April held on to her mother, but Danny hugged his great-grandmother who glared at Jeane.

"Why are you wearing shorts?" she said. "When are you ever going to grow up? Don't you know it is wrong to show off your bare legs? You are a terrible example for your children."

"Grandma, this is what all my friends wear where I live. We are different out there. You look wonderful. We will be here a month and I'll see you often, but now we have to go. Grandad Graham is expecting us."

Her Grandad Graham lived in an apartment on Main Street next to the Royal Cafe. His apartment had been a barbershop when

Jeane

Jeane lived in Almena. When she saw her grandfather, he looked years older. It seemed strange to see him in an apartment on Main Street. He was sitting in his old oak rocking chair which Jeane remembered from when she was a little girl. She remembered the story of how her grandmother bought the chair before baby Ethel was born and without telling her grandfather. Now her grandfather sat in the chair quietly and watched the children for a few minutes, then he asked Jeane how soon her mother would be there. She told him her mother couldn't come today and tears began to roll down his cheeks.

Jeane didn't know what to do and she was delighted when she saw her Uncle Gilbert come in the door. He saw his dad was crying and he suggested they all go next door to the Royal Cafe and have lunch. That seemed to please him. When everyone in the cafe admired Jeane and her children and he beamed with pride.

After lunch Jeane took the children to see her Uncle Gilbert's family. Jeane had adored him from the time she started school and he wrote her short letters. Now Gilbert and Opal had four children: Joan was sixteen and wanted to know everything about California, Gil was twelve; Gayle ten; and Arnold eight. It was a busy happy household.

Next they saw her Uncle Dan and Aunt Nell Brown for a few minutes. Then they went to see her Aunt Faye who was pleased Jeane was there for the wedding of her son Robert to Donna Hagaman in Trinity Episcopal Church in Norton.

As always, Jeane's mother wanted her to see all her friends in Norton. She invited them to come and bring their children for coffee on the Browns' patio. Everyone talked about the new swimming pool and park on the edge of town.

Her friends asked if she liked living in California. She told them she did, then she described in detail their apartment and the playground in their backyard. She described La Jolla with the beaches where the children played in the surf. She mentioned the Miramar Officers' Club and how the children had learned to swim last summer. Jeane enjoyed herself until she looked around and found her friends talking to each other or getting out their car keys.

Jeane was shocked. "Please, don't go! I haven't gotten to hear about your last year." She realized she should not have talked about

Jeane

herself. "You know I loved living here but Curt was ordered to go and we had to follow. Remember when we moved back to Norton in 1948? You made me feel wanted. I will know all of you for the rest of my life. Please, I want to take your pictures with your children. I do miss you.

"Every Navy family move every three years, *We have no choice*. I miss all of the good times we had together here. You are all special to me and I want to remember each of you while I am away."

During the next few weeks she saw them again. It was hard for them to appreciate what Jeane had told them. When someone asked her if she missed her big house on Grant Street, she always said yes. When she convinced them she still loved Norton everyone relaxed. Her friends knew and loved Norton. Jeane was still a newcomer after twelve years. Now she knew why Curt would never live in Norton again.

Time passed quickly. Curt took a bus from Columbus, Ohio to Norton two days before Bob and Donna's wedding. Jeane's mother always insisted on buying new clothes for all of her family. Soon after Bob and Donna arrived in Almena, he brought Donna to meet his favorite aunt and the McLyrres.

Jeane knew her cousin, Joan, would like to see California. She had asked questions about California every time Jeane saw her. Curt finished at Ohio University and was back in Norton when Jeane told him how much Joan would like to see California. He said, "why didn't you invite her to go home with us?" Joan was delighted.

When it was almost time for the McLyrres to start back to California, Ethel had mixed feelings. She adored her grandchildren, but it had been hard for her to live with them for a month. They ate all over the house.

Ethel liked a spotless house, but she made one concession: if it rained the children could eat popcorn in the living room. All the children wanted for lunch was a sandwich. After lunch Jeane took the children to play while her father napped. He was tired by noon every day, but he still went to Friendly's every morning for coffee, and then he stopped at the shop on his way home. Now it was Jay's Shop. Maurice taught Jay how to design and build beautiful cabinets

Jeane

and other furniture. Now, he sat on a sawhorse and watched Jay.

This summer the wheat harvest was early. The children were fascinated with the huge combines that crawled through town en route to ripe wheat fields that needed to be cut. Day and night the big trucks loaded with new wheat rumbled past the Browns to one of three elevators a few blocks away.

After Bob and Donna's wedding, the McLyrre family and Joan left Norton. They planned to pay a short visit to Curt's parents in Hugo, Colorado. Jeane never realized how demanding Curt's father could be until they got there. He expected the children to behave as adults. He ordered his wife around as though she was a hired maid. There was little for the children to do in Hugo and Curt was anxious to get back to his squadron. After two days they drove to Denver and spent one night with their friends, the Adams.

Jeane knew Joan had never seen any of the famous sights in the west so after they left Denver they drove west through Glenwood Springs and on west to Salt Lake City, where they toured Mormon buildings. The second day they drove south to the north rim of the Grand Canyon, but Curt was anxious to get back to Miramar so they stopped on the north rim for less than thirty minutes. Jeane could hardly look down into the chasm to see a narrow line that was the Colorado River. She held April in an iron grip as they walked toward the rim of the canyon and back to the car. Curt carried Danny to the overlook and stood there without saying a word for several minutes.

Curt felt he had been away from Miramar too long and he insisted there would be no other sightseeing on this trip.

When they crossed into California everyone was excited, but the temperature was over 100 degrees so they took a motel room and slept until nine that evening. It was still miserably hot but nothing like it was during the day. After they reached San Bernadino it was a little cooler so they drove west to the Pacific Coast and took US 101 south to La Jolla where the waves were breaking over the rocks in La Jolla Cove. All of the trees and flowers were in bloom. Jeane was happy and Joan was overwhelmed.

The morning after the McLyrres got home Jeane called Faith

Jeane

and a strange woman's voice answered. Jeane was told Faith was visiting her family in Illinois

For Jeane the next two weeks were full. She took Joan and the children to Balboa Park and the zoo; they all rode the miniature train around the park before going back to La Jolla. Joan took care of the children several times during her visit and Jeane wanted to do something special for her so she took her to her favorite fabric store and let her choose material and a pattern to make a skirt. When they got back to La Jolla, Jeane helped her lay out the pattern on the material, pin it down, and cut it out. Then she showed Joan how easy it was to use an electric sewing machine.

The two weeks went quickly and Joan boarded the train from San Diego to Los Angeles where she changed to another train to Denver, then east on the Rock Island Rocket to Norton, Kansas.

Curt's shop had run smoothly; nothing had changed during the month he was away. Chief Brock had kept everything just as Curt had planned. Curt's Radar Shop was important because of their photographic and radar work. Curt might be gone any time for a few days or weeks.

Soon after Curt was back in the shop, Chief Brock asked him if he would like to bring his family for a picnic at the Brocks home. Curt felt it was an honor to be invited and when they arrived they were welcomed by the whole Brock family. Their home sat back in a stand of palm trees and behind their house was a grove of lemon and orange trees. Ron Brock was able to keep everything in order at work and at home.

On the way home Jeane turned to Curt. "Was it unusual for us to visit the Brocks?"

"Yes, Jeane it was, but I consider Ron my best friend. He helped me get started last year. He was anxious for us to meet his family and see his home. I think it would be better if we don't talk about what we did today. The Navy prefers the officers associate with other officers."

In late August, Curt packed his bag and was gone. It didn't worry Jeane this time. She knew she would know where he was after she saw the other wives in a few days. Curt had become so cranky and demanding she thought it was nice when he was gone.

Jeane

When Joan left for home, Jeane called Faith again and this time she answered. "Faith, when did you get home from Illinois? I called last week but you weren't there. It seems like a long time since I've seen you." Faith interrupted Jeane and urged her to come for coffee. Jeane asked Connie if she would watch April and Danny and she didn't mind because the children were glad to be home and busy with Tinky and their friends.

Jeane and Faith exchanged news of the summer then Faith handed a small white envelope and handed it to Jeane. "These are tickets for the Leonard Bernstein concert in late September. We want you and your husband to join us for the concert and supper in our home later. Our guests will all be seated together at the concert. Basil and I often sponsor events for talented artists. You will enjoy Mr. Bernstein's concert, I'm sure. He will also be a guest in our home after the concert."

"Thank you, Faith. We have never attended anything like that. I'm sure you know Navy pay, even for officers is low. Curt and I are usually broke even though he is an electrical engineer specializing in communication. He feels he helps protect our country from the situation in Korea. He never tells me what he does. He says he is happy keeping his squadron's electronic equipment in perfect order, but I wonder why he has to be gone so much. Most of the Naval Officers believe they are helping save our country.

"We all know what everyone earns so no one pretends to have more. It is a good way to live if you like people. We are lucky; my mother buys most of our clothes and my dad gives me money. I don't mean to say we are hurting, but extra money is always welcome. I'm glad I can make most of the children's clothes and mine, too."

"Jeane, I understand, but do plan to come to the concert and supper; we really want you. If Curt is away, you come and ride with us. I don't have close friends here and I feel comfortable with you. We are both from the Midwest where people say what they think."

"Faith, is Basil away a lot? I don't ask questions, but sometimes I wonder. I have never even seen a picture of him."

"I don't talk much about Basil; I think you know he is a physicist. We lived in Las Alamos for several years in the early 1940s. I'm

Jeane

sure you know that is where the atomic bomb was developed and perfected. I'm like you, I never know what Basil is doing, just like you don't know where or what Curt is doing."

Faith stood up and smiled. "Let me run upstairs and get our wedding picture." She was gone only a minute when she came back with the picture. "Don't you think Basil is handsome? Yes, he is away a lot, but sometimes he is here when you come for coffee. Basil is not a friendly man. His parents are Russian and quite wealthy. Basil is their only child.

"They had planned to leave Russia and come to the United States for years before they finally came in 1914. They had invested their wealth in United States and British bonds and they had the earnings deposited in the United States and Swiss banks. By that time they were afraid to wait any longer. The Communists were becoming more powerful every day.

"Basil was two years old when the Markovitch family left St. Petersburg by train to Helsinki, Finland. There they boarded a ferry to Stockholm, Sweden. Their next step was on a train from Stockholm to Copenhagen then on to Bergen, Norway where they took a ferry to Harwich, England. They had left Russia in October when it was dark all but a few hours a day. Their last step was to take an ocean liner from Southampton, England, to New York. Their name was Markovitch, but at Ellis Island the man who registered them couldn't spell Markovitch so he shortened it to Marko. Basil grew up in New York and was educated at Harvard. His family still live on Park Avenue in New York City."

Faith smiled as she looked at their wedding picture, then she handed it to Jeane. "I met Basil when I was in my third year at the University of Illinois. I was taking organic chemistry and Basil was working on his doctorate in physics. He wanted some experience in teaching so he became an assistant professor in the chemistry department. I hated the sciences, but I was required to have five hours of chemistry for my degree in dietetics. Basil offered to help me, and I tried hard to learn. With his help I managed a C for the semester.

"When I graduated in 1940, I was only nineteen. Basil and I were married that summer in my parents' home. My parents knew

Jeane

Basil, but for some reason they were never comfortable with him. I heard my mother tell my grandmother he always looked fierce, but I knew he was really gentle. His eyes were sharp and seemed to bore into anyone he looked at. Mother told my grandmother she had never seen him smile. I guess he didn't understand the friendliness of the Illinois farmers.

"Over the years he has seemed intense about everything. After we were married he never visited my family again, but he expects me to visit his family with him at least twice a year."

"Faith, that doesn't seem fair."

"Jeane, it is fair. I'm about to tell you something I've never told anyone. In 1942 I became pregnant while we were living in Los Alamos. Basil and his parents didn't want our baby to be born anywhere but in New York City where one of Basil's cousins was an obstetrician. I was willing to do anything Basil wanted. When my time was near, Basil took me to New York to be with his family, but he had to go back to Los Alamos where he was needed.

"Our baby boy, Brian, was born in the Markos' home. Dr. Otto, Basil's cousin told me our son should be examined by a specialist who would come to our home. I thought that was strange but I didn't say anything. I thought our little boy was perfect! I could hardly believe it when I was told he was a Down's syndrome child and would never develop like other children. The tests proved this to be true.

"Basil came to New York and he told me Brian, our son, would have to be placed in a special home near New York where he would have the best care. Basil's parents would see him every few months, but he probably would never know them. Basil told me a child like Brian had been born to his cousin in Moscow before the Marko family came to New York.

"I wanted to take my baby home and care for him myself, but Basil refused. He wanted me to be available to do things with him. He told me I would never believe our son couldn't learn if he was with us. He felt this had happened because of the Marko genes. He told me he would never father another child. I cried for days. I was heartbroken. I had to agree or he would have divorced me. That was ten years ago, now I don't think of my son often. The reports we get from the home tell us the doctors knew what was

Jeane

best. Basil wants everything to be perfect. He loves me and he knows I still want to have another child, but he tells me it will never happen."

Jeane and Faith had been sitting on the kitchen balcony. When Faith stopped her story, Jeane could see she was crying. She dried her eyes and stood up, then she walked over to the railing on the balcony. She looked down for several minutes as the surf crashed against the rocks below. She brushed away the tears, then she looked up and smiled. She picked up the picture of Basil. "Jeane, wasn't Basil a handsome bridegroom?"

She didn't know what to say so she smiled and nodded. Faith still seemed caught up by the surf breaking on the rocks. She stared down over the side of the balcony. It was like she had forgotten Jeane was there.

Jeane smiled at Faith. "You two were a handsome couple." She picked up the picture and looked at it again. She was surprised when she saw that Basil was no taller than Faith, but he had broad shoulders, black hair, and eyes that were so intense it was hard to look away even in a picture. His hair was long and bushy, a style seldom seen in 1940. He wore horn-rimmed glasses and stared straight into the camera.

"Basil has changed very little in the past ten years. I am not sure he ever looks in the mirror. Today, he is here, but no one will see him before evening. We had this house built two years ago. It includes a laboratory in the basement. It has no windows and only one door that he keeps locked all the time. His laboratory is complete with a bathroom, air-conditioning, heat, and extra plumbing. He even has his own telephone. I have never been in that room. I believe he is the only person who has ever been in there.

"He is not friendly and he never wants to be interrupted when he is working. It is like he lives in a different world."

When Jeane left the Markos her head was spinning; what she had heard was almost unbelievable. She felt she knew things no one else knew, but Jeane would never talk about it.

After supper Jeane told Curt about their invitation to the concert and supper. He was furious. "Did you tell her we don't associate with Communists or Communist sympathizers no matter how much

Jeane

money they have? Are you trying to ruin my Navy career? You can do things other than be friends with Communists."

"Curt, I'm positive Faith is not a Communist."

"What do you know about Communism?" Curt was angry. "How do you know she isn't one?"

Jeane ignored him. She handed him the white envelope. "Curt, did I tell you Basil Marko worked at Las Alamos while they were perfecting the Atom Bomb. He is a physicist and he has taught at Cal Tech. I have never met him, but Faith told me his parents left Russia in 1914 to get away from the Communists. How can you believe he is a Communist?"

Curt looked at Jeane and shook his head. "Don't you know he has been on Senator McCarthy's list for several years? You still don't understand how the Navy works do you?

"<u>WE WILL NOT TAKE CHANCES</u>! If I am going to have a successful career in the Navy, you will not see that Communist again." Without telling Jeane, Curt had ordered a background security check on Basil Marko and his Communism. When the report came back, there were still questions because of the McCarthy report, but nothing else had been found.

He was angry with Jeane. He thought she simply must do what he told her, no matter what she said. He vowed he would have a successful career as a Naval Officer regardless of her independence! He said to himself, some day she may go too far and I will have to do something about it..

He glared at her. "Is going to this concert and supper worth my Navy career? You have no idea how Communism is spreading in this country. Even receiving this invitation could be bad for me. Think about it. Is that worth it?"

"Curt, I didn't know! Of course, no occasion is worth that. I would not do anything to harm your career. I don't always understand what I have done, but I want you to be happy with me. When I see Faith tomorrow, I will tell her we can't come. I'm sure she will understand."

Later after Curt and Jeane were in bed, Curt turned toward Jeane. "I know you are trying. I know you are bored with some of the officers' wives' activities and you never ask me anything about

Jeane

my work. I appreciate that."

"Curt, we both know we want you to have an opportunity to work in your field."

"I want you to know, Jeane, I'm leaving tomorrow. I will be gone a month. Like before, if anything happens call the skipper."

Jeane called Faith the next morning. "Curt will be out of town and he doesn't want me to go to the concert without him. Faith, it is hard for me to understand the secrecy Curt thinks is so important, but I try to do what he wants. Where I grew up there were few secrets, probably because the town was so small. If a teenager misbehaved, the parents knew about it before the culprit got home. For you I expect it was about the same."

"Jeane, you're right, but I am older and I have married a man who has been in highly secret work all the time. You learn to accept it because we wouldn't understand. I'm sure your Curt is a conscientious young man. He may be an admiral some day and you will know you helped."

"Faith, you don't know how much I appreciate what you have said to me this morning. I'm not used to having to think before I speak. Remember that Curt said I talked too much when we paid our first courtesy call on the skipper."

"Yes, I remember your telling me. My best advice to you, Jeane, is to support your husband. Sometimes it isn't easy. I never talk about it, but you must know my husband's name is on Senator McCarthy's list of suspected Communists. There was never anything that showed his name should have been there.

"That was the reason he built this laboratory. He hopes to be a consultant again. He feels sorry for the fine entertainers who are suffering because McCarthy has them on his list. Now I see McCarthy is having library books burned if they hint of capitalization. He insists every book about the Russian czar must be destroyed and he claims the librarians hide books that should be burned. He claims most college professors are sympathetic to the life style of the Communists. A person can be fired even if he has gone to a Communist meeting just once."

Curt came home at the end of September. He was pleased to find that Jeane had been elected president of the Miramar Officers'

Jeane

Wives' Club and she had decided training the Sigma Kappa Pledges was taking too much time away from her family. She smiled at everyone and supported every Officers' Wives' Club activity. She helped with Danny's Sunday School class and volunteered to be a room mother in April's second grade.

During the fall, Jeane never mentioned Faith at home, but Curt remained bitter. When they went to the Miramar Officers' Club on Friday night, he spent his time at the bar near Carol Conway. She was never far from her Scotch, and she demanded the attention of the young officers, especially Curt. He laughed and teased her as long as her husband wasn't there. Jeane noticed Cdr. Conway spent most of his evenings bragging about his golf game. Jeane was never sure what she was expected to do. Often she sat alone in a corner or in their car most of the evening.

All the McLyrres were excited. The Browns would be there for Christmas and the children were counting the days. Both Curt and Jeane were disappointed when Curt drew officer of the day duty on New Year's Eve. They had been invited to several New Year's Eve parties and they were anxious to go to all of them. Three of the parties were with people in their building. Curt insisted she accept them, and since Connie was alone he suggested the two women go together to all of the parties. April and Danny would spend the night with their grandparents in their apartment.

1953—Happy New Year

Connie's mother and aunt had spent Christmas with her and had gone back to Chicago on December 28. Connie was ready for a party so she invited everyone in their building to come to her apartment at five o'clock on New Year's Eve. The two families upstairs in the building wanted to continue the party idea. Connie decided to serve only orange blossoms at her party since they were easy to make. Jeane was anxious to try them so she went to Connie's early and have her first drink. She had never tasted anything so good. She was helping Connie serve and found it was easy to refill her cup. In less than thirty minutes she was dizzy. She went to her

Jeane

apartment to take some aspirin and decided she must be coming down with a cold.

When Jeane got back, everyone was ready to go up to the Monroes. Dr. Monroe was a dentist, and his favorite drink was a martini. Jeane had never heard of a martini, but she thought the first one tasted awful. When Dr. Monroe refilled her glass she thought it was much better. Jeane and Connie were a little foggy when they left Clarimar for the Conways' party. Jeane drove slowly down back streets until they were close to the skipper's house. Connie wasn't seeing well.

"Jeane, do you think it is foggy this evening? I rolled down my window, but it didn't help. Maybe we are out in a boat in the fog."

"Connie, you're right! Maybe we should get in the mood for the next party." Connie started singing "Row, row, row your boat" and Jeane joined in. Fortunately, the Conways lived near Clarimar and there was no traffic on the road. Connie and Jeane continued singing until they reached the Conways, but neither of them were quite themselves.

Jeane had not forgotten her experience at the skipper's house so she was very careful. When Carol Conway greeted them, Jeane smiled and introduced Connie. She wanted Curt to be proud of her so she drank only the punch she saw on the table. She thought it was fruit juice. After a half hour, Connie and Jeane thanked their hostess and said they needed to get home and check on their children.

They walked into the night air and stood still. "Connie, does everything seem to be swaying, even the moon?"

"Jeane, I'm not sure what I see. Are you sure that punch wasn't spiked?" The friends held on to each other until they found their car all alone down the block. Connie was weaving as she put her hand on the car to steady herself. "Now, which of us is going to drive home?"

Jeane was fighting with her stomach, but she was determined to get home safely. "I will do it, Connie. I know the way. I will drive near the curb and I'll stop at each corner and wait until we can across the street." Jeane was dizzy, but determined not to ruin their car. All four car windows were open and the women watched the curb as they crept back to their apartments. It was hard to stay beside the curb in Clarimar. Jeane stopped the car, got out, and

Jeane

walked around the car three times. She nodded her head and told Connie they were less than a block from home.

Jeane parked the car and staggered up to the front door, where she waited for Connie. The last party of the evening was upstairs in Nora Brady's apartment. She met Connie and Jeane at the door. "Ladies, I have never seen either of you like this before. How about a roast beef sandwich right now?" Nora had good solid food and soft drinks. Jeane left the party at ten minutes before midnight and went to her apartment to wait for Curt's call. She sat on the floor with the telephone and an empty waste basket, just in case.

Curt called on the stroke of midnight. "Happy New Year, Jeane. I hope this is the first of many for us here in California. Jeane, are you listening? Jeane, what's the matter?" Jeane should never have sat on the floor. She put down the telephone, grabbed a chair leg and stood up. "Happy New Year, Curt! I'm sorry we are not together, but I am not feeling very well. I guess I have the flu." She hiccuped loudly and smiled. She had not understood a word Curt said.

"Jeane, YOU ARE DRUNK! Don't you know that? Can't I trust you at all? Did you go to the skipper's party? I hope you didn't make a fool of yourself there. I have never known you to take more than two drinks; I am truly disappointed!"

By then Jeane was crying and sick. "Curt I really didn't know the punch was spiked. I drank orange blossoms at Connie's, martinis at Monroes, and punch at the Conways. You told me to go to all of our parties. I'm sorry but I feel like I better get off this telephone."

Curt was furious. He had never expected this from Jeane. She seldom drank at all but now she was drunk at the skipper's house. He came home early on New Year's Day and made a pot of coffee, then he sat down at the table. Jeane heard the noise in the kitchen and she slipped on her robe and slippers and went to the dining room table. She could tell by the expression on Curt's face he was still furious.

"Curt, I feel awful. I never want to see another orange blossom in my life!" He glared at her, but he didn't say a word.

About eleven her parents came with April and Danny. Jeane smiled and wished them Happy New Year. She had a splitting headache, but she had lunch ready. Her mother thought Jeane looked a little pale and Curt seemed to be in a bad mood. Jeane admitted

Jeane

she wasn't feeling well. Her mother decided the children should spend the afternoon with them in their apartment. Curt was still angry, but the Browns ignored him.

This year the Browns would be there all of January. Jay Fawcett owned Jay's Cabinet Shop now and Maurice had very little to do.

One evening when Maurice and Curt were watching the evening news the reporter talked about Communism and McCarthy's lists. Curt turned to Maurice, "How did that program compare with those in Kansas? Are those people concerned with the growth of Communism?"

"Curt, no one I know is the least bit concerned about Communism and McCarthy. In my opinion he has found something that makes him feel important and it gives him publicity. You know he is an alcoholic, don't you? He is afraid he won't be elected again if he doesn't keep people believing he is smoking out Communists.

"At home there is very little interest in what happens outside of the Midwest. We feel secure and think we will be safe for many years, if not forever. Russia talks big. They keep reminding us how successful Communism is for them and how successful it would be for us. None of us believe it. We may be wrong, but in Kansas we are more concerned about snow and sleet during the winter so we will have a big wheat crop."

Curt could hardly believe what his father-in-law had said. "I think we should watch those Russians. They claim it is the Russians who converted the Koreans and the Chinese to Communism and now Russia wants to rule the world. Russia is dangerous, and the Baltic countries and most of Spain have joined them."

Maurice was surprised with how much Curt had told him about Communism. He thought of how little interest there was in world news in Kansas.

"Jeane feels like you do, Dad. She isn't interested in learning what is happening around the world. Here we can see and hear it in the newspapers and on television. The Russians claim to have perfected an atomic bomb and they claim their v-bombs can reach any city in the United States. They talk of how soon all the world will be Communist. We know Communism is spreading, but in my opinion we have to stop it now. I am glad the people in Washington

Jeane

are investigating."

Jeane and her parents watched the inauguration of Dwight David Eisenhower on television.. It had been a long time since the country had had a Republican in the White House. The public felt Eisenhower was a fair and honest man. There were celebrations around the world; it seemed that almost everywhere General Eisenhower was admired and respected. Most of the public looked forward to peace for the next four years.

The picture on the television screen was small and fuzzy, but Maurice enjoyed it. He decided that when he got home he would buy the best television that would work in Norton. He knew they would have to have a big antenna put on their chimney to get decent reception.

The Browns started home at the end of January. Jeane picked up Tinky and told her how glad she was to be alone with her family again, and Tinky started purring. No matter how much Jeane loved and wanted her parents to come, but Curt relaxed when they were gone.

Jeane wanted to be a good Navy wife, but she found it was hard. Curt insisted she smile and he told her every senior officer's wife expected to be complimented. Jeane learned to use double-talk. "You always know exactly what is right for you. I wish I could do that." It was not easy for Jeane, but she had to do it for Curt to make his promotions. Jeane kept reading *The Navy Wife*. It said a wife should always put her husband first and be sure to speak to every senior officer and his wife.

Only a week after her parents left California her mother called and she was crying. Jeane asked her mother, what was wrong. "Jeane, I'm all right, but your Grandfather Graham is critically ill in the hospital. He has pneumonia. When we got home, we found Gilbert had left a note on our backdoor to let us know. As soon as I saw the note, I went to the hospital.

"Jeane, he is very sick. They are keeping him sedated, but he is not breathing as he should. The shots they gave him haven't helped. Don't even consider coming home to see him. He wouldn't know you. When I see Gilbert I will know more.

"After I saw my dad, I asked the nurse what had happened.

Jeane

She told me a farmer from Almena was going home about nine o'clock last Saturday night and saw him lying in a ditch about ten miles north of Almena. He was unconscious; the farmer and his wife got him into their car and brought him to the hospital. Pray for him."

Jeane was stunned. She couldn't believe something like that could have happened in Almena. She knew her grandfather was old and confused, but she thought anyone who had seen him outdoors on a cold night would have taken him home or called Gilbert.

Less than a week later, Jeane had another call from her mother. "Your Grandad Graham died early this morning. He had been in an oxygen tent since I talked to you last week. He became weaker every day. I wish I knew what happened, but maybe it is better this way. I spent every night at the hospital with him after I got home."

She wrote Jeane and told her no one knew what had happened, but when people asked about him she said he had pneumonia and it didn't respond to medication. The *Almena Plaindealer* ran a news story that told how Bert Graham had been a respected businessman. It continued by saying how much business he had brought to Almena with his livestock, farms, elevators, and stockyards. No one would ever forget his smile and his big laugh.

Ethel missed her father. She wondered how anyone could have taken him out of town when it was so cold. In the letter she told Jeane she never discussed anything about their father's death with Gilbert. It seemed too painful for either of them.

She tried not to think about it. She was sure her dad would have wanted it that way. She knew more than anyone that he wasn't himself any more. She was sure there were rumors about what happened, but since she was in Norton she didn't have to listen. She missed her father and thought how could anyone have taken him out of town when it was so cold. He hadn't been himself since his fall from the railroad car the past summer. Now he was gone. She hoped everyone would remember him as a happy, healthy man who loved everyone.

Ethel saved his obituary from the Norton County Champion for Jeane and her children. It said Bert Graham was born August 7, 1878 in Norton County. He had lived there until his death, February 18, 1953 in the Norton Hospital. It told how he had unfaltering faith

Jeane

in Norton County. The obituary said his father, Gil, brought his family to Norton County in July 1878 where he homesteaded in Grant Township. The Grahams farmed but they preferred buying and selling cattle, hogs, and sheep in the big city markets like Kansas City or Omaha. They were among the first livestock buyers in Norton County. The article told of his fair dealing. Ethel hoped he would be remembered that way.

In the next letter Ethel told Jeane there would still be Graham cattle in the pasture of the homestead just as before their father died. Gilbert said they should not settle the estate for at least a year and he would run the Graham cattle and keep the elevator open.

Jeane didn't think much about her grandfather. She was so busy with all the Miramar wives' activities. Kansas seemed far away.

Jeane wrote to her mother more often. She knew there was very little she could do, but she knew her letters helped a little.

In March Cdr. Conway had orders to the Naval Air Station in Penscola, Florida, and he was to report early in May. Jeane was anxious for them to be gone. All her life she would remember that courtesy call in 1951. Transfer orders were usually written during the summer months when the officers' children were not in school. Most tours of duty were for three years. In the Navy people never said good-bye, they just said good luck. Their paths would cross again.

The ceremony was in late April. Jeane's friends had told her this was a time for parties. She didn't know what to expect. One of her friends explained first there was a parade on the parade grounds. There was a reviewing stand for local politicians and their wives. In the rows of seats behind the guests were seats for the Naval Officers and their families. The enlisted men paraded back and forth in front of the officers and dignitaries. Everyone who watched wore their best dresses, hats, gloves, and dress shoes. The officers were in full dress blue uniforms or white dress uniforms in hot weather. Jeane wondered how many years the same ceremonies had been carried out across the country.

After the ceremonies everyone went to the Miramar Officers' Club where the skipper turned over his squadron to the new skipper,

Jeane

Cdr. Harold Howell. The Conways stayed only long enough to introduce the new skipper.

Next was the welcome aboard for Cdr. Howell and his wife, Marjorie. She was about five feet tall with short black curly hair and big blue eyes. The Howells had three children between the ages of four and ten.

Cdr. Howell announced that instead of the courtesy calls they would give a cocktail party. Jeane was delighted, she still remembered their call on the Conways. Now they were gone and she could quit thinking about them. When she thought about that day she realized that was the day Curt became a different person.

After that courtesy call he never mentioned anything about his work and his life when he was away from home. Jeane wondered if he would ever relax and be like he once was. All of this past year he had been secretive.

Jeane had avoided Carol Conway since that first day for fear she would say the wrong thing again, and Curt had made up for Jeane by giving Carol more attention at the bar. Often he would spend most of the evening at the bar and Carol expected it. She expected Curt to be close so they would drink, dance, or talk. Carol knew Curt was a good dancer and she constantly reminded him how good they looked on the dance floor. Jeane hated seeing them dance together until it was a relief when Curt packed his bag and went away again.

Jeane was glad the Conways were gone and she was careful of the new skipper's wife, but she was so friendly and relaxed they became friends.

Curt left early in April. He wrote Jeane short notes and sent them through the skipper. He told her he was lonely and he missed his family, but he was very busy. The letters told her nothing. After receiving one of those letters Jeane needed to talk to someone. She called Faith and ask if she could come over.

She was in tears when she rang Faith's doorbell. She handed Faith the letter Curt had written. "Faith, do you think Curt will ever be like the other officers? I never mention that I don't know where he is or when he will be home. It is hard for me to understand this secrecy he claims is so important."

"Jeane, I think Curt is eager to be a success in the Navy. He

Jeane

will not take any chances. I remember you telling me his father has never approved of what he did. Maybe he is trying to get approval from his father. Does Curt write him?"

"I don't think so. His father never approved of Curt's choices. His father was angry when Curt refused the appointment to West Point that had been arranged for him. His father never approved of me. Remember, we were married during WW II. My folks were hurt, but they have always helped us. When we were in college at Colorado University the McLyrres gave us venison that was so strong I couldn't eat it. They have never come to visit us even once before Curt was called to active duty. You could be right, but Curt always insists he doesn't care what his father says."

Curt seemed happy when he was home. He saw that Jeane had learned to put the Navy first. She helped with Danny's Sunday School class while Curt slept. He lay awake nights and tried to find a way to stop her from seeing Faith Marko.

For Jeane, Happy Hour on Friday night was miserable. She tried to get Curt to go alone, but he told her that it would make him look bad, He would not let her stay home with the children so she sat alone, at the officers' club. She had never thought Curt would cheat on her, buy now she wasn't sure. She didn't mind the attention he gave the other senior officers' wives. Now Carol was gone and she could quit worrying.

While Curt was away in May, a new executive officer, John Martin, and his family, joined the squadron, and they rented a Clarimar Apartment near the McLyrres. Their two children were the age of April and Danny. The Martins were experienced in Navy life and always made friends quickly. John Martin realized how much Curt had contributed to the squadron. The Martins had come from Jacksonville, Florida where it was hot and muggy all summer so they were happy to be in California.

The first Friday the Martins were in their apartment, Doris called Jeane and invited all of the McLyrre family to come for pizza. Jeane was delighted to have an invitation that included their children. The evening was such a success that Friday night pizza become routine. The men would go out and bring back hot freshly

Jeane

baked pizzas from a small shop near Clarimar.

One evening in May Doris told Jeane she was going to drive east in June. She asked Jeane if she would like to drive to Kansas at the same time. She explained that they would both drive their family cars, Doris to Kentucky and Jeane to Kansas. Jeane didn't comment, but after they got home that night Jeane asked Curt if he thought she could drive all the way to Kansas. He didn't answer, he wasn't pleased, but he said they should think about it. After a few weeks Curt agreed it would be safe if the wives stayed together.

Jeane was worried about the three or four days to drive to Kansas. She had never changed a tire or put gas in the tank or water in the radiator of the car. Now she would have to drive even when she was tired. She wished Curt had said no when Doris asked her. Now she had to drive across country with only the children. It was more than two thousand miles they would be alone. She kept telling herself she couldn't say no now.

Jeane never followed the Navy wife routine of golf, tennis, and lunch at the Miramar officers' club. She would rather visit museums and explore the history of San Diego. She loved to haunt antique shops, even though she had very little extra money to spend. She enjoyed the small art galleries in the Green Dragon Colony, a part of La Jolla near the cove. Faith enjoyed the same things so they went together, but since Christmas Faith had seemed nervous and detached.

In June when Jeane called Faith, she was told Faith was in Illinois. Two weeks later when she called, a strange voice answered and said she would give Faith her message. Jeane wondered if Faith was there.

Curt was happier when Jeane spent time with Connie. He wished she would not spend any time with Faith Marko. He still worried about the possibilities of Basil being an underground Communist.

Jeane hated to go to Kansas without talking to Faith, but she called the Markos several times and was told Faith wasn't there. Now it was time for Doris and Jeane to start. The women were to stay close together. At the last minute Doris's cousin from Los Angeles decided to go east with them and Doris was delighted to have company on the long trip.

Both women had their cars packed and ready to start at three

Jeane

o'clock the morning of June 20. Doris had done this trip before, Jeane would follow her. Jeane made a bed for the children in the back of the station wagon. She was nervous about the trip, but she wouldn't admit it.

They arrived in Las Vegas in the afternoon the first day. Doris told Jeane they were going to stay there overnight. She assumed Jeane and her children would do the same. Doris said her cousin wanted to try her luck in the casinos.

Jeane was shocked. "Doris, I don't have the money to stay here; I didn't count on stopping this soon. I knew we were going to travel U.S.66. I have very little experience with driving alone, but I'm sure we will be fine."

Doris got out maps and gave them to her. "I should have told you that when my cousin went with me last year we stopped here. I'm sorry you want to go on alone. I would be glad to loan you extra money."

"I don't want to stop now. I'm anxious to get home. I don't want to go in a casino." Jeane and the children got in her car, she folded the map, waved, and they were gone. They followed U.S. 66 east until dark, and then she stopped at an old motel that was clean and cheap.

Jeane got the children up early and they were on the road by six the next morning. All three of them sang songs and watched for white horses as they drove. Jeane told them the horses were a sign of good luck. About nine o'clock Jeane felt the car swerve and she knew something was wrong; she stopped on the side of the road. She got out and walked around the car. She saw the left rear tire was ruined.

Alone on Route 66

Two cars whizzed by and kept going. Jeane stood behind in back of her car almost in tears. She wished she had stayed in California. Very soon she saw a man walking toward the car. As he got closer she realized it was an Indian; she told the children to stay in the car.

He was wearing Levis, cowboy boots, and a Stetson. He was

Jeane

weaving and smiling as he came closer. He looked her up and down. "Good morning, Miss. I see you have a problem. Would you like me to help you?"

Jeane was shaking. "Would you? I have never changed a tire. We have a spare tire and jack in the back of the station wagon." The man grinned as he looked at Jeane, but when Jeane opened the back of the station wagon he saw the children and he looked down at his feet. Then he started looking for the car jack. Jeane took the hand of each child and walked down into the ditch to wait.

The Indian had trouble with the jack, but finally he blocked both front and back wheels so the car couldn't move. When he tried to get the spare tire out of the car, Jeane saw his knuckles were bleeding, but he was still smiling. Jeane told the children to stay where they were, and she went to the back of the car and loosened the lug bolt on the spare tire. After the Indian saw how Jeane had loosened the bolt he finished and took the tire out. He had gotten the jack to hold up the wheel with the ruined tire so he could put on the spare. His hands were bleeding and his Levis were covered with dirt.

Jeane took a ten dollar bill out of her purse.

The Indian stepped back, "No, no. You should not be out in this desert. You are a brave girl. Do you know there are dangerous men along this highway? I'm glad I could help you. God speed, little girl! Let God protect you on your way." He walked away, then turned and waved as he heard the car start. Jeane was still shaking, but she had to go on.

In Albuquerque she bought a new tire and had it put on, then she went to their friends, the Owens. Jeane had written them before her trip east and when they replied they had urged Jeane and the children to spend the night with them.

Jeane waited until all the children had gone out to play before she told the Owens about her day. Jim was shocked. "Jeane, this doesn't sound like Curt. Why didn't he come with you?" Jeane said she expected to drive through with a woman friend, but it didn't work out. Jim told her never to drive east on U.S.66 alone. He told her there had been car thefts and one murder already this year on U.S.66.

Jeane

By the time Jeane got to Norton, she decided not to tell her parents what had happened, but the next morning when she got up she heard April telling her grandmother about their adventure in the desert. Later, Ethel cornered Jeane and insisted on hearing all the details.

The children looked forward to their visits to Norton, and this year they could walk to the drugstore alone. April had two friends near the Browns and Danny had friends almost next door.

Every summer was the same. Jeane went to visit her Grandmother Brown alone. The children felt strange in their Great-Grandmother Brown's house with the big oak table, a spring rocker, and the old-fashioned wall clock that chimed every thirty minutes. Jeane remembered all of them for as long as she could remember. Her children had never seen anyone dress like their great-grandmother who wore dresses loose and down to her ankles. When they started home April asked her mother if her great grandmother was a witch, she said her book had a picture of a witch that looked like her great grandmother.

After that the children didn't go with Jeane, and she enjoyed her grandmother more. The two weeks went quickly with visits to relatives and old friends, then Jeane was ready to go back to California. The Browns planned to keep the children the rest of the summer, then bring the children to California in time for them to start school.

Jeane met Curt's plane in Denver. They drove to Hugo, Colorado, where they planned to visit there for two or three days. Curt and his father had never been close, but he adored his mother. Curt's father asked him many questions about his work at Miramar which Curt couldn't answer. Then Curt's father started telling Curt about his brother, Charles, who had just been promoted early. Now he was a Lt. Commander.

Curt's father smiled at him. "What do you think now? Don't you wish you had gone to West Point. You don't need to answer. You refused that appointment because you wanted to show me. Look, now you are married and have two children. You had better be careful. I will not help you with any of your debts. Ask the Browns if you need money." Luther McLyrre sat back with a satisfied smirk. Curt didn't answer, but they left Hugo the next

Jeane

morning for Denver.

Curt was steaming. "Jeane, what did I do to get that lecture last night? I don't think my father has ever been proud of me. He has thrown my brother in my face since high school. Why doesn't he stop?"

"Curt, forget what he said. You know yourself; you can't be pushed around by anybody. Now let's look forward to the next week when we can do what we want. We will be in Denver before noon and you know we always have fun with Carroll and Bob Adams. Let's treat them to dinner and dancing at the Top of the Park." That was the place to go when we came to Denver for your Naval Reserve weekends and we stayed with Carroll and Bob and her parents. The four of us always had fun."

Curt looked at Jeane and smiled. "OK, we are going to have a vacation of our own until September." After two days with the Adams, they drove west on U.S. 40 into the Rocky Mountains. Their first night out of Denver they spent in Glenwood Springs. Their next stop was Salt Lake City, then they continued west past the Great Salt Lake and through Elko, Nevada west on U.S. 40 and on into Reno late that night. Since they had a limited budget they left Reno without seeing the gambling houses.

When the Browns decided to keep the children the rest of the summer, Curt suggested they take a slow trip to California. Jeane ordered a set of travel books that were a bonus from Book-of-the-Month Club. Curt and Jeane studied the books and learned what would be interesting for them to see. They followed US 40 out of Reno, where it joined U.S. 395 south to Virginia City.

Jeane and Curt were excited when they reached Virginia City. Jeane had learned that both silver and gold had been mined there as early as the Civil War. The city had been built of stone and restored with the help of the Works Progress Administration that was active during the 1930s.

In the Crystal Bar they found the Ace Gambling Casino. The roulette wheel was six foot across. Slot machines stood along one wall. Jeane put five dollars in the nickel machine and lost it all. Curt put in the same amount and won enough for their day and a room that night. The Miners' Dance Hall and Pipers Opera House were ornate with red velvet curtains and gold tassels on the stage curtain.

Jeane

St. Mary's on the Mountain was one of the most beautiful Catholic Church Jeane had ever seen. The interior had rosewood pillars and a powder blue ceiling. They were told by the guide it was copied from a church in Rome. There were old mansions and a huge cemetery where many claims were settled with pistols. Visiting there was like time had stood still. All the people who worked there wore costumes from the 1860s.

After lunch they drove on U.S. 395 to Carson City, Nevada where they turned into Yosemite National Park. It was a beautiful drive through high mountains and clear icy blue lakes, then back to U.S. 395 south to Bishop, California and a motel where they could see the mountains.

After driving five days, Curt were anxious to get home. The next morning they were on the road by three, since they had to cross the Mojave desert before the heat of the day. Inyokern was where the U.S. Navy had increased its experimental development program of new weapons after World War II. It was still 150 miles to San Bernardino, so they decided to stay in Inyokern. The next morning at four they got up in the dark and headed into the desert one more time. At noon they reached San Bernardino and had lunch before the last leg of the journey. Both Jeane and Curt were exhausted.

As they drove into the Clarimar Apartments, they felt they were home When they unlocked their door there was a note from Connie. Her husband, Jim, had surprised her and was home to stay. He was again assigned to Balboa Naval Hospital and he had two weeks leave before he reported for duty, so they had flown to Chicago to visit their relatives. Connie had added that Faith had called and wanted to know when Jeane would be home, and Tinky was being cared for by Catherine Holder.

The next morning Jeane called Faith after Curt went to the base. Faith answered on the first ring. It sounded like she was crying. "Faith, I want to come over right now."

When Jeane saw her, she was shocked. Faith had lost weight and her shoulders curled inward like she was protecting herself. It made her look small and lost. Her whole face was puffy, as though she had been crying for weeks. Her eyes looked dead as she stared

Jeane

into space. She was dressed in a faded clean cotton dress. Her hair fell straight around her face.

"Jeane, I'm so glad you're back. Basil has been called to Washington again. The Atomic Energy Commission, AEC, wants to do further interrogation. They decided that he was a security risk because of his refusal to work on the H-bomb.

"He has started another appeal and will try to find some proof that hasn't been used before. The committee stated there was no doubt of his loyalty to this country, but as long as he supported the policies of people in the entertainment field he would have trouble proving he is not a Communist. I don't understand how this happened. I'm sure the committee knows his parents left Russia because of their fear of Communism. I think those people in Washington must be crazy."

Faith had tears in her eyes. "I needed someone to talk to. The people Basil and I know are not my friends; I could never talk to any of them. Most of them are selfish and self-centered. They only look at what shows, their big homes, their designer clothes, and the two Mercedes in their driveway. Those things mean nothing to me. I know you and I don't need those things; we were taught not to show off. While you were away, I was lonely since Basil was in Washington and I needed help so I called Father Glasson and he came here to see me. We had tea on the balcony and I felt like a different person. He told me I would be better if I found something just for me. He suggested our Altar Guild at St. James-by-the Sea. He said the ladies were eager to help anyone and they would welcome me."

"I'm glad you called him. Faith, I think he's right. He said if you helped someone away from this house, you would make new friends. I have always thought those Altar Guild ladies looked so peaceful. I think all of us should give more to our church. I know this will be hard for you, but just remember other ladies at St. James have had problems, too. Will you volunteer?"

"Jeane, would you go with me? It has been so long since I've done anything but sit in this house and feel sorry for myself."

"I will go with you for awhile, but if I can't for some reason, call Father Glasson. He will help you."

"Faith, I didn't tell you earlier, but when I didn't hear from you

Jeane

in March I called here. A woman who sounded young answered the telephone and said you had gone to Illinois. She didn't even ask my name."

"Let's go out on the balcony. Do you mind?"

Jeane didn't know what to say. She knew Faith was upset. She looked toward the ocean, then turned toward Jeane. "Yes, I did go to Illinois, but I stayed only a week. I wasn't aware there was anyone in the house."

"Faith, I kept calling and all I got were brief messages. Somehow I felt there was something wrong. I didn't know what to do; I thought maybe Basil was back in Washington. Faith, could someone have been in here trying to prove that Basil was a Communist?"

"I don't think so. I haven't told you everything." Faith stood up and gripped the railing on the balcony as she stared at the rocks below. She was crying, Jeane put her arms around her and led her into the kitchen.

"Jeane, I have been sick, very sick. Three months ago Basil had a call from his father. Brian was dead; he tried to stand alone and fell head first down the stairs. He was dead when they found him.

"Basil told me, yet I couldn't accept it. I wanted to go to my son, but it was all over, Brian had been buried in the family plot in New York. I felt guilty. I was sure if he had been with us he would be alive and happy. I didn't want to live. One morning I went out on the balcony and tried to crawl over the railing, but Basil stopped me; he insisted he couldn't live without me.

"He arranged for me to have medical help, but I didn't want any help. I wanted to end my life, but I couldn't. Basil knew one of the best psychiatric doctors in New York, Margaret Handel. He knew her at Columbia University when they were both students there. She came to our home and examined me. Basil was home then and he spent time with me every day. He told me Dr. Handel specialized in mental illness, and she was willing to come here and take care of me while he was in Washington. He didn't want me alone with just a nurse.

"Basil had called Father Glasson and told him of Brian's death. Father Glasson came that afternoon. He told me he knew what it

71

Jeane

was like to lose someone you loved. After that he came every week to remind me that God loved me. I was so depressed I just sat and listened. As I got better, I noticed sometimes he seemed quiet and a little sad. Once I asked him what was wrong, but he just shook his head. He kept telling me my life was not over. He repeated when I was stronger he wanted me to work with the Altar Guild."

"Faith, does Basil need you?"

"I'm not sure; sometimes I wonder if Basil is tired of my poor health and my begging for a baby. When Dr. Handel was here, Basil didn't work in his laboratory. Now it seems he is not here even when he is away from the house. I know nothing about what he does here in La Jolla, but now he seldom spends long days working in his laboratory. I think he's avoiding me."

"You are a strong woman, Faith. This has been a terrible time for you, but now you are better. Do you think you could volunteer to work in the church? I would like to, but I need to be home with Danny. Your friendship has made me appreciate my own life. You must start leading a life that helps you be happy. I know your church is important to you."

Jeane still worried about Faith, but now she was expecting her children and her parents in September. Her mother's favorite cousins, Orval and Grace Stewart, were coming with them. When they arrived, Jeane wanted to show them all the places she liked best in San Diego. She started with the Mexican Village in Old Town and lunch in Ramona's Wedding House's garden. Next they took a ferry ride across to the island to Coronado; on their way back to La Jolla she showed them Father Serra's Mission Church that was a museum now. On another day they visited the Cabrillo Lighthouse at the point beyond Point Loma.

On Saturday Curt drove everybody to Los Angeles. Everyone wanted to visit the RKO Studios where so many cowboy movies were made and they saw Roy Rogers. When they left the studio, they drove around Hollywood using a map that showed where the movie stars lived. Later they had supper in the famous Farmer's Market.

They found a motel in Long Beach near where they took a day ferry to Catalina Island. The ferry took two hours to cross to Catalina, but it seemed like being on a real cruise. When they docked at

Jeane

Catalina they explored until lunch time. After lunch they walked around the town near the wharf until time for the return trip to Long Beach.

It was evening when they reached Long Beach and almost ten o'clock before they reached La Jolla. The McLyrres said good-bye to the Browns and the Stewarts, since they were anxious to start north early Monday morning en route to the state of Washington where they would visit Orval's sister and Ethel's friend.

Two weeks after school started, April awakened with a headache and she was slightly nauseous. Danny had cramps and didn't want to get up. Jeane kept them both home the next two days. Danny was still throwing up on Wednesday morning but by Thursday morning he felt fine. April still had a low grade temperature and felt no better. Jeane called Connie and asked if her husband, Doctor Jim, would check April before he went to the hospital.

When he came he said, "Jeane, why didn't you call me sooner? You know I never mind checking your children." He looked at April and took her pulse and temperature. He listened to her heart and finally checked every joint in her body.

When he came out of April's room he told Jeane he wanted to see April at Balboa Hospital for further tests this morning. He said Connie would look after Danny. Jeane got April out of bed and helped her dress, then they drove to the hospital. While April was being examined, Jeane called Curt and told him they were at the hospital where Dr. Jim was having tests done on April. Curt arrived in less than thirty minutes.

Curt found Jeane in the waiting room. A nurse had just told her they were running more tests. Curt was impatient, he demanded to know why more tests had to be run. Jeane sat as though she was in a trance. She realized this fall there were more cases of polio across the country than ever before, but she thought San Diego had had only a few cases yet. Curt fumed while they waited.

An hour later Doctor Jim came out and asked them to step into his office. "Jeane, I am glad you asked me to examine April this morning. What I have to tell you is frightening, but you must know she has poliomyelitis. I am sure you know something about it. I was suspicious this morning, but I hoped I was wrong. Now you must take her to the San Diego County Hospital where they have facilities

Jeane

for children with polio. Balboa only has facilities for adults. We will call and alert the hospital you are bringing April and the test results. That hospital has the top polio specialist in this area.

Shock

Curt went for the car, as a nurse wheeled April out the front door. Jeane walked beside her. Curt had directions to the hospital, which was less than fifteen minutes away. They were met at the emergency room doors with a wheelchair for April. They took the test results and gave Curt the papers to fill out for April to be admitted.

The hospital staff worked quickly. The doctor in charge told Curt and Jeane they were welcome to spend as much time with April as they could. The doctor believed a child of eight would do better if she wasn't alone and frightened. After April ate a little of her lunch, she dropped off to sleep.

Curt and Jeane went home and Jeane called her parents. "Mother, we have bad news; this afternoon April was admitted to San Diego County Hospital. She has polio. She didn't seem very sick, but this morning I asked Doctor Jim, Connie's husband, to examine her because she had been home for three days and wasn't getting any better. He suspected polio and had me bring her to Balboa Hospital for tests. There are very few cases here now, but no one knows how anyone gets polio.

"I know you are exhausted. Did you get home yesterday? I will call you when we know more."

"Jeane, we are tired but you need us. Your dad heard the conversation and said to tell you we will fly from Denver tomorrow morning to be there with you."

Jeane handed the telephone to Curt. "Do you want to call your folks?"

"I guess we should, but if I know my father he won't do one thing."

Curt was right. When he called his father he was told that school had just opened and he absolutely had to be there. He said he was sorry, but it was probably not serious. He said the Browns

Jeane

were retired, let them come.

Curt was angry, Jeane was crying. "Jeane, that man who considers himself my father is the most selfish man who ever lived. I don't care whether I ever see him again."

The next morning Curt took Jeane to the hospital, then he went to Miramar to asked for emergency leave. When he returned to the hospital, Jeane was in the waiting room outside April's room. She was pale and shaking.

"Curt, when I got here this morning April was in an iron lung. The night nurse came out in the hall and told me April had had a very bad strangulation during the night and they were lucky to have pulled her through. They need our permission to perform a tracheotomy as soon as possible." The nurse told them that if she had another attack like the one she had last night it could help save her life.

The tracheotomy was done at noon. Curt walked the floor. He accused Jeane of not getting help for April. He accused her of talking to Faith and neglecting their daughter. Curt kept Jeane in tears. He told her she was a poor mother. He accused the Browns of taking her into a dirty motel when they brought the children home.

Jeane walked away from Curt when she saw they were taking April back to her iron lung. She went into the bathroom and washed her face with cold water before she went to April. She could put her hand through a hole in the side of the iron lung where she could reach April's hand. She smiled when she squeezed April's hand. She couldn't talk after the surgery. They had told Jeane even if she couldn't speak the operation would help April breathe. Now the nurse could force oxygen into her lungs through the opening in her throat. It would help even if her muscles were partially paralyzed. The iron lung would help too, but the opening in her throat was the very best way of getting air into and out of her lungs.

Jeane and Curt sat with her until she awakened. Even though she had been told she couldn't talk after the surgery, she was frightened. She fought the restriction of the iron lung. When she tried to cry out, mucous flew out of the breathing tube. She was angry and frightened and her upper lungs were almost paralyzed.

During the surgery the hospital patient service employee had come to Curt to fill in the forms. While she was there, a nurse came

Jeane

to tell them April had to have special nurses around the clock. The woman from patient services told the McLyrres one of the best polio nurses in San Diego County was free and she would take one shift now; the woman told the McLyrres she would get two more nurses. She told them the March of Dimes would pay all the expenses if needed. Curt had called the bank in Norton and explained they would need money for hospital expenses. Their friend, Bill Smiley, said not to worry; their checks would always be honored.

April was frightened; she could not breathe with the iron lung. The nurse had to fasten her arms down to her sides so she couldn't hurt herself. A special nurse came at five o'clock. She sat down and started to talk to April in a soft smooth voice and she started pumping positive oxygen into the tracheotomy tube in her throat. When April attempted to exhale, the green phlegm was thrown out.

During that awful day, Jeane prayed harder than she had ever prayed in her life. Curt didn't pray and he continued to chastise Jeane for not getting help for April sooner. He was angry, and he wanted someone to blame. When Jeane cried, Curt told her to dry up. He was hurting too; he loved April as much as Jeane did.

Jeane sat staring into space. She prayed for help. She called one of their squadron wives and ask her to call everyone she knew to pray for April. Then she called Connie. She told Connie where to find her address book and call her Aunt Opal Graham in Almena and ask for prayers for April and call her friend, Wanda Heaton, in Norton and ask for prayers for April in all of the churches in Norton, and then she asked Connie to call Faith.

Curt stayed at the hospital all night with April and the nurse. The only thing that happened was April's anger. She couldn't understand why she couldn't move. The special nurse helped her inhale by forcing the positive oxygen into her lungs, so when the lungs were full they had to exhale and force the phlegm out. That night a five-year-old-boy who had been in the hospital for a week with polio died. April never knew.

The Browns reached San Diego about noon on Saturday. They had driven to Denver, then flew to San Diego. Ethel wanted to go to the hospital immediately, but Maurice said he would not go into

Jeane

the hospital because he might have a heart attack if he saw April like she was now. He found his place by taking complete care of Danny.

The McLyrres' telephone rang at five o'clock Sunday morning. Jeane answered and was told by the hospital that April's temperature had gone higher, which was not a good sign. Jeane called Faith and asked her to call Father Glasson to see if he would come to their apartment. Curt and Jeane got dressed. Curt wanted to go on to the hospital, but Jeane wanted to see Father Glasson first. Jeane called her mother and asked if she wanted to go to the hospital. She said she would be ready.

Curt respected Jeane's need for prayer although he thought she was silly. Faith had gone for Father Glasson and they were at the McLyrres in thirty minutes. Father Glasson prayed with Jeane and Curt and sat with them for several minutes after the prayers. He tried to reassure them God was with them. During the prayers Faith held Jeane's hand. Father Glasson promised to have someone call all the churches in the area and ask for prayers for April.

Ethel was exhausted, but she was dressed by the time Curt stopped at their door. When they got to the hospital, April's fever had left her more fearful than ever. Her eyes showed the fear she felt. It was like she was begging them for help and there was nothing they could do. The nurse was still helping her breathe. Doctor Movius, the leading polio specialist in San Diego County, came in at seven and said April was about the same. The nurse said he had been there all night.

The Movius family lived in La Jolla near Bird Rock and had twins in April's class. The girls were friends and in the same Brownie troop. He knew April, but not well.

The nurses changed shifts at seven in the morning and the night nurse talked to Jeane in the waiting room while Curt stood beside the iron lung. The nurse took Jeane's hand. "I watched April every minute last night. I don't think she is any worse, but she is very tired. I think she has helped herself by fighting so hard. Continue your prayers for her; she is a strong-willed little girl. I believe she will live a long and healthy life. She is a real fighter."

About noon that Sunday, April's fever broke. It was a miracle. She was more comfortable, but she still fought the iron lung and it

Jeane

was not helping her. The doctor came in every few hours. He watched her as she fought for breath.

"You know," Dr. Movius told Jeane and her mother, "This little eight-year-old girl has fought harder than anyone I have ever seen. I believe she has helped herself by trying to scream. Her lungs are working, certainly not enough, but with the oxygen she inhales her lungs have to exhale."

Curt stayed all night; April was wearing herself out fighting. The doctor decided the iron lung wasn't helping her, so before night he ordered the staff to take it away and put her back in bed. Her breathing was shallow, but the nurse helped her inhale most of the time. She relaxed and slept for awhile. All of the morning tests showed she was stable. She ate a little breakfast and smiled when her grandmother came into the room.

Within a few days, April learned to cover the air hole in her throat with her finger so she could talk. Dr. Movius was pleased with her progress. He said she had been strong and healthy when she was stricken and that would help with her recovery. There were very few minutes she was alone with only the nurses. The three people who loved her most divided the day into three shifts, just like the nurses. Curt took the night shift and slept part of it. April's grandmother liked the morning shift and Jeane the afternoon.

April was in the hospital three weeks and she progressed every day. After two weeks the tracheotomy had been closed and the nurses were not necessary. In another week she was able to go home.

Jeane kept her as quiet as possible. Since it was near Halloween, Jeane asked her what she would like to be. She answered a ballerina. Jeane went out while Connie watched April and found sky blue net and taffeta plus 500 sequins. April was delighted. Her mother sewed the 500 sequins all over the skirt while April sat beside her petting Tinky and choosing each sequin to be sewn on next.

Faith came almost every afternoon for a little while. She always found something April would enjoy. One day it was a hand-painted Cinderella doll, one day a set of hand painted paper dolls with costumes from different countries. Faith knew April loved to read, so she brought different books almost every day. Martha, April's special friend, came after school every day. If Faith was there

Jeane

when Martha arrived, the girls went to April's room and whispered together. One afternoon Christine Holder prepared a special tea for the girls and served it on the Browns' dining room table overlooking the playground.

One day Jeane looked at Faith and realized she looked like a different person. Her eyes were sharp and she smiled most of the time.

"Faith, what has happened to you?"

"I'm happy. Those ladies in the Altar Guild are so nice. One day soon after I started helping on the Altar Guild, I heard a lady say Father Glasson seemed happier than any time since his wife died. I asked her if Mrs. Glasson had died recently and they told me she died in 1949 and Father Glasson was lost without her. She said now he seemed better."

"Faith, you are better. Your eyes sparkle, has Basil noticed?"

"I don't know. He is gone most of the time and he seems restless when he is home. I wonder where he goes when he is away."

Jeane thought Faith didn't seem to care. Now she was building a life for herself. She was young when she married and she never had a life of her own.

On Halloween, Martha was a fairy and came early to see April in her ballerina costume. Connie had planned a surprise party for April. Her friends met in Connie's apartment and waited for April and Martha to arrive. When Jeane saw how excited April was; she felt tears running down her cheeks. It was a wonderful party.

Jeane could hardly believe April was so well; she went back to school after two weeks and narrated the Thanksgiving story on the last day of classes. Tears ran down Jeane's cheeks as she listened. She said a prayer of thanksgiving to God for the miracle of April's recovery. Faith sat beside her and held her hand.

When April was released from the hospital, the Browns decided to go home. They were tired and anxious to get some rest. They were thankful they could have been with her when she needed them, but they decided not to come for Christmas.

Christmas was special: April was healthy and Danny was just himself. He was busy exploring and chasing Tinky until she stopped and spit at him.

Jeane was at peace. She was sure she was pregnant. When

Jeane

Curt and Jeane had planned their family, they wanted four children; first a boy, then a girl, and when they were in school, they wanted another boy and girl. She hadn't told anyone, but now she wanted the world to know. She hoped the baby would be born in California.

On New Year's Day, Connie and Jeane prepared lunch and their families celebrated together. Jeane brought a bottle of champagne and before dessert Curt uncorked the bottle and filled the glasses. Jeane couldn't wait, she held up her glass. She said, "Welcome baby number three for the McLyrres."

Connie and Jim were delighted, Connie smiled, "Your new baby will have a playmate in Illinois. Jim will be back to reserve status by that time. We are expecting, too." The children didn't care. They just wanted to play outdoors in the 72 degree weather. The men watched the football game and Jeane and Connie continued to work on a jigsaw puzzle.

1954—We had no choice

The second week of January, Curt came home with orders to Wright-Patterson Air Force Base in Dayton, Ohio, to join a small Navy contingent called the Bureau of Aviation General District (BAGR). It was made up of a small group of experienced engineers. He would be stationed at Wright-Patterson Air Force Base with a group that did liaison work between the federal government and various companies that have contracts with the Navy.

Jeane, as usual, didn't understand what Curt was to do, but that was no surprise. She guessed the school he had attended the summer of 1952 prepared him for this assignment. He was to be detached from the squadron and Miramar on March 1, 1954. He had two weeks leave time before he reported to BAGR, March 15, 1954.

She started to cry. "I want to stay here. Does the Navy always send orders in the middle of the school year? I have made a place for myself, but now you say *we have no choice.*"

Curt look disgusted. "That's right, *we have no choice..* When orders come we smile and prepare to go."

"Curt, most of these last three years have been wonderful. I

Jeane

worked hard to learn to be a Navy wife, but I still hate to kowtow to the senior officers' wives. Even first lieutenants wives want special favors."

Curt said, "The next assignment will be easier. I will not be away as much. I feel very good about these orders."

"Why are these orders special?"

"Have you forgotten already? Do you remember *the need to know*? I have not forgotten. You know I will not talk about my work at home. Come on, Jeane, it's time for bed and yes, you have learned to be a Navy wife." Jeane was pregnant and happy in California. She thought about all that had happened in the past three years, but it had been hard for her to accept Curt and his need for secrecy.

The next morning Jeane called Connie. "I need to talk. May I come over?"

Connie put on a fresh pot of coffee. Jeane repeated the news of the move to Ohio. "Connie, I don't want to go. I am happy here and I won't know anyone in Ohio."

"Curt said *I have no choice*. Just hold up your chin and smile. The world is not coming to an end. It sounds like Curt has a very special assignment, so be happy for him."

The word about the McLyrres orders to Ohio were out. The squadron wives were on the phone. It seemed some of the wives had friends there now and they would write and tell them the McLyrres would be there in March. That was the Navy life line. On every move there was someone who would help the wife.

Jeane's telephone rang all morning, she made notes about their friends who were with BAGR now. Orders were exciting to most wives. They felt it was a challenge to meet new people and live in new places plus seeing people they had known before. When Jeane thought about it, she admitted to herself she was a Navy wife.

Everyone loved living in California, but new assignments were necessary for promotion. Jeane had not thought of that. When Doris Martin heard about their orders, she called Jeane and told her they had good friends in Dayton and she would write them immediately.

Jeane called Faith to tell her about the new baby and the new duty station. Faith reminded Jeane to take extra care of herself during the months ahead. Faith seemed happier than Jeane had ever seen her.

"Jeane, I'm delighted that you will have a new baby next summer. You are truly blessed. I have just learned Basil will be doing medical research at Yale after the first of March. You remember the young woman doctor, Margaret Handel, who helped me so much, has encouraged Basil to stop fighting with McCarthy and his fanatics on Communism. She told him he would be appreciated at Yale and she got a grant for him to assist her for six months. She has an important research project under way now. Basil listed the house for sale today."

"Jeane, I don't want to leave La Jolla. He assumes I will go with him, but I want to live by myself for at least a few months. Basil and I don't think alike anymore. He keeps telling me how important Dr. Handel is at Yale. He has changed so much since we moved to La Jolla I hardly know him. I think it is time for me to live alone. I want to see what it's like.

"I thought of going back to Illinois, but at thirty-three I think I should learn to take care of myself. I have some money from my father's estate. It should be enough for me to rent a small apartment and live quietly. I want to be near St. James because those ladies in the Altar Guild are my friends. We work together and sometimes we go out in the evening." Jeane was surprised at how determined Faith seemed to feel about staying in La Jolla alone.

Faith continued, "Jeane, I'm sure you will like Dayton. It is so much like Illinois and very different from here. The landscape is beautiful. It is farm country and there are wild fruit and nut trees along all the back roads. Every June my brother and I picked wild plums and my mother made jelly and jam. There were lots of black walnut trees growing beside the road and we collected the nuts. I haven't been in Kansas, but I'm sure Ohio will be a lot like Kansas and you make friends easily. Be careful and take care of yourself for that new baby."

"Faith, this has been the most wonderful three years of my life; you have been a special part of it. I feel that we will always be special friends. We both needed a friend and Sigma Kappa helped us meet."

"Jeane, we will never say good-bye, that is too final. I promise you even if we live across the country we will never forget we are

Jeane

friends. I will see you next summer when I go to Illinois."

Jeane had written her parents about their new baby who would be born after they moved to Ohio. The next week she had a letter from her mother.

> January 20, 1954
> To my dear family,
> Why didn't you tell me about the baby? How do you feel? Now don't you lift those boxes. Let the moving company do everything. Have you told the children?
> We are both happy for you.
> Your dad is taking better care of himself now. Every morning he drives to Friendly's then on to Jay's Shop. That keeps him busy all morning. In the afternoon he naps until almost four. The new TV antenna is fastened to the chimney and we are getting good TV reception. We both enjoy the music, and he listens to the news every evening.
> I haven't been to Almena since Christmas. It's just too cold to be out on the road. I call your Grandma Brown every week to check on her. Faye and Nell both check on her, get her mail, and any groceries she needs.
> I haven't seen any of your friends since we got home. I won't drive the car in this weather, but not everyone is snowbound. You remember my next door neighbor? Now I see her employer, Doctor John, picks her up about nine every morning. Sometimes he doesn't bring her home until very late at night. I don't know what is going on there, but your father tells me I should mind my own business.
> We can hardly wait to see you in March. Maybe the children can stay with us and go to school until you find somewhere to live. You know the elementary school is less than a block from us. I'm so glad you will be closer to us.
>
> Love,
> Mother and Dad

Jeane was busy. She was confirmed at St. James by-the-Sea early in February. She resigned from all her activities, first the Sigma Kappa alumnae, then room mother for April, and last she resigned

Jeane

as teacher for Danny's Sunday school class. It was hard to leave. Curt was eager to get to Ohio and his new work. Curt and Jeane had both grown up a lot in the past three years.

Book Two
East to Ohio

1954-1957

East to Ohio

On the third of March, the station wagon was packed and ready for the McLyrres to start their long drive east to the new duty station. They had planned their trip carefully; Jeane had worked hard even though she was four months pregnant, but when she saw her doctor for the last time he said she was fine. Curt got everyone out of bed and they left La Jolla promptly at four in the morning. Curt knew this way they could have breakfast in Barstow, California, two hundred miles closer to Ohio.

As Curt planned it they joined U.S. 40 and continued east for two days or more until they reached Amarillo, Texas. There they would turn north and be less than three hundred miles from Norton.

Curt knew they must drive through about three hundred desolate miles across a desert where neither man nor beast could survive in the summer. All they would see after they left Barstow was wind, dust, sand, tumbleweeds, and sagebrush. The first one hundred miles were easy because the children were looking at their new books.

Jeane's doctor said she was fine, but this morning she had cramps and felt a little nauseous after they left Barstow heading into the desert. The wind and the weeds crashed into the car from all directions. They drove through Needles entering part of the desert where the highway went south and crossed into Arizona. The strong wind continued and Jeane started chilling. At Kingman, Arizona, Curt stopped for gas. Jeane was anxious to continue on.

The road east from Kingman continued through the desert. The hard bitter wind still threw tumbleweeds and sagebrush at the side of the car. Jeane was worried. Curt gripped the steering wheel as he watched for the next dead sagebrush to slam against the car.

Jeane's cramps were almost unbearable. When the next one came, she could hardly breathe. All of a sudden she screamed,

Jeane

"CURT, STOP THE CAR!" He knew she had been very quiet for the past fifty miles. Now he saw she was in pain. He stopped. He didn't ask what happened, but when he looked at her he knew she was suffering. He turned to the children and told them if they looked out their window, they could see a herd of deer.

Jeane opened her car door and put her feet firmly on the ground, then she slipped down into a sitting position with her back against the car seat. Another cramp hit her and before she could do anything she felt blood gushing down her legs and over her shoes. The icy wind blew in her face with no relief. She sat in the cramped and helpless position.

When Curt saw what had happened, he ran to the back of the station wagon and opened the door. He told the children to hop into the front seat and he grabbed a blanket and wrapped it around her as he carried her to the back of the station wagon. She was shivering as he put her in the children's bed. He was frightened; he hurried to cover her with another blanket, then he reached down and kissed her.

She sobbed as she clung to him until he closed the backdoor. She was frightened and she thought she couldn't move. Even with the extra blankets she was still shaking. She had never experienced anything like this. When she felt the warm blood on her legs she shivered and clung to the blankets, then she prayed for the bleeding to stop. The cramps were not as severe when she got warm.

Curt started the car and called to her. "What shall we do? On the map I don't see any town except Kingman."

"Never go back to Kingman! Just keep going east!"

Curt kept the children in the front seat singing songs with them and telling them jokes. When Jeane realized the heavy bleeding had stopped, she felt better. She told Curt not to stop until they reached Flagstaff, Arizona where it would be easy to find a room. Late that afternoon they reached Flagstaff. Curt registered at a motel, then he helped Jeane out of the station wagon and into the room. He kept his arms around her while she clutched the blanket. Curt turned down the bed and helped her lie down. He asked if he could call a doctor and she said no. She told him to get food for himself and the children.

When Jeane was warm, she sat up and finally made her way to

Jeane

the bathroom door. She turned on the hot water and stepped in the shower. The hot water felt soothing as it poured over her. She was weak, but she clung to a bar in the shower. She almost fell as she stepped out of the shower and quickly turned off the water before she slipped back into bed. Immediately she dropped off to sleep. She heard nothing until Curt and the children came in, then she realized the bleeding had almost stopped.

"Curt, I have to have Kotex. Will you go to the drugstore and get it for me?"

He didn't know what to say. "Jeane, are you sure you have to have it?"

"Yes, Curt, I have to have it." He tucked his head and before he left he asked Jeane again if she was sure she didn't want to see a doctor. She refused. He ran back out into the cold night, but it wasn't long before he was back with the Kotex and hot soup for Jeane. He looked worried when he sat down beside her. "If you won't see a doctor here, I think we should leave early in the morning. Do I remember you filled a box with fruit, graham crackers, canned juice, Vienna sausages, and cookies before we left La Jolla?"

"Yes, I did. They will come in handy in the morning." Curt wasn't listening. He was worried and anxious to get Jeane to Norton so she could be seen by Dr. Bennie whom she had total confidence in. Again they were the only car on the road when they left Flagstaff. Curt started the car early so it would be warm when he carried the sleeping children to their bed in the back, and then he helped Jeane put on her heavy jacket. She sat in the front seat under a blanket while the children slept soundly until almost eight o'clock. When the children awakened, they were hungry and ready for breakfast. Curt stopped at the first cafe he saw. Meanwhile the children found things they liked in the snack box. Jeane saw them watching every move she made. They couldn't understand why she was so quiet.

Curt drove fast, there was no one else on the road. They were through Albuquerque early in the afternoon and Jeane said to go on as far as they could. By the time they reached Tucumcari, New Mexico, all of them were exhausted, so they took a room for the night. Jeane couldn't sleep; she was still frightened and she didn't know what might happen next. All she wanted was to see Dr. Bennie.

Jeane

Curt had everybody ready to leave Tucumcari by six the next morning and they were in Amarillo, Texas, before breakfast. The shortest road to Kansas was U.S. 60 that angled north just over one hundred miles before they turned north on to U.S. 283 for the last two hundred and twenty miles.

They reached Norton late in the afternoon. When Curt drove in the driveway, Jeane was relieved. April and Danny jumped out of the car and dashed into the house. They told their grandparents their mommy had been sick all the way from California.

Ethel hurried out to the car and saw that Jeane was pale, but she was able to walk. Before they got to the door, she told her mother she had a miscarriage in the desert. Her mother immediately called Dr. Bennie. He told her he had to see Jeane as soon as he could get to the Browns' house.

Her mother insisted Jeane stay in bed and lay quiet.

Dr. Bennie was there in less than thirty minutes.

He said, "Let's see what has happened here." He gave her a thorough examination and told her everything seemed normal. He said the uterus would cramp for several days even though the birth canal and uterus were both clean. He said there seemed to be no infection, but he wrote a prescription for Curt to have filled immediately, just for her protection. Jeane's parents were relieved.

Everyone was worried about Jeane and her mother kept her in bed for two days. By then she felt fine and was ready to go to Ohio.

"Jeane, please leave the children with us until you are settled in Ohio. You know our school is less than two blocks from here. It will be hard to look for a house with them. You take care of yourself. If the children stay here, Tinky will stay too."

Snow was predicted for north central Kansas so Curt and Jeane left Norton early the next morning. They hoped to keep ahead of the snow by driving east on U.S. 36 to St. Joseph, Missouri. Curt hoped they could reach Hannibal before dark.

"Jeane, tell me if you get tired; we can stop anywhere. If we get to Hannibal tonight, we can get to Indianapolis tomorrow evening and be in Dayton on the afternoon of the third day." Jeane was exhausted by noon, but she didn't complain. They didn't see any

Jeane

snow in Kansas. She was relieved when they arrived in Hannibal before six.

After two nights of sound sleep, Jeane felt fine, and she was anxious to see Dayton. Even though it was still winter the trees were budding and the fields were showing some spring green. After they left Indianapolis snow covered the hills and the big white houses with red barns. The winter scenes looked like they should be on a calendar.

"Curt, do you know what Dayton is like? I had never been east of the Mississippi River until today."

When the McLyrres reached Wright-Patterson Air Force Base, Curt was anxious to let BAGR know he had arrived in the area. The full name of his new assignment was Bureau of Aeronautics General Region. The car was warm so Jeane waited for Curt to come back. When he returned he told her only twelve officers and twenty enlisted men were assigned to BAGR, and he was the youngest. He was excited when he realized the commanding officer was Admiral Clifford Wells whom he admired from the time he studied at Ohio University in 1952.

Curt was anxious to get settled so as soon as he had checked in with BAGR, then he checked with the housing office. He was told Wherry Housing Project in Fairborn was available for all families stationed at Wright-Patterson. Fairborn was close to the Wherry Project and that was where most of the military lived. The Navy and Air Force shared the commissary, post exchange, and military hospital. Most of the military were Air Force and several thousand men were stationed there.

They checked into a hotel in Fairborn so they could see where most of the service families lived. The town of Fairborn close to the base was dedicated to the military. Curt drove Jeane around the area until dark and saw only a few trees and no grass. To Jeane the Wherry Housing seemed desolate. She saw clothes hanging on lines behind every building; motorcycles were parked everywhere, including on the sidewalk. The side streets were full of modest houses without city sidewalks. Jeane told Curt the whole ugly place must have been built in a hurry. Dogs ran in the streets and children threw mud at the passing cars. After living in La Jolla, they were shocked and Jeane began to cry.

Jeane

"Curt, I don't want our children playing in the street or around those apartments; they look like barracks. Even most of the little houses were neglected. I saw children playing in the street. I wondered what kind of parents do they have. I'm sure the schools are crowded. What are we going to do?"

Curt answered, "First, we will buy the *The Dayton Sun Tribune*. Rentals have to be available somewhere in the area. Let's go to the Post Exchange and see if we can find a good map of the city. Surely the housing office could have given us that. You know I would rather drive further and have good schools for our children and I don't want our children to stay in Norton longer than necessary."

"Curt, don't be so cranky! In Norton our children have good care and are happy. I think you are tired and need to rest for awhile before you go back to your office to talk." Later Curt talked to the BAGR officers. He learned most of them drove thirty minutes each way to live in a nice neighborhood. One man told Curt about a builder named Huber who had bought a large parcel of land in Kettering and was building affordable homes for young families. He said Kettering was on the south edge to Dayton about thirty minutes from the base.

He said Huber had built a few sample houses with John Mansville siding before he found people wouldn't buy them. Now he builds only small brick houses that are so popular buyers wait six months for a brick house.

The man in BAGR told Curt he thought the best place in the Dayton area to live was in Kettering. He said that the new elementary school had excellent teachers and his children loved school. He said there were new shops being built in Kettering all the time. His family was happy there and he couldn't suggest anything else.

No one suggested they call a real estate company. No one mentioned the G.I. Bill of Rights that allowed a veteran to buy a house with no money down. All the McLyrres knew was to read the newspaper, ask questions, drive, and look.

The next day they read the paper and found a map of Dayton. Jeane wanted to live in the older part of Dayton that had big trees and paved streets. In an area near St. Paul's Episcopal Church

Jeane

were some beautiful old stone houses, but none the McLyrres could afford. Any of them would have pleased Jeane. They watched for signs that said for sale or for rent, but they never saw even one. Finally they gave up and drove south on Far Hills Road until they saw a sign that said, "Welcome to Kettering." They turned east on Stroop Road where they saw stores along both sides of the road and most of them were new. A few blocks further east they saw another big sign on the left that read "Huber Homes are Best." On the right there was the new elementary school called Oak View. All the houses around the school were neat and clean..

They drove through the Huber Homes subdivision several times before they continued east to meet Hank Marsh's wife. Hank was the man in BAGR who had told Curt about Kettering and the Huber houses. When Curt and Jeane found Mrs. Marsh, she insisted they stay for coffee. She told the McLyrres her boys went to Oak View School, and she was sure it was the best school in the Dayton area.

When they left the Marshes, Jeane turned toward Curt. "I hate moving. I still wish you had taken the job of city engineer in Norton. I look around here and all I see are strangers. I admit I loved La Jolla but this is different. It's cold here, and everybody looks angry except Mrs. Marsh. I don't think I was meant to move so often. We were doing well in Norton and now look at us: we have no home and no money." Curt didn't answer; he never wanted to live in Norton again. They drove up and down every street in the Huber Homes subdivision more than once before they saw the little gray house with a sign in the front window that said "for sale".

The Little Gray House

Curt drove in the driveway and parked. Jeane hated the looks of the house, but Curt wanted to be settled. He hated house hunting and he wanted their children with them. "Jeane, don't turn this down until we know more about it. Let's look in the windows; there's no one living here." He got out of the car and found the house unlocked. They walked into a big bright living and dining room with a fireplace and two walls of glass. It did not look like any house they had ever seen. From the front door they could see some of

Jeane

every room except the bathroom. The house had three bedrooms, all small. One redeeming feature was the large walls of glass.

"Curt, this house is tacky. My dad would never have built a house like this. I wish we lived in Norton now. I look out these windows and I see motorcycles next door and behind us. This big yard is nothing but weeds and trash. I'm a stranger here and I will probably stay one. All I see is work in this ugly little house!"

"Jeane, just think a minute. In this house we would have a new clean house with new appliances that include stove, refrigerator, hot water tank, washer, dryer, furnace and fireplace." Curt was ready to buy.

The house was small, and Jeane hated the gray John Mansville panels that covered the outside of the house. Jeane said it looked like a prison. They went to the shopping center, where Curt called the Huber Construction Office to ask if the house could be rented. They told him no. The sales representative told him the price of the house was $7,500 which was a bargain. She told him the smallest brick houses were selling for $11,000, and people had to wait at least six months for delivery. The agent who answered the phone was eager to sell the Johns Manville house and she came quickly. She knew this house had been hard to sell. Two of the John Mansville houses were finally sold, and she was anxious to get rid of the last one.

Again, Curt went to the shopping center and called the First National Bank in Norton, where they kept their checking account. He asked to borrow $1,000 to buy a house and was told the money would be in their account when he hung up.

Curt looked over the house and yard while they waited for the Huber agent. "Jeane, I think this is the best we can do. You know we have very little money to put down and we like the neighborhood because Oak View Elementary School is less than a block away. You will be able to choose your friends here. I'm sure you will be involved in a half dozen things in less than six months.

"Neither of us like the gray panels on the house, even though they are fireproof. Maybe we can buy some shrubs and get some color around the house later in the spring. When the grass comes up and that tree in the front yard leafs out it will look better. When we drove around this neighborhood, it looked like there were children

Jeane

in every house. You know this carport will be a perfect place for our children to play on rainy days. Don't forget the big storage room at the end of the carport, we will need that. If that woman from the Huber Office doesn't get here soon, I will call her again."

"Curt, this yard is a mess. I don't think we should buy here unless Huber will grade and clean up both the back and front yard and sod the front yard. We should make a list of things that have to be done."

When the next door neighbor saw someone looking at the house, he walked over to say hello. Curt was anxious to ask him how they liked their house. He explained they needed a house quickly but they didn't like the Johns Manville siding either. Curt ask him the price of the houses and he told him they paid $7,900 and that included having all the yard sodded.

The agent was all smiles when she arrived. She had the contract written, and all she needed was their names and the amount of their down payment.

Curt glared at the agent. "Just a minute, you haven't even told us the price."

The agent was angry. "This house is a bargain at $7,500."

Jeane interrupted her. "We are new here, and we might be willing to buy this house if you show us what is included." The agent glared at Jeane as she handed the contract to Curt. The contract listed all the appliances and stated the house was ready to move in immediately.

"Curt, I won't sign that contract unless the whole yard is cleaned up and graded and the front yard sodded."

The agent was angry, but she continued to smile.

All Curt wanted was to close the deal. After more discussion the agent called her office and got approval on the contract. The front yard would be sodded.

In Ohio, the $1,000 Curt borrowed was enough to close the sale because of what was called a land contract. The title of the property would be escrowed until the last payment on the property was paid. This method of ownership helped lots of young people own their home. The McLyrres had very little cash and they would have accepted almost anything near a good elementary school. Curt was eager to bring the children to Ohio.

Jeane

The contract was firm and the painting was finished. The next day the grading of the front and back yards was started. It was completed in less than a week, and the sodding was completed in one day.

On the first of April the Browns met the McLyrres in Hannibal, Missouri. Curt was delighted when Tinky wasn't with them. Ethel decided to keep her until everybody was settled in their new home. Jeane had written her parents and described the house. April and Danny were anxious to see their rooms, and Curt was eager to start his new assignment. He insisted they head back to Kettering after lunch. Jeane drove the first four hours and Curt the rest of the way. It was six o'clock in the morning when they arrived at the new house in Kettering.

Life in Kettering was different than life in La Jolla. Their next-door neighbors on the right were Jack and Arlene Thomas from Philadelphia and both had graduated from Pennsylvania State College. They had twin girls six years old. Jack told Curt there were two Johnson families, one on the left side of the McLyrres and one behind them. He said it was a father and daughter who owned two Kawasaki Motorcycle dealerships, one in Fairborn and one in Xenia. Curt didn't mention any of this to Jeane.

Call Me Flo!

The day after the McLyrres moved in, someone knocked on their door. Jeane answered and she saw a big gray-haired woman. Jeane thought she looked German. The woman smiled and walked in.

"I'm Florence Johnson," she said. "I'm your next-door neighbor. Just call me Flo." She was wearing a cotton house dress covered with red and yellow roses and she had a white scarf tied over her unruly gray hair. She closed the door and pulled off her head scarf. She pulled back a dining room chair and sat down. Jeane didn't know what to do or say. She wasn't sure she wanted to know this woman. Mrs. Johnson took charge.

She smiled, "Dearie, we are so glad you are here. I know you

Jeane

are anxious to meet all your neighbors. My hubby is Pete, and our daughter Fern lives behind you with her husband, Ralph, and their two boys. Her boys are a little bigger than your boy.

"Fern knows all the young people around here and I know she will have you acquainted in no time! Oh, yes, you and your hubby have a standing invitation to come to our house any old time. We always have lots of company and lots of fun." Jeane was tongue tied when she saw that Mrs. Johnson had pushed back her chair and slipped off her shoes, smiling as she wiggled her toes.

"There girlie, I feel better. I'm lots more comfortable barefooted. I grew up on a farm south of here and I didn't have a pair of shoes 'til I went to school." She stood up and pulled down her corset. "Look at me today. You may never see me in a corset again, but since I didn't know you I decided to dress up. My folks came to the United States when I was ten. They had enough money to buy a few acres of bottom land down south near the river. My grandfather paid for all of us to leave Germany. He felt sure the first World War would be fought in Germany and he wanted his son and his family safe in the United States."

Mrs. Johnson picked up her basket and sat it on the table. "Jeane, yes, of course, I'll call you Jeane! I'm gonna be your friend." She was busy unpacking her basket on the table. "These eggs are from my folks' farm; I'll bet you never ate fresh farm eggs. I know your children will love my cookies. Tell them there are lots more just like these in my freezer. Now, I've got something special for you and your hubby. Here's two cartons of good Budweiser Beer."

Jeane wished Mrs. Johnson would go home, but she seemed to be having a fine time.

"Girlie, I'll bet you'll really like my daughter, Fern; like I told you, she knows all the young folks around here. I'll bring her over here one day soon. This is a real friendly place to live. Have you met the Salernos? They are nice folks even if they are from Italy. All us folks say live and let live. I think you will fit right in. Joe Salerno came to the U.S.A. after World War II. He came to Dayton to join a cousin who worked for Huber Construction Company. In only three years he was able to bring his wife and little gal to Ohio. Everybody in the Salerno family works for Huber now.

Jeane

"Oh yes, someone else lives next door to the Salernos who I haven't met. It seems it is one man alone. I guess he is waiting for his wife. Joe Salerno told my son-in-law, Ralph, the strange man told him he was looking for work.

"While the man was gone last Saturday, my grandson slipped over to that house and peeked in all the windows. There were no shades. He told his mother there was almost no furniture in the house. I guess he must be poor. Maybe he's too proud to ask Joe Salerno again to help him find work. If I know Joe, he will take that poor man to the hiring office and he will recommend him.

"Honey, you're gonna be happy here! Every Sunday afternoon the Salernos have a picnic with their big extended family right there in Joe's yard. The men sit outdoors and drink beer or wine and tease and quarrel with their cousins. They enjoy themselves. Oh yes, honey, we have a right good time in our yard every Sunday too. Lots of our bike riders live in apartments and they love to congregate in our yard.

"Well honey, I better git home now. Don't want to wear you out. I'll see you again soon." She picked up her basket and hurried out the door.

That evening Jeane told Curt about her visitor who wanted her to know everybody in the neighborhood.

"The Johnsons are friendly people. Jeane, I think you may have become a snob. "Did you see Mrs. Johnson jump on that motorcycle and speed down the street to the grocery store last night? She had one of her grandsons sitting behind her and he could hardly get his arms around her. You know anyone who stops at the Johnsons' are welcome to their cookouts of beer and hamburgers." Curt would have gone if Jeane hadn't refused. When Curt had to go and bring Danny home, he always talked with some of the motorcycle owners. He told Jeane one of the fellows he talked to was a doctor who specialized in brain surgery. He told Curt the picnics relaxed him.

Jeane always found an excuse not to go to the Johnsons. She hated those nights because as they drank the beer, the noise got louder. Often she called the police and they came, but that didn't help because the policeman had a beer and the noise level become louder. The motorcycles were revved up and often there were races up and down Kenosha Road. Danny told his mother the men put

Jeane

money in a hat and the winner got it. Danny loved to be at the Johnsons when a new motorcycle appeared. Jeane hated it, but even when she spanked him he would slip away as often as he could.

In less than two weeks Curt joined a car pool with two other BAGR officers who lived near them. Jeane was delighted. Now she could have the car most of the week. First, she found a fabric store that sold monks cloth so she made drapes for the living and dining room, then she made sheer white curtains for the bedrooms. She painted the kitchen pale yellow to cover the original blue gray spatter paint that had been sprayed in every room in the house. She put two coats of enamel on the walls and cabinets. Next she painted the rest of the house with antique white paint and it took her almost a month to finish. She planned to paint the inside of the carport and by May she was anxious to start her new flower garden.

Jeane had worked hard, but she hadn't been able to make any new clothes for herself. Every morning she looked at herself in her standing mirror in the corner of their bedroom. The bedroom was so small it was seldom she could get far enough from the mirror to see all of her. During the time she had been painting, she pulled her long dark hair back and held it with a thick rubber band. She wondered if she would ever have time to curl it again.

The backyard was bare; Curt needed to plant the grass now. The Huber people had sodded the front yard, cleaned up the trash, and graded all the back lot, but nothing more. Without grass Danny was dirty all the time. Jeane was thankful for the new washer and dryer that came with the house. Every weekend Curt was busy working in the backyard. He planted perennial rye to cover the dirt quickly. Jeane watered it several times a day, and she was delighted to see how fast it grew. They knew it was hard to mow, but it would keep Danny clean.

Jeane had been so busy she hadn't written anyone, but she did write and send their address and telephone number to her parents and Faith. Faith had a different life now and Jeane missed her more every day, but as Curt said, *there was no choice.*

When Faith got Jeane's letter, she called. "I am so happy to hear from you. I'm fine, Basil has gone east and is doing research

Jeane

at Yale. You remember the young woman doctor who helped me? She managed to get the grant for him.

"I have an apartment near St. James. Dr. Margaret wrote and reminded me it would be best for me to stay in La Jolla for at least six months to let Basil adjust to his new research project."

"Faith, that sounds wonderful. From what you have told me moving is hard for you. I understand, but as long as Curt is in the Navy we will have to move every three years! I hate the moves, *but there is no choice*. I have worked hard since we moved in late March.

"Sometimes I wonder if Dr. Handel really believes it is better for you to be in La Jolla. I miss you every day. I miscarried the day we left California, but now I'm fine. Some day I will write and tell you all about my new neighbor.

"This is nothing like La Jolla. We bought this ugly little house and I have worked hard making curtains, painting the inside of the house, and watering the new grass three times a day. We had very little money to buy a house, but this one was close to a new elementary school and that was important to both of us. The children are happy and have already made friends."

Monday Morning Calls

Faith interrupted. "Jeane, it means a lot for me to talk to you even if you are more than two thousand miles away. I would like to call you every Monday morning about this time. Shall we plan to be home then?"

"That would be wonderful. I will wait for your call every Monday. You asked about Curt, he seems happy. He is gone part of every week but usually just overnight and he enjoys playing with the children every evening." Jeane decided she would not tell Curt that Faith had called. He hoped Jeane had forgotten her.

Curt was delighted with his new assignment. Most of the BAGR Officers had been in the Navy for about fifteen years and they were experts in their field. Again, Jeane never knew what Curt was doing, but he did tell her when he was going to Washington. He

Jeane

didn't talk about his work, nor did she hear gossip from other Navy wives. They didn't talk about their husbands' work. All of them had been Navy wives for a long time.

Jeane found the activities for the BAGR wives were more formal than the squadron affairs in California. For the morning sherry hour at the Wright-Patterson Officers' Club the ladies wore hats and gloves. The evening parties were usually dinner and dancing in formal dress. Curt and Jeane attended every event BAGR sponsored, but they never went to the Wright Patterson Officers' Club alone, they couldn't afford it.

In May it was time to plant flowers. Jeane put on her old clothes and started planning her garden. She was preparing the soil when Mrs. Johnson appeared beside her.

"Jeane, may I give you some advice." Before Jeane could answer Mrs. Johnson continued, "I see you are planting flower seed, but you can't eat flowers! I would suggest you take part of your backyard and make a vegetable garden. Every year we plant sweet corn and watermelon. It may not be pretty, but it tastes great."

"Mrs. Johnson, our backyard is for our children. I like flowers and that is what I am going to plant here. By the way, I saw you talking to Joe Salerno Sunday morning. Did you learn anything more about his neighbor?"

"Yes I did. That man asked Joe if he could find any kind of a job for him with Huber Construction Company. Joe met him at work the next morning and took him to the hiring office. It turned out he couldn't do anything but push a wheelbarrow or dig a hole. Joe said it seemed all he did was talk about Communism to anyone who would listen. He would ask them if they were earning as much as the men who were sitting in the office. Most of the men shook their heads and walked away. He didn't give up. He would walk around and ask any man if he would like to go to lunch with him where everybody got hamburgers and beer free. The men learned to stay away from him. All he talked about was how to make this a better world.

"Joe told me he was fired in less than a week and that night he packed his car and was gone. He didn't even thank Joe for getting him a job. I think that man must be crazy or a trouble maker. I'm

Jeane

glad he is gone. He didn't mix with any of us.

"Jeane, I'm tired. Why don't you come home with me and we will have a good cold beer?"

"Thank you, but not today. I must plant these plants my mother sent me. The little violets are out of her yard and they are wilted now. She sent me some of her daylilies plus four o'clock and sunflower seeds. I have to hurry. It's almost time for me to start dinner."

When school was out, Jeane wanted to go home and visit her mother. Danny was in the Johnsons' yard more than he was at home. She called her parents and asked if they would meet her and the children in Hannibal, and they agreed immediately. Curt was willing to take his family any day. Jeane's mother called back, and they arranged to meet on Wednesday.

Jeane felt good as they got close to Hannibal. She couldn't tell her parents she was lonely in Ohio. She hadn't made friends with BAGR wives. Jeane was younger than most of the wives and only two of the families lived in Kettering. In Norton she felt at home again. She saw all her close friends and their children several times.

After two weeks she was ready to go back to Kettering. The Browns drove to Hannibal again and Curt was waiting for them.

Soon after they were home, Curt handed her a white envelope. They were invited to a special party for the new executive officer and his wife. Captain and Mrs. Steel. She wrote an acceptance note the next morning. The night of the party she was surprised to see every BAGR officer and his wife there to meet the new executive officer and his wife, Captain and Mrs. Steel. It was more formal than most BAGR parties' and everyone was dressed in formal clothes.

Jeane looked around and saw Susan Steel standing alone and she wanted to be friendly. "Mrs. Steel, I have been admiring your dress all evening. The color is perfect for you." Mrs. Steel smiled and thanked her. Dorothy Kline joined them and asked if the Steels still enjoyed a good bridge game. Mrs. Steel answered that they did, then she turned to Jeane and asked if they played bridge, and Jeane said "Yes". There was no way to continue the conversation since this party was for the Steels.

Jeane

After the party Jeane realized it had always been important to her to be dressed properly. She still studied Vogue every month, but she soon realized the BAGR wives didn't wear the newest fashions. Most of them dressed more like Faith had dressed in California. Jeane began to make simple dresses that helped her blend in with the other wives. She was only five feet tall and had to fight gaining weight constantly. Finally she realized the simple dresses were more attractive on her.

In the fall Jeane's flower garden was so pretty she forgot how Mrs. Johnson had wanted her to plant vegetables. She had planted everything her mother had sent and they all flourished. She looked up one day and saw Mrs. Johnson coming.

"Jeane, I have to tell you how much I have enjoyed your flower garden. I'm glad you didn't listen to me and plant vegetables.

"For some reason today, I don't know why but I thought about that man who lived beside Joe. Did you know Joe left Italy to get away from the Communists? He had told his boss he knew all good Communists were dead Communists. Joe is a gentle man, but he hates Communists. He told me he thought that man who left here so fast was a Communist.

"Jeane, what's the matter, didn't you hear me? I called you twice and you didn't answer. I want to sit down and put my feet up. Why won't you come home with me, and we will both have a good cold beer."

"Thank you, but why don't you sit down here and have a cold glass of lemonade."

"My feet are killing me, Jeane, even with my shoes off. Usually when I go barefooted my feet feel good, but not today. Yes, I will sit down here in one of these chairs with a footrest." The children loved Mrs. Johnson, and soon they had her playing a game with them and Jeane finished her watering.

Jeane continued her promise to write her family once a week. She knew they looked for letters that told them all about their grandchildren. She wrote them that April was reading books constantly and always had good grades and Danny was happy in his kindergarten class.

Oak View was a new school with all new equipment and April was always eager to excel, even in the second grade. Jeane wrote

Jeane

her mother about their neighbors who had twin girls April's age. The children drew pictures to put in the letter for Tinky. Ethel thought it was best for Tinky to stay in Kansas.

After school started Jeane was lonelier. She realized her only friends were Mrs. Johnson and Arlene Thomas. She went to all the activities for BAGR wives. She enjoyed the ladies, but none of them lived near them except Sally Marsh who was expecting her third baby any day.

Faith called Jeane every Monday morning, and Jeane always waited by the telephone. She was excited when the call came. "Faith is it you? I feel like you are here when I'm talking to you. Has anything happened this week?"

"Yes, Jeane, a lot has happened this week. Basil called to say Cliffside Drive had been sold. He told me he had signed the papers in his lawyer's office and I must go there and sign, too. I took a deep breath, I was glad the house was gone and I could start my new life. Now I have a wonderful feeling of freedom. When I moved into this apartment I took what I wanted from the Cliffside house. I don't want to remember that house. I want to build a new life.

"Did I tell you Father Glasson helped me find this apartment? I have no regrets. I just hope Basil is happy too. I know I am alone here in La Jolla, but since I moved into the apartment I have made some good friends at St. James and I could be busy every day."

One Monday morning in early July Faith called Jeane and told her she was in Illinois and she wanted to come to Kettering and spend one day. Jeane told her they didn't have a room for her to stay with them. Faith laughed and said she planned to rent a hotel room and she would be there on the 10th of July. Jeane called her favorite baby sitter and asked if she could stay with the children all day the 10th of July.

On the evening of the 9th of July, Faith called Jeane from the Princess Hotel and asked if she would be ready to come away with her by nine the next morning. Jeane hadn't told Curt Faith was coming to see her. Faith found their little ugly gray house near the school the next day.

Jeane

Jeane, you look wonderful. Do you like living here? Is Curt any different than he was in California? Let's go! We can talk on the way."

Jeane got in the car and waved good-bye to her baby sitter and the children. "To answer your first question, Faith, I'm not sure I do like it here, but we have only been here four months. Our neighbors are from all walks of life. I don't seem to have much in common with most of them.

"You asked me about Curt. Yes, he is different. He likes what he's doing and he even tells me when he goes to Washington. Faith, have you decided what you want to do since Basil is back in research work?"

"Yes, I know I will never live in a big eastern city. I haven't seen Basil since he started work on Dr. Handel's project, but I can't believe he will do medical research for long. Basil has to be working in his own field, but after all the problems he has had with Senator McCarthy it will be almost impossible for him to work in defense. I worry about what will happen to him, and I wonder why he followed Dr. Handel to Yale. That was unlike him.

"He has been a different man since Margaret Handel came to help me. I will never know what happened. As I was getting better it seemed like both Basil and Dr. Handel were not in the house. That was when I called Father Glasson and he came. It seemed he always has time for me. He told me I was getting better every day and he knew I would be helping at the church soon."

"Faith, you are better! You have taken control of your life. If there is something between Dr. Handel and Basil, you will soon know."

"I may be wrong, Jeane, but I wonder if he went to Yale because she wanted him there while I was recovering. I noticed she smiled every time he entered the room. He was almost never in his laboratory when she was there. He said she was there to help me, but I'm not sure."

Jeane wanted Faith to see some of the pretty parts of Kettering and Oakwood so they drove down Far Hills Drive to Faith's hotel. "Jeane, I feel like I could talk all day. I want you to know how happy I am now. I have never lived alone and now I want to see what it is like. You know Father Glasson has made a difference in my life. I know I can depend on him." Faith's eyes sparkled.

"Faith, when I hear you talk about Father Glasson, you are like a different person." Faith looked at Jeane and smiled. "You know he lives in the St. James parsonage, only a few houses from my apartment. About ten every morning he knocks on my door and asks for a cup of coffee. I look forward to seeing him then, or any time." Jeane could see Faith was happy; she looked ten years younger and she enjoyed every minute of their wonderful day. She promised to come back next summer.

When Faith took Jeane home, Curt was there. The children told him their mommy had been gone all day and Mrs. Cook had stayed with them. Curt had paid her and thanked her for staying so long. He glared at Jeane when she came in, but he didn't say a word.

After dinner he took the children out to play ball. Jeane knew he was angry. The children went to bed at eight o'clock. After he kissed them good night, he came back and sat down at the dining room table where Jeane had been sitting.

"Jeane, why didn't you tell me Faith was in town? Are you afraid of me?"

"Yes, Curt, I admit I am afraid of you. In La Jolla you were angry every time I said her name. As I told you then, I will never give up my friendship with Faith. We need each other."

"Was Basil here, too? Did you see him?"

"I have never seen Basil and I did not see him today. If you want to know, he is doing research at Yale, and Faith has rented an apartment in La Jolla for at least six months. She called when she was visiting her family in Illinois. Let's not quarrel. We are in Ohio now and I don't want to talk about this anymore."

"Jeane, I respect you for your strength, but sometimes you should do what I want. I was taught a wife should honor her husband in all things."

Jeane didn't say a word. She got up from the table and went back to their bedroom. She undressed and went to bed. A little later when Curt came to bed, he whispered in her ear. "Do you still love me?"

"Of course I still love you, but I will never be pushed around like your mother has been for the last thirty years." Curt snuggled down beside her. He mumbled something but she didn't bother to ask him

Jeane

what he said.

In September, Jeane had a call from Dorothy Kline, who had been nice to her at BAGR wives' activities. Dorothy ask Jeane if the McLyrres would like to join a bridge group to make two tables of bridge. One of the couples in the group had been ordered to Washington, D.C. and Dorothy remembered that the McLyrres liked to play bridge. Jeane accepted immediately. All of the husbands were part of BAGR. Dorothy told Jeane they played once a month, and each couple prepared cocktails, appetizers, and dinner every fourth month. Jeane was delighted. Very soon she learned most of these people had traveled all over the world. The Klines were just back from a tour of duty in Egypt and the Davisons had spent three years with the American Embassy in Rome before they came to BAGR.

Jeane could see she needed to try new recipes. She started looking in Gourmet magazine at the library, and she copied some recipes to try at home. Curt and Jeane looked forward to their first evening of bridge.

The hosts that evening were the Steels, Capt. Steel was the executive officer in BAGR. Cocktails and appetizers were served before dinner; Susan Steel passed a silver tray of smoked salmon on tiny rounds of bread spread with cream cheese. Also on the tray were tiny hot biscuits filled with ham, and in the middle of the tray surrounded by parsley were thin rounds of something Jeane had never seen before.

She didn't say a word, but she avoided eating it. She listened to the conversation and soon heard one of the men say to another, "This is the best rattlesnake meat I ever tasted, I wonder where Mark found it." Captain Steel told them he had brought it home from Paris last week. Jeane's head was spinning. She realized they were included in this group of sophisticated people who had played bridge all their life. Jeane had been playing since she was twelve and she had taught Curt the basics of bridge when they were first married and lived in Santa Rosa, California. They continued playing when they were in college at CU. Later in Norton they played often. Bridge had always been popular, during the depression years bridge helped people forget and it didn't cost a thing to play.

Jeane

When Curt had been called for active duty at Miramar they played with neighbors at least once a week.

Jeane enjoyed being a room mother so she volunteered for both April and Danny's class. One day the other mother in Danny's class mentioned there was a new Episcopal Church was being built in Kettering, but it wouldn't be finished for a year or more. Now their Sunday services are held in the auditorium at Oak View. On Sunday Jeane took the children to Sunday school there and she met the young priest, Father John David. She offered to help if she was needed. He wanted her to help him form an Altar Guild and member of the Altar Guild from St. Paul's would come and help for several months when they were ready.

In early September Jeane had a letter from Faith with a postmark from Illinois. She could hardly wait to read it.

September 15, 1954
Dear Jeane,
I'm sorry to be so long writing to tell you how much our day together meant to me. I'm still visiting my family, and they say I am like the happy girl I was before I met Basil. Isn't that wonderful? Late in July Basil told me he planned to accept a position at Columbia University this fall. He said it was in medical research and a great opportunity for him. It seems when I was so ill Dr. Handel gave notice she would resign from Yale this fall. Now she has an important position in the medical school at Columbia. Basil told me she was responsible for him receiving his appointment.

Since the six months are up, I suspect he assumed I would move with him. He is in New York now trying to find an apartment so he can start there in September. Of course, his parents are delighted.

Jeane, I wish you were here to talk with me. I don't think I could ever live in a busy city like New York. Since I moved into this apartment, I have been helping at St. James and I feel at peace. I never want to live under pressure again. Truthfully, I don't think Basil would care. Every time he mentions Margaret, he seems excited.

Jeane

What shall I do? I am happiest when I am helping at the church. I'm happier than I have been in the past seven years. I need to stand alone and make my place in the world. When you get this letter, call me. I need you. You have the phone number here.

Love,
Faith

Jeane sat down. She didn't know what to think, but she knew Faith needed and wanted help. She picked up the phone and called. Faith answered the phone.

"Faith, I have just finished reading your letter. It sounds like you are a different person and you know what is best for yourself. Tell me honestly, what do you want to do?"

"I want to stay in La Jolla, I have made more friends among the Altar Guild ladies. Those people have begun to depend on me. I am myself and I will never entertain entertainers again. I don't want to wonder where Basil is anymore. I just want to hear what you think is best."

"Faith, why don't you tell Basil you want to stay in La Jolla for at least another nine months? Both of you know these past seven years have been difficult. Wait until next summer to make your final decision. I think he needs time, too. His work at Columbia will be different than defense work. You will know by next summer if you like living alone.

"Since you were married, he told you what you could and couldn't do. You need time to be sure you want to plan your own life. Wait, don't act too quickly."

"Thank you, Jeane, I knew you could help me. Now I am going back to La Jolla and my apartment."

Jeane was amazed at the changes she had seen in Faith. She knew Basil had always been demanding, but now Faith wasn't afraid of him and she was ready to take care of herself.

In September, Jeane's mother wrote they wanted to see their grandchildren and the little gray house. Jeane was delighted and wrote back as soon as she found a motel near them so her dad could have somewhere to rest. When they came, she could see

Jeane

that her dad seemed tired most of the time. He didn't play ball with the children, but he sat in the carport and cheered the ball games. After a week her dad decided it was time to go home. He didn't say much about the house except that the workmanship was terrible. He showed Curt how to fix the windows so they would open in summer and close tight in winter; then he showed him the best way to put up shelves in the storage room.

Jeane's parents watched her all the time. They were delighted that she was expecting another baby, but they worried about her. She told them she felt fine and was anxious for the baby to arrive.

October, 20, 1954
Dear Jeane and Curt,
    Your dad had a thorough examination and Dr. Kennedy told him if he lost twenty pounds he would feel much better, but you know him. He refused. Now after dinner, he sits down in his easy chair and I can see he is having trouble breathing. Then he gets up and lies on the bed where he can breathe a little easier. I don't mention it because it makes him angry. I try to pretend he is fine. I don't want him to blame me.

    The shortness of breath is a worry, and I don't know how many digitalis pills he has to take now. He still drives to Friendly's every morning for coffee. I'm glad he still wants to do that. He always goes unless it is icy outdoors.

    I hate to worry you but the Brown men have had bad hearts as long as I have known them. I know you remember that your Grandpa Brown died in 1942 and your Uncle Lewis Brown died about the same time. I think your Great-grandfather Brown had a bad heart, too.

    We had such a nice time when we were there. Danny is growing up; how is he doing in school? I noticed he always tells you what you want to hear. April is such a good little girl and smart, too. I have always felt like she was almost mine.

Love,
Mother

Jeane handed Curt the letter when he got home. He sat down

Jeane

and read it through. For a moment he was quiet. "Jeane, I noticed your dad seemed very tired and short of breath when they were here. I know he didn't feel well most of the time. How would you feel about us going to Norton for Christmas? I feel this will be his last Christmas, but I know you will be very uncomfortable by then."

"Curt, I will ask the doctor, and if he says it is all right we will go; we won't mention it to them yet."

Christmas in Kansas

December was warm, and the doctor told her to go home and have Christmas with her parents. They started west on the 18th of December. Curt had packed the car and all the boxes of old Christmas ornaments were on top. He thought a Christmas tree with those three little birds near the top plus the other ornaments would remind Jeane and her parents of all their Christmases together. After Jeane and Curt moved back to Norton in 1948 when Curt graduated from C.U. and went to work with his father-in-law. That first Christmas her parents insisted Jeane take all the old ornaments to keep the traditions of the past. The Browns had decided they didn't want a tree just for themselves.

As the McLyrres drove west Jeane prayed this would not be their last Christmas together. She thought about the little celluloid birds and knew they would be near the top of the tree again in Norton and on other trees for many more Christmases.

Jeane thought about the surprise she had for April. She had worked hard on a wardrobe for a six-inch girl doll that all the little girls wanted for Christmas this year. Jeane knew she wouldn't have time for such foolishness after the new baby arrived.

When they got to Norton her mother was anxious to buy each of the McLyrres new outfits for Christmas. She liked to see her family well dressed.

Jeane remembered how her dad always did his shopping on Christmas Eve and he did the same thing this year. Her mother had tears in her eyes when he came in with his arms full of packages. He bought Danny a Lionel electric train and April a child's electric typewriter. His eyes shone with happiness as he watched the children

Jeane

unwrap their gifts.

When the packages were all opened and the children were busy with their new gifts Maurice had tears in his eyes. "Curt, thank you for making this a special Christmas. Jeane, I know you are miserable but you and your family have made this our best Christmas since we sold the motel in 1946 and moved here."

Christmas afternoon the Grahams came to celebrate the day. Everyone sang the old Christmas favorites and Ethel popped lots of popcorn. April and Danny were surprised because it wasn't raining and they got to eat popcorn in the living room anyway. Joan and Gayle had beautiful voices and they led the Christmas carols. Late in the afternoon Jeane brought in a bowl of punch, with plates of cookies and fruit cake she had made in Ohio. Her dad sat in his platform rocker and enjoyed the day. Jeane was uncomfortable, but she knew they were where they belonged, if only for a few days.

The day after Christmas, a blizzard was predicted for northwest Kansas. Curt packed the car, and the McLyrres were on their way east before noon. They promised Jeane's parents they would stop the moment they saw the first snowflake. April and Danny were tired and slept most of the afternoon in the back of the station wagon. Curt drove to Hannibal for the night. The desk clerk told Curt no blizzard was predicted there.

Curt was anxious to have his family back in Ohio as soon as possible. During January and February, Jeane felt as if every day was a week. She worried about herself and she wished she were back in Kansas where Dr. Bennie could deliver this big baby she was carrying. Her feet and legs were swollen even though she had gained only four pounds since the doctor prescribed Dexatrim. Her doctor assured her this would be an easy delivery. She smiled when she remembered she had never looked nicer than after Danny was born. She hoped she would be that thin after this baby was born. Jeane loved to cook and taste. It seemed like it was impossible for her to keep her weight down.

While she waited for the new baby she decided she would make a princess line dress like she had seen in Vogue. The magazine assured its readers the princess line was the choice for spring.

Jeane

Jeane looked in her standing mirror and laughed out loud. She looked like a big rubber ball with arms and legs. When she saw herself she couldn't believe she would ever wear the princess line dress she just finished. During the time she worked on it she held it in front of herself and she looked in the mirror and smiled. She hoped it would be her Easter dress.

Curt asked Adm. and Mrs. Wells if they would be the new baby's godparents and they said yes. During the past year the McLyrres had become friends with most of the BAGR Officers and their wives. The McLyrres wanted all of them to come for the new baby's baptism and reception. In February she prepared all the food for the reception and arranged it on separate trays stored in their new freezer in the storage room.

Preparing for the party helped make the time pass. She didn't admit it, but she was worried because she was so big. She remembered Dr. Bennie had to induce both April and Danny. When she went to her doctor early in February she asked about being induced, and her doctor told her the policy in the hospital was not to induce. He promised her it would not be necessary with a third baby.

The morning of February 22, 1955, Jeane awakened with strong contractions. She awakened Curt and called Arlene Thomas, who was there before they were ready to go to the hospital. Curt was nervous. He helped Jeane into the car and sped toward the hospital as her contractions became stronger and more frequent. He broke the speed limit, hoping a patrolman would stop him because then they would have a police escort all the way. No patrol car saw them and Jeane suffered; she twisted and turned until she was almost on the floor of the car. When they reached the hospital emergency entrance, they were met by a young enlisted man with a wheelchair. Jeane was exhausted.

Patrick Brown McLyrre was anxious to be born and by eight o'clock that morning he was screaming and kicking. It was only an hour after Jeane had been admitted to the hospital. Curt called the Browns. They told him their car was packed and they would be on their way east by nine o'clock.

Jeane

They stayed in the same motel as before because Jeane's father was comfortable there. On the third day the Browns arrived and Curt took them to see Jeane and Patrick. They had never been in a military hospital or a big ward in any hospital. Curt had not told them that all the new mothers were in one ward. The Wright-Patterson Air Force Hospital had only wards for women patients. In the military all women were treated the same unless they were critically ill. When the Browns went into the ward, Maurice was shocked. There were women of many races and his daughter was in a bed next to a woman from Africa. He yelled for the nurse to move his daughter. Curt and Ethel pushed him out of the ward. He told the nurse he was going to move his daughter to a private hospital. After that Curt took them back to the house.

Jeane was embarrassed and she apologized to the new mothers. The woman in the bed next to her was the wife of an Air Force Sergeant. She told Jeane not to worry. She insisted most parents, unless they were in the service, would have acted the same way.

Jeane's parents stayed only one day after she brought Patrick home. Both of her parents were pleased that Patrick would have Brown as a middle name.

The day Patrick was born Jeane asked Curt to send Faith a telegram with the news they had a son whose name was Patrick Brown McLyrre.

The day her parents started home she had a special delivery letter from Faith.

February 26, 1955
Dear Jeane,
Congratulations! I can't wait to see him.
I have wonderful news too! I went over what was in the Cliffside house before I signed the final papers. I have been in my apartment more than eight months now. Basil couldn't have been nicer while he was here. He urged me to go over the house again. I went back and found several things that meant a great deal to me. When we were married, my parents had given me an old painting of our farmhouse. Now it is on the wall in my dining room. I had forgotten a quilt my grandmother made when she was seventy years old. It is very old, but it means

Jeane

home to me. My parents had given us silverware for a wedding present and I'm not using it now, but some day it may be precious to me. I'm sure you noticed the pearls I wear. They belonged to my grandmother and I will wear them always. I don't want the Oriental rugs or the huge oil paintings. I don't know what Basil will do with them, but I don't want them.

Basil agreed it was a good idea for me to stay in La Jolla for a year. He told me when the sale was final he would put half the money in my account. I told him it wasn't necessary, but he insisted it was fair. He told me Dr. Handel agreed that it would be best for me to stay here for the rest of the year, then we should reach a final decision.

Basil found an apartment and started his work at Columbia University last September. He told me he was called in October to go through another interrogation by the Atomic Energy Commission. They told him he would never work for the AEC again. Senator McCarthy with his list of probable Communists have ruined Basil's hopes of ever doing defense work again. I don't think he will ever be the same. I am happy Dr. Handel has helped him more than I ever could.

We took what we wanted from the house and Basil sold the rest. He had his car driven to New York. He flew back east the day after the house sale was final. I feel like a new person. I can look past St. James through the park and see the cove every day. When I was settled in my apartment I invited my new friends for my house warming. It was fun and I have never been happier than I am now.

During the time Basil locked himself in his laboratory and we lived in the big house life was painful for me. You seemed to know I was lonely. Those strangers we entertained were there only for publicity. I didn't want to know them. When you sat down beside me at that Sigma Kappa Alumnae meeting I felt you wanted to know me. Those months when we saw each other often were wonderful. I knew you would always be my friend. Basil never mentioned our friendship, he didn't care as long as I helped him with his entertaining. He felt sorry for those entertainers that were on Senator McCarthy's list. Nothing was right with us after we moved to La Jolla. I have to believe

Jeane

Dr. Handel has helped both of us. I am fine now and I hope Basil is happy too.

Father Glasson has helped me even more. He knew of this apartment and took me to see it. He told me he felt I had made a good choice. He said I was still a young woman and now I must find what is right for me. He told me I had helped him too. When I remember how sick I was two years ago I can hardly believe how well I feel now. I am a different person!

Jeane take care of yourself. I am so anxious to see you I will come back and visit my family and you next spring. You have my address on the envelope. Write when you can.

Be Happy,

Love,
Faith

While Patrick nursed, Jeane sat and pondered the letter. She hoped Faith was really happy in her new life. It amazed Jeane that Faith still appreciated Margaret Handel. Jeane suspected Maragret Handel was anxious to have Faith's marriage ended. Jeane was sure Faith would never be happy in New York. Jeane had never met Basil, yet she wondered if it wouldn't be better for him to have a friend like Dr. Handel. She hoped Faith would never be lonely again and it would be wonderful if she met a kind gentle man some day. Faith was thirty four and that was not too old to have a baby. She looked down at her new demanding son. She had little time to worry about anything, but keeping things in order at home.

All the BGAR Officers and their wives were invited to Patrick's baptism on March 17, 1955 at St. Paul's Episcopal Church in Dayton, since the new Kettering Church wasn't finished. The celebration was a success. The guests could hardly believe Jeane had prepared all the food before Patrick was born.

Curt and Jeane had begun to think BAGR was better duty for them than Miramar. Curt was less tense; he went to Washington often, but he was usually gone only one or two nights. They were happy in their ugly little house and Jeane had discouraged Mrs. Johnson from coming while Patrick was asleep.

By April the McLyrres had saved enough money to buy some flowering bushes that would bloom later in the spring. When her

Jeane

parents came to see Patrick, her dad had brought her four wooden flower boxes for the carport. Jeane decided to fill them with red geraniums and white petunias that bloomed all summer.

In the backyard she planted the cosmos and four o'clock seeds her mother brought from Norton. The backyard was like a carpet, with grass and flowers. Jeane suggested April's class could have the last day of school picnic in the McLyrres' backyard since that location was only a block from Oak View School. April loved school and had done well. Danny was a dreamer; he would agree to anything and then ignore it.

Peace

When summer arrived, Jeane was even more unhappy with the Johnsons. After school was out and the windows had to be open even more motorcycles were going up and down Kenosha Road until midnight. She called the police almost every night, but the Johnsons always talked the policeman into eating hamburgers and checking out one of the new bikes. They knew Jeane called the police but never mentioned it. Danny slipped over there whenever he could escape his mother. Jeane was shocked by some of the language he brought home. One Sunday Ralph Johnson invited Danny and Curt to the motorcycle races. Jeane was shocked when she saw Danny riding in the sidecar of a motorcycle.

After that Jeane decided to take the children to Norton before her mother's birthday and stay there the rest of the summer. She wanted Danny away from the motorcycles. Curt liked the Johnsons, but he knew Jeane didn't want Danny over there.

On the second of July Curt drove his family to Hannibal, where the Browns met them. When Jeane saw how tired her dad seemed she insisted she wanted to drive. She could see her dad had lost weight and his eyes had lost their twinkle.

By the time they reached St. Joseph, Missouri, Jeane suggested they stay in a motel for the night; everyone was tired, and it would be easier to get to Norton early the next day. Her mother agreed Maurice needed to relax and rest, and the children could run around and play until dark.

Jeane

After supper Maurice sat down beside the swimming pool. Jeane could see he was having trouble breathing. She suggested he stand up for awhile, but when she saw how hard it was for him to stand she walked with him to his room. The next morning Jeane drove on to Norton, and Maurice seemed relieved to be home.

The children were happy with their grandparents, but they were noisy. Every afternoon Jeane took them some place so her father could rest. Some days they went to Elmwood Park, another to the school playground, and often to the swimming pool. Sometimes one of Jeane's friends invited them to their home.

Maurice played with his grandchildren every morning. He had built a cradle for April's doll and he let her decorate it. He took Danny to the hardware store and bought him a tool box. When Danny went through the tool box he found a hammer, measuring tape, carpenter's pencils, screwdrivers, saw, and a drill with extra bits. His grandfather took Danny to the shop so he could watch Jay use each of the tools. Maurice seemed to feel good in the mornings, but at lunch he ate very little and napped all afternoon.

On the fifteenth of July, Wanda Heaton invited Jeane and the children to her house to play with Diane and Janice. About three o'clock Wanda's telephone rang and when she answered she immediately handed the telephone to Jeane. It was her mother and she was sobbing and hard to understand. "Jeane, your dad is dead! I didn't know. It happened so fast. I don't want you to bring the children home until later."

Wanda heard enough to know Jeane's father was dead. She insisted Jeane go home to be with her mother and she would bring April and Danny later. Jeane picked up Patrick and hurried home. Her mother sat on the sofa sobbing as she looked into space. She didn't say a word for twenty minutes.

"Jeane, I walked through our bedroom, and he sat up. I asked him how he felt and he said fine; then he fell back on the bed. Somehow I knew it was serious. I ran to the telephone and called for an ambulance, which was here within minutes. They examined him quickly and put him on the stretcher. They said I should come, too. They took him to the hospital, and it wasn't long before they

Jeane

told me he was dead. The doctor on duty told me he had died instantly. I don't know who brought me home, but I am glad I was here and I'm glad you weren't. It would have frightened the children."

The news passed quickly. Ethel's neighbors came to help although there was nothing anyone could do. Wanda brought the children home about five and Jeane told them what had happened. Danny was sure it was a mistake. April wanted to comfort her grandmother.

Supper appeared, Jeane never knew who brought it. In small towns whenever there was a death the food kept coming. Friends and family came with more food and stayed through the evening.

Both Jeane and her mother wanted April and Danny to go to the funeral; it was the way to say good-bye. Jay Fawcett's wife, Vida, took Patrick home with her for the morning.

The funeral was at the Scott-Brantley Funeral Home. Jeane was amazed how many people were there. She vowed she wouldn't cry during the funeral. She kept feeling her father was there. He had always insisted flowers at a funeral were wasteful, but there were so many flowers at his funeral it seemed like they were in a garden. Jeane thought her dad was watching from above and shaking his head. Ethel had requested no flowers, but no one listened. The chapel was crowded, every seat was taken, and people stood in the back. Some people waited outdoors under the canopy standing on both sides of the driveway until the hearse drove away.

When the funeral procession reached Mount Olive Cemetery in Almena, the hearse drove to a newly dug grave. The pallbearers carried the coffin to the frame over the grave. The mourners took their places. The undertaker led Ethel to a seat beside the grave. Her eyes shot sparks as she held him there. She gasped, "Stop this burial! This is not where Maurice will be buried." The undertaker glared at his assistant who was in charge of digging graves. He saw that Ethel was angry. She told him this grave was in the wrong place. The undertaker urged Ethel to let the services be completed. She was furious, but she agreed. The mourners did not wait for the coffin to be lowered; they spoke to Ethel and her family as they went to their cars. When everyone had gone, they were alone in

Jeane

the cemetery.

The gravedigger twisted his hat in his hands. "Now, Ethel," he said. "This has been hard for you, but I am sure this is your grave site."

"You listen to me! Don't you tell me I don't know what I am talking about. When my mother died, we bought the grave site next to my parents. I will show you exactly where it is. You will not bury Maurice where he is now."

"Ethel, I bury people every day and I have never made a mistake."

The caretaker of the cemetery had appeared in time to hear the argument. He immediately stepped forward and asked why the grave site was not on the Browns' plot. The gravedigger turned red. Apparently he had not checked with his boss who had assigned a new employee to dig the grave. Ethel never forgave him.

The undertaker told Curt the funeral car would take them back to Norton and bring them back to Mt. Olive at six o'clock to be sure everything was in order. Dinner had been brought to the Browns and some of their relatives who came from far away. Everyone wondered what had gone wrong at the cemetery, but no one asked. The family and friends relaxed when Ethel, Jeane, Curt, and the children got to the house. Ethel was in control of herself and made everyone feel comfortable.

Ethel was surprised and delighted when she saw her cousin, John Graham. She didn't know Gilbert had called him in Sterling, Colorado, and he had driven almost four hours to get to Norton in time for the funeral. During lunch Ethel realized Maurice's clothes would fit him. After dinner she insisted he take all of Maurice's clothes home with him.. She said she would feel better if she knew someone was wearing them. Jeane was pleased that all the Brown family were there for the services. Maurice's mother refused to stay for the dinner so Dan took her home. Lewis and Clarence's families were all there.

Curt came for the funeral, and returned to Dayton the next day. He agreed that Jeane should stay with her mother until school started. April sat beside her grandmother every minute she was awake. It seemed like she was afraid she would lose her grandmother if she wasn't right there. Danny was unusually quiet;

Jeane

he took out the big wooden blocks his grandfather had made for him when he was three. He sat on the floor and built houses and barns, then he kicked them down as though he was angry. He did it over and over.

Ethel cleaned house as though her house was filthy. It was her release so Jeane didn't try to help. She knew her mother wanted time to be alone so Jeane took her children out until noon every day. Ethel knew Maurice had not been well for a long time, but she never accepted it until he was gone. She knew she could never have changed him. He had to do it his way.

Jeane took the children to Almena and left them at the Grahams while she visited her Grandmother Brown. She realized she knew very little about her father. She wanted to know where they had lived when he was growing up. She realized she could never speak to him again. Her grandmother told her he was born near Prairie View and had lived in Almena and Norton all of his life.

His mother was blessed with a wonderful memory, but she wanted to talk about her own childhood and Jeane wasn't interested. Every evening Jeane would sit in her father's platform rocker and mull over what she had learned.

Ethel was restless; she wanted them to go somewhere every evening. Usually they went to Elmwood Park and the children played on the play equipment, then they would go to the Dairy Queen and have ice cream before they went home and to bed.

Jeane knew her mother had found solace from being near her farm homestead where she was born. It had given her solace when her dad died, and now she looked there for peace again. The roads into the farm were rutted and sometimes muddy so many evenings they just sat on the edge of the road in the car and remembered times past. This was the only time she talked about the past, but she looked to the future every day. Another of her sayings.

"Yesterday is gone, tomorrow may never come, so live for today."

By mid August, it was evident Ethel was ready for her peace. The children had been good a long time, but now they resented

Jeane

being told to keep their toys in place and not run in the house. Patrick had pulled up in his playpen. It was time to go home. Jeane called Curt and he came for them the next day. Jeane had worried about their ugly little house; but now she thought it looked like a mansion. Curt had watered her flowers all summer, and he was ready for her to take over.

Patrick was a spoiled baby. He had been handled and pampered all summer and he didn't like to be alone. He cried when she put him in his crib. She found he was happiest in his baby seat on the washing machine as he watched her cook and wash dishes.

Jeane was restless. She felt the world that was so important to her would one day be gone. She knew the children would grow up, but now she felt tied to the house. She missed going to the officers' club to play bridge. She never told anyone she felt sorry for herself when she should be happy.

She needed something she could do at home. She had always wanted to learn to paint. When school started she saw in the Oak View News someone was going to give oil painting classes at the school. She enrolled immediately. Her first picture was of the old barn on the Graham farm. She could see it in her memory. It wasn't a great picture, but she was proud of it. She put it in a frame and sent it to her mother for Christmas.

Her next picture was a covered bridge like so many still in Ohio. She was anxious to try because she had a picture to copy. She quickly learned oil paints were slow to dry so it was easy to improve her picture.

Christmas was quiet; Jeane begged her mother to come, but she refused to be away from home in bad weather. She promised she would come in the spring. Jeane helped with the Girl Scouts, and the meetings were at the McLyrres' house. When the girls saw Patrick they were eager to earn a Girl Scout badge for giving him a bath. Patrick wasn't pleased at being used for the Girl Scouts' lessons.

Jeane tried again to get her mother to come to Ohio for Christmas and again she refused. She wrote that the Grahams urged her to celebrate with them and she accepted, if there wasn't snow and if it wasn't too cold.

Before Christmas, Jeane dressed all three children in red

Jeane

sleepers and Curt took their picture in front of the fireplace. Jeane sent a picture to each of the grandparents and smaller ones to their friends. Patrick didn't quite understand what was happening but on Christmas morning he learned to tear open packages as well as his brother and sister.

The McLyrres' income allowed one special gift for each child so Jeane wrapped pajamas, socks, and underwear separately in Christmas paper. The children played with the packages two weeks before Christmas and counted the packages every day to be sure each had the same number.

Jeane sent Faith a picture of the children before Christmas and told her how happy they were in their little gray house. She didn't mention the reason they were so happy was because she did nothing to annoy Curt. She stayed home and took care of her baby. She helped at school and went to all the BAGR coffees, teas, and luncheons. Jeane was not unhappy but she knew this was not the exciting life of her dreams. She hadn't made close friends because she had to stay home with her baby and most of the BAGR families had older children. She closed her letter asking Faith to write her a long letter soon.

December 20, 1955
Dear Jeane,

I have been so busy I hardly have time to think. I had your letter from Norton telling me about the sudden death of your father. You must have been glad you were there when he died. I'm sure you and your active children did help your mother, but I am sure it was hard for you, too. I hope to see you next summer. It has been more than a year since we have seen each other. I always go home to Illinois every summer or I would be lost, and my family wouldn't understand.

When I think of you, I wish you still lived in La Jolla so we could go shopping and out for lunch. I wish you could see how happy I am now. I still think I might not be alive if it hadn't been for you.

Jeane, I didn't know how busy and happy I could be. I volunteer to help take care of the babies during Sunday School. They are so sweet. I guess I will never forgive Basil for not

Jeane

letting me take care of our son. John scolds me when I say that. He says I must forgive Basil because he thought it was for the best. By now you must wonder who is the John I mention so often. It is Father John Glasson.

After he helped me find this apartment last January, he asked if he could call me Faith. It surprised me. I felt my face turn red, and I looked down at the floor. That embarrassed him. He apologized and said he wanted me to be his friend. He looked at me and asked again if he could call me Faith. He told me that after his wife died, he wished he could die, too.

I looked straight at him and said, "John, please call me Faith; I want to be your friend. I am so happy here, and you have made it possible. I enjoy making coffee for you every morning and we are friends even more since I live in my own home."

Jeane, you know how hard it is for me to make friends. Now I know I have two friends.

I am busy where ever I am needed. So many wonderful things are needed to be done at Christmas time.

Last week when John and I were having our morning coffee, and I saw he had a far away look in his eye. I asked him if he was well. He smiled and said he was thinking about the Christmases in his childhood homes in Indiana and Michigan. He told me now his parents live in Florida. His only child is a son, David, who lives in Connecticut. It was then I realized we would both be alone on Christmas so I decided to ask him to have Christmas dinner with me.

Pray for me,
        Faith

The year, 1956, came while all the McLyrres slept soundly. The church bells rang, fire crackers went off, and motorcycles raced up and down Kenosha Road, but everyone in the little gray house slept. Jeane dreaded the long and snowy winter in Ohio. The children loved the snow, and Jeane appreciated the big windows in their house so she could see where they were playing. Eleven-month-old Patrick wanted to be outdoors too.

Jeane continued her painting classes. She found a new calendar

Jeane

with a picture of snow, a rocky stream, and lots of trees. Since she had to be home, she worked on her painting every day and the time went quickly. She never missed her painting class that met once a week at Oak View. Curt knew the cold weather was hard for Jeane so he was willing to take care of the children when she went to painting class.

Patrick was busy every moment and Jeane had to resign as a room mother since he was into everything. She continued with the Girl Scouts even though they chose projects to do on the McLyrres' dining room table. Every month she and Curt anxiously waited for the BAGR bridge group.

Jeane even enjoyed having Florence Johnson come on cold snowy mornings when she had to stay in the house. Patrick loved her. She would open the McLyrres door and holler. "Hey Patrick! Where are you? Come on, let's have fun!" No matter where Patrick was he ran as fast as he could. Mrs. Johnson picked him up and whirled him around, then she reached in her pocket and pulled out a cookie. Immediately he wanted down to get down to eat it. Jeane made fresh coffee and Mrs. Johnson sat down at the table.

"Mrs. Johnson, sometimes I think Patrick likes you better than he likes me."

"That's easy. If you carried cookies in your pocket, he would follow you. By the way, I am going to be a grandmother again. Fern is having a baby in May. I told her that was very bad planning. May is when we sell the most motorcycles in both stores. Oh, well, if I know Fern that baby will be in their store before he's two weeks old. Maybe it will increase our sales.!

"Wow, won't that be fun to have another baby in the neighborhood. You won't let me keep Patrick, but I bet I can keep Fern's baby any old time."

Jeane looked up and smiled. "I just had a letter from my mother. She is going to keep her word and come for Easter. I know you will like her. She talked to some of her friends in Norton and they suggested she take the Trailways Bus to Dayton. She will only have to change in Kansas City."

When Jeane's mother arrived before Easter and Mrs. Johnson knew she was there, she was anxious to meet her, but she waited until nine o'clock before she knocked on the McLyrre's door with

Jeane

fresh breakfast rolls. As soon as she knocked she opened the door and called out, "Where's Patrick?"

Patrick ran to her and tried to reach in her pocket. His grandmother picked him up, but immediately he started to cry and he squirmed down to the floor. Mrs. Johnson squatted down to Patrick's size and he knew he would find his cookie. Patrick liked to be the center of attention, but first he wanted to eat his cookie.

Mrs. Johnson sat down at the table with Jeane and her mother. "I'm glad to meet you, Mrs. Brown, please call me Flo. All of your grandchildren have told me you were coming. I guess you know you are a very important person. When Mrs. Johnson finished her coffee, she slipped out the door.

Ethel looked at Jeane. "Is that woman clean? I guess she must be. I saw you enjoyed her breakfast rolls. Did you see she was barefooted? She is different than I expected. I'm sure she wants to be friendly. I'm surprised you let Patrick eat what she brings over here. Does she always bring cookies for Patrick? Now I see why you get annoyed with her. Why do you put up with her?"

June said, "At first I was annoyed, but, *I have no choice*, as Curt would say. She comes when she wants and she is good to all of us. The children treat her like another grandmother. Patrick has a short memory. If you show him a cookie in your pocket, he won't leave you alone."

Ethel helped the children dye their Easter eggs and Curt hid them in the backyard so the children could find them Easter morning. While Ethel was there she wanted to do something for Curt and Jeane. She saw they had only a bedframe and a box springs and mattress on legs. So she had Jeane take them to find a complete set of matching bedroom furniture. Jeane was thrilled. All they ever had was a chest of drawers her dad had built for the motel over fifteen years ago. Both Jeane and Curt were proud of their new set of furniture.

Jeane was thrilled with the new furniture, but her standing mahogany mirror now looked out of place with the limed oak bedroom furniture. She bought a pint of white enamel and painted the frame with white enamel.

Jeane hadn't done much sewing since Patrick arrived. He demanded all her time, but now since he could walk he was much

Jeane

easier satisfied. Jeane had to put a hook high on all the outside doors to keep him from slipping out.

Jeane needed a break when school was out. She called her mother to ask if she would like company for two weeks. Of course Ethel was delighted. Curt drove his family to Norton on Saturday and returned to Dayton on Sunday. For Jeane it was a relief to get away from the motorcycles. Curt didn't mention how often he ate hamburgers and drank beer at the Johnsons.

When they were back in Kettering, nothing had changed at BGAR and life was good. Curt liked his work and Adm. Wells suggested he apply for the regular United States Navy and Curt agreed. He remembered several Naval Reserve Officers who had sixteen years of service and had been forced out of the Navy with no retirement. Curt worried that it might happen to him since he was Active Duty Naval Reserve, too. Adm. Wells wrote the selection board an A-1 recommendation for Curt.

Early in October Curt came home in a bad mood. He had been refused for the regular United States Navy. Adm. Wells told him it wasn't unusual to get a first refusal. He said the reason was because the Navy wanted to be sure the applicant was serious about a life in the Navy. Adm. Wells told Curt to wait until next spring and apply again. Curt refused, he told the admiral that if the Navy wanted him they had to ask for him.

Adm. Wells knew Curt would have been an asset to the Navy, but he knew the Navy never asked anyone. If Curt has listened to Adm. Wells probably he would have been selected the next year for regular Navy, but he was too stubborn.

In 1956 Curt's brother Charles invited Curt and his family for Thanksgiving. Curt's brother, Charles was an Annapolis graduate earning his masters' degree at the University of Michigan in Ann Arbor. Neither Curt nor Jeane really knew Charles and his family, but when Charles wrote Curt and invited them for Thanksgiving Curt accepted immediately. Jeane hadn't seen either Charles or his wife Beth twice since they were married.

Beth was a lovely lady who had grown up in Boston. Jeane, had never been in Boston, but she was intimidated by Beth. She hoped some day she could be more like Beth, quiet, thoughtful, and efficient. The brothers wished they could spend more time together,

Jeane

but since it was a four hour drive between their homes it never happened, except this once. Charles house was small so Curt's family stayed in a motel. Charles' family included Michael, six, and Cindy, four. Curt admired Charles and how well he had done in his career. The brothers and their families had been together in Hugo, Colorado only once before Charles family moved to Ann Arbor.

New Years Eve 1957 was just another day. Most of the BAGR families had children at home and all of the families lived far apart. There was one new family who had come to BAGR during the summer. They loved to have people around them. Cdr. Ed King and his wife, Betty, encouraged their friends to stop in often. Their three children and the McLyrre three were similar in age. Ed was a pilot with flight pay, so they could afford a house in Oakwood and have lots of parties. Jeane envied them their traditional house and all the people they had around them. The McLyrres' loved to go to the Kings because it was always party time and their children were always welcome. Most of the Kings friends were pilots.

Ed loved a party and he loved to cook. He didn't care how many people were there, young or old, they were always welcome. Ed would not let Betty in the kitchen when he was cooking.

Everyone who came to the Kings slipped in and out with beer, wine, or food. The children seemed to be every where. They tormented Zipper, the Kings dog. It was hard not to have fun with the Kings. The children raced through the house, but most of the people ignored them. Patrick's legs were shorter than the others he was furious because he couldn't keep up with the others; being with the Kings reminded Jeane of La Jolla and Miramar.

New Year's Day was typical of the Kings' parties. The McLyrres were there before noon and others came and went all afternoon. Jeane had brought snacks and soft drinks for at least a dozen children. Most of the men watched the football game on television. People started coming just after noon to get a head start on the big day. On the party days there was food all day, plus good television and good company. Ed cooked, and he didn't want help, but what he prepared was fit for a king.

Jeane

1957 Orders—There was no choice

Jeane knew their three-year tour of duty was almost over. She was exhausted from chasing Patrick. She hoped by summer they would be gone. She knew nothing would ever change the Johnsons and their motorcycles. Jeane was happiest in the winter when there was very little activity at the Johnsons. Jeane made a New Year's resolution. She would quit calling the police, but Pete Johnsons' brother was the chief of police now and he would be there most evenings. Jeane thought she wouldn't have to worry. They would soon be gone.

In January Curt came home with orders to report for Naval Air Training School in Olathe, Kansas on March 15th. He was being trained in Ground Control Activity. The Navy would provide quarters for his family in Olathe or in Norton, Kansas. The Training Program was for four months. At the completion of the training Curt would receive final orders to proceed to Japan and report to the Commanding officer of NAS Atsugi. Both Curt and Jeane had mixed feelings. They were happy in Ohio except for the motorcycles. The children were doing well in school, but *there was no choice.* The training was for officers ordered to a various GCA facility somewhere around the world.

Neither Curt nor Jeane were pleased. Curt spent his last six weeks in Ohio painting the living room, dining room, and kitchen. Jeane cleaned the windows and sorted what should go into storage. Every day Curt brought home more instructions about life in Japan and they were advised not to take any major electrical appliances because of the difference in current. They were instructed to have their furniture put into storage. The Army Depot in Japan would issue the furniture they needed when they got there. They hoped for quarters on base, but they would probably have to live off base in a Japanese house approved by the housing office at Camp Zama, a big Army base near Atsugi.

Their little gray house was listed for sale, $12,500. They had learned to love it but they couldn't afford to keep it. Their agent insisted it would sell immediately, but that didn't happen, it wasn't brick. Jeane was busy planning what they should take to Japan and

Jeane

what they should send to storage. They had been advised to take no furniture or electrical appliances. She decided to take all their clothing, cameras, radio, clocks, and pictures for the walls to make it seem more like home and she was sure they would need the children's bicycles, roller skates, and toys. Jeane needed her sewing supplies and sewing machine. She wanted to take her mirror, but the movers refused to promise it would get to Japan in good condition so she let it go to storage. She packed all the bed linens, dishes, silverware, glassware, pots, and pans to take with them.

The storage pieces were picked up the morning of the fifth of March. The express shipment was picked up that afternoon. After both shipments were gone, the house didn't mean so much to them.

They packed everything else in the station wagon, told their neighbors good-bye, and drove away. They drove to Indianapolis and stayed all night at a Ramada Inn on the west side of the city. Curt telephoned their agent just before they left. He told her if the house wasn't sold by the first of June they would have to rent it. In May a couple made an offer to buy if the McLyrres would accept a loan where the new buyer paid the McLyrres, and the McLyrres paid the lender. The new owners were expecting their house to sell soon so their agent urged Curt and Jeane to accept the offer. The new owners moved in on the first of June.

One of the last things Jeane did before moving was to call Faith. She told her they had very little time to get ready to leave Kettering, but it would be six months before they sailed for Japan. Jeane gave her their address and her mother's telephone number in Norton.

Jeane's mother was delighted; she would have her family there again. She was working one day a week at the Norton Sale Barn where she managed the office. Frank Sellers owned the sale barn, and Ethel had known the Sellers family for a long time. She soon realized Frank worked with all the farmers she knew and more. She had to be busy and Frank didn't like to do book work. For Ethel it was like being back in Almena surrounded by stockmen and farmers she had known all her life.

She loved to work with the public. Everyone knew her, and soon she was asked to help solicit funds for a Senior Citizens Center in Norton. It would be a meeting place for people over fifty. She

Jeane

was excited and worked hard to get generous donations. She and a friend concentrated on local businesses and successful farmers. The federal government would match each dollar that was donated in Norton.

Ethel was able to get big donations from the bankers and merchants. She knew all of them well and she pushed them to give more. Many of the retired farmers donated generously when they were called because they were bored and they had no where to go especially in the winter. They needed a place to play cards and meet their friends. A nice building on West Main Street was for sale and the Senior Citizens Center was able to get financing to buy it. Jeane remembered when people in Norton from different churches seldom spoke to each other and now they all worked together.

Jeane had forgotten how cold it was in March in western Kansas. One week after they arrived there was a blizzard. It came fast with strong winds. The children wanted to go out and play, but they didn't realize there was ice under the snow that made it dangerous.

Jeane and the children lived in Norton as if they would be there forever. Jeane filled in at various bridge groups and Ethel gladly kept Patrick even though he was two and into everything. After school when April and Danny came home cold, Ethel even let them eat popcorn in the living room.

It had been less than two years since Maurice died, and Ethel was still lonely. When Jeane told her she and the children would be with her for over four months she cried. Now she would be busy every minute. Ethel adored her grandchildren, and April followed her everywhere.

Ethel was a strong woman. She had helped care for her mother through her three years of suffering before she died. Ethel literally lived beside the telephone when her father lived in his apartment that had been a barbershop and was next to the Royal Cafe in Almena. She remembered the many mornings the cafe owner called to say her father needed her. She never talked about that, but she remembered how her niece Joan often came in when she saw her Aunt Ethel's car and helped her take care of her granddad.

She told herself this was her family's hardest change yet. She hated to think of her family being in Japan for three years. She

Jeane

thought about another of her favorite sayings.

What can't be cured must be endured.

She decided not to think about it yet. She would just enjoy her family for the next four months, then she would stay busy for three more years until they were home again. She suggested to Jeane that it would be best if she and the children stayed with her, since she was sure Japan was full of disease and filth.

Jeane was upset. She knew her mother needed her, but she knew her duty was to go with Curt and make the best home she could. Curt came to Norton every weekend; he couldn't wait until his course was finished and they were on their way to Japan.

While they were in Norton, Jeane was busy. She received packets of information and requirements from the Navy that had to be taken care of before they could leave the United States. They were scheduled to sail no later than the twentieth August.

When the time to leave came nearer, every day someone gave a farewell coffee, tea, or bridge party for Jeane. She had enjoyed her old friends during the six months in Norton. On the last day her Aunt Faye had dinner for all of them and included home made ice cream for dessert.

Curt's GCA school was over on Friday the twenty sixth of July. He graduated first in the class. When he arrived in Norton, he told Jeane the car had to be checked and prepared for the trip. Before they left Dayton they had bought a new white Ford station wagon with red trim. It had three seats and storage space behind the third seat. Curt had been told that car was the kind the Japanese Police Force in Kyoto wanted to buy and they would pay $5,000.00 more than the price in the United States.

All their shots had been completed; including yellow fever, malaria, and cholera. Dr. Kennedy had ordered the serum and gave them their shots. Jeane hated to see Patrick take them, but Dr. Kennedy assured her it was absolutely necessary. Their last instructions required any dependents coming to Japan have all their dental work completed and a complete physical examination before they sailed.

The passport with Jeane and the three children in one picture

Jeane

arrived in time. The last instruction Jeane received was that everyone in the family must have a year's supply of shoes. Now that had been completed and they were ready to go. Jeane had many misgivings, but she didn't talk about it. Jeane had missed hearing from Faith during the summer, but on the fourteenth of July she was delighted to find a fat letter from her.

July 10, 1957
Dear Jeane,
It has been a hectic spring this year. Basil won't give up. He has been out here twice. He brought me pictures of his new apartment. He seems to like his work, but Dr. Handel has been telling him he should get his divorce. She doesn't know him as well as she might. Basil is used to getting what he wants. She even suggested he go with her to a Communist meeting so he would know what it was about. He wondered why she said it, but he was furious. He told her he had heard enough about Communism to last him a lifetime.

Jeane, he was truly angry. I wonder what she is trying to do to him. He will not be pushed around by anyone.

The last time he knocked on my door I didn't know he was in La Jolla. He told me he wanted us to adopt a baby, if I would come to New York and live with him. He still looks terrible with his weight loss and his hair long and bushy. I told him it was too late. I told him I was happy and secure living in my own apartment. I told him our marriage was over and he should talk to my lawyer, not to me.

Maybe I was wrong, but I can't give up the peace I have had for these last months. Japan seems so far away I can't imagine what it will be like. It will be hard for me to realize you are halfway around the world for the next three years. Maybe I will come and see you out there. I have your address and I will write.

Love,
Faith

While he was still in Olathe, Curt had received new orders that told him and his family to sail from Seattle on the *MSTS O'Hara*

Jeane

the twentieth of August. When Curt called his father to tell him they were sailing from Seattle, Washington, his father didn't comment. His mother grabbed the telephone and insisted that they must stay with them until they sailed. The McLyrres didn't know their grandchildren and they had never even seen Patrick.

Curt and Jeane planned a leisurely trip to Washington. They started north from Norton on U.S. 283 north through Nebraska and the Sand Hills where they stayed in an old cabin camp the first night. The next day they continued north to Mount Rushmore in the Black Hills of South Dakota. From there they would follow U.S. 14 west to visit Devil's Tower, where the Indians congregated every summer for prayer and ceremonial dances. Curt had been there often when he was a little boy in the 1930s.

In those depression years Curt's father taught school during the winter, and summers, he sold encyclopedias he carried all over the north country. He took his whole family with him and they all slept in a tent. Curt and his brother Charles thought those were wonderful summers. They ate rabbit, squirrel, and fish. They bought milk and eggs from the farmers and explored every town where they stopped. Curt told his children the stories of those summers while he drove.

He wanted their trip west to be perfect. Jeane had spent hours planning with the children so they could see things that interested them. Their map was marked so Curt didn't bother to remember which highway to take.

On the second day they were in South Dakota. They were surprised it was hard to find a room even before five o'clock. During the day they had been forced to drive on fresh tar, and their new white station wagon was a mess. They finally found a room in an old fashioned cabin camp again. Curt found a service station that would clean off all the tar on the car for twenty dollars. The children thought this town looked like a cowboy movie. Very few people were on the streets and April and Danny explored everywhere while the car was being cleaned.

Curt had budgeted thirty dollars a day, but he found that wasn't enough. The motels were busy and their price had gone up from ten dollars to fourteen dollars a night. Breakfast was about four dollars and fifty cents for all of them. For lunch they picniced beside

Jeane

the road in the shade so the children could run and play. Their dinners varied, but they were usually hamburgers and French Fries.

Neither Jeane nor the children had been in the North Country so they were surprised when they had trouble finding a room at any price. The second day they drove through the Pine Ridge Indian Reservation where they saw herds of bison on either side of the road.

They were almost to Mt. Rushmore National Memorial when they saw advertising for Rocky Caverns, claiming to be more beautiful than any in the world. April and Danny begged to see them. Curt hated to stop, but they were so anxious that he did. The children were awe struck, Jeane was miserable in any cave and this one was damp. She hated to walk over the slippery rocks and sticky mud.

Less than an hour after they left the caves they were at Mt. Rushmore. The children saw the faces of George Washington, Franklin Roosevelt, Theodore Roosevelt, and Abraham Lincoln. Danny wanted to go back to the caves. Curt had wonderful memories of Devil's Tower near Sundance, Wyoming, but it was nearly evening before they got there. Curt saw it stood alone, tall and stately against the clear blue sky, but he realized they could not stop or they would be very late getting to Cody the next day. They spent the night in a motel in Gillette, Wyoming. The motel was run down but clean. There was a counter in the office where the only food they sold was vegetable soup and hamburgers.

The next morning the little cafe offered a breakfast of cereal, milk, juice, and coffee. Curt was anxious to be on the road again so he had filled the car with gas the night before. As they drove across the grasslands they saw big herds of bison, sheep and cattle.

Curt smiled to himself. "Jeane, do you remember when I tried to talk you into living up here? I wanted to work with Uncle Bert Crossan and some day have a ranch of my own."

"Curt, you know as much as I loved you, I could never live there. From the time I met you and we fell in love I told you I would never live on this windswept prairie. It was after Christmas 1945, when you took me to your uncle's ranch. Your aunt and uncle were nice to me, but I was miserable. April Anne was only six months old, and the room where we slept had a feather bed under us and

Jeane

one on top. I was afraid April would freeze in the crib so I took her into bed between us. You got up early and went to the barn with your Uncle Bert. He suggested you two go for a ride and look at the bright stars before breakfast. When you got back you stood in front of the big iron range for thirty minutes. After that visit, you never talked much about being a rancher."

When they reached Cody no rooms were available. They had to drive into Yellowstone National Park where they had reserved a cottage at Old Faithful. It was dark and they were exhausted, but they were in the park. All summer they had talked about the bears who were so friendly they would come up to the car. They wanted to sleep in a log cabin, build a fire, and keep warm. This was the first real vacation they had ever had. Danny wanted to fish in Yellowstone Lake, April wanted to see Old Faithful erupt, and Patrick didn't care what they did just so he could go, too.

They had planned to spend a week in Yellowstone, but Curt felt he should check with the message service, when they checked in at Old Faithful. He learned there was mail service at Mammoth Hot Springs where there was an emergency telephone. The next day they watched Old Faithful erupt and rented a boat and fished in Yellowstone Lake.

As Curt rowed the boat away from the pier. He said "Jeane, I have never rowed such a heavy boat." He dropped his fishing line beside Danny's.

April looked up at Curt. "Daddy what is this rope back here in the water? It won't move." Curt laid his pole down and went to the back of the boat. He realized in their hurry to get the boat out in the lake he had forgotten to raise the anchor. The children thought it was a marvelous joke and teased him for a long time.

So after Danny was tired of fishing, Curt suggested they drive over to Mammoth Hot Springs and look for messages. The mail clerk was glad to see Curt. He said Luther McLyrre had left three messages for his son to call immediately when he checked in. No one was home when Curt called, so he decided they should start west immediately after they went back and loaded the car. When they were leaving the park a Yellowstone Patrolman stopped them with the message to hurry on west because the O'Hara would sail the fifteenth of August which was five days earlier.

Jeane

They were all disappointed but they realized, *there was no choice*. They had planned to see Glacier National Park, but now that was impossible. They still had three days of hard driving before they reached Auburn, Washington, and Curt's parents. Curt had not visited his parents since they moved to Washington.

They had done everything the children wanted and more. They had eaten breakfast in the Old Faithful Inn early that morning after they had stayed in the log house. Danny had awakened early and looking out the cabin window he saw a big black mother bear and her two cubs rummaging through the trash near the outside toilet. Danny decided he didn't need the bathroom.

Days of Dread

As Curt drove out of the park, he thought about his father who had become disenchanted with his teaching in 1956. He had found a rebellion among the students when he used harsh discipline. One of the boy's father threatened him with a law suit. He was discouraged with the students that didn't respect him. He was the principal of the high school and had taught chemistry for thirty years. He loved his work, but he was afraid of more problems with the students.

In the spring he had been offered a job with Welch Scientific Company who sold science equipment to high schools. The company was opening up the Northwest and wanted him to develop that area and sell their science equipment. He discussed the offer with his wife, Molly, and they agreed it was a good offer so he resigned at the high school, sold their house, and left for Washington state. He never wanted to teach again. He had written Curt and told him they were moving to the state of Washington.

Neither Luther or Molly knew anything about Washington and they learned together. He decided Molly should travel with him and be his secretary. It was necessary because he had trouble turning his head more than a few inches and he needed her to watch traffic.

When Curt sent his parents a telegram after Patrick was born, he got a letter ten days later that said congratulations, "You have a big family now. You are young, you may have a dozen more children,

Jeane

don't look to me for support, and since you are just a Naval Reservist you could be released without notice. You would have a real problem then." Curt was angry. The letter sounded like his father hadn't changed.

The last leg of the McLyrres' trip west was dismal. The roads were good and there was very little traffic, but it was still late when they reached Spokane. The children understood they had to rush through the beautiful scenery that all looked the same. Even two-year-old Patrick seemed to understand; he slept most of the time.

Jeane had written her friend LaVora who lived in Almira, Washington that they would stop when they passed through her town. Jeane called LaVora from Yellowstone and arranged the meeting. LaVora had married a man she met in college who had grown up in Almira, Washington and he wanted to stay there forever. After World War II they went to Washington where he completed his education with the help of the G.I. Bill. Both Mel and LaVora were teachers. Curt agreed with Jeane that they could drive a few miles off their route to see her friend. The two girls had played together in Almena and were almost like sisters. Jeane felt she would never again be able to visit LaVora in her home if it wasn't now.

After lunch they left Almira and drove around the south end of the Coulee Dam, then through Dry Falls State Park and Sun Lakes. By then it was three o'clock, but Curt insisted they had to get to Auburn that night. Traffic was light and they drove into Auburn at one-thirty in the morning. Luther McLyrre answered the telephone and directed them to the house.

The next morning Curt called San Francisco to check on their express shipment that contained things they needed until their household shipment reached Japan. No one knew anything about the express shipment, but they told Curt they would try to find it.

Jeane was miserable; she felt the grandparents, especially Luther McLyrre was annoyed with the children and their noise. She heard their grandfather suggest they should go outdoors and run around the block. Curt was shocked when his father seemed to want to get the children out of the way. It seemed he didn't want to talk or play with them. Curt thought his father was more interested in bragging about Charles instead of talking to his grandchildren. He

Jeane

reminded Curt, that Charles had just made Lt. Commander ahead of his class. Curt's mother, Molly, was a lovely lady who tried to make everyone happy, but it was impossible because Luther wanted everything his way. Curt didn't answer his father. He turned and walked into the kitchen and hugged his mother. Then he went outdoors to play with the children.

Curt, Jeane, and Patrick slept in the basement. It was not a pleasant place but, there was a bathroom there. They were close to the washing machine with several clothes lines strung across the basement. Curt and Jeane slept late the first morning, but when they went up for breakfast, Luther had a plan.

"Hey, kids! Come in the kitchen a minute. I just saw in the paper there was a new aquarium in Tacoma. Who would like to go?" Molly and Jeane were doing the breakfast dishes and Luther had been reading the paper. Luther had already found three active children were not easy for him to live with. The children were ready to go and all of the family got in Curt's station wagon.

Curt realized Jeane was having a bad day. The express shipment had not been found, and she thought Curt's parents were not enjoying any of them. After they saw the aquarium, Curt's father suggested they have lunch at the Top of the Ocean Restaurant where they served all kinds of fish. Jeane urged her children to order tuna fish, the only fish they knew.

Since that day had worked so well, Curt's father decided they should do more sightseeing. The children were restless, but it seemed their grandfather felt more relaxed when they were all out of his house. Jeane felt sorry for Curt's mother. She was a gentle lady, but it was hard for her to please her husband and her grandchildren. Curt had told his father they needed to go to Bremerton and the Navy Shipyard, then to Seattle to catch the ferry across Puget Sound in order to check in at Fort Lawton.

When they went downstairs after dinner to go to bed, Jeane saw a stack of letters on the table. "Curt, we have several letters. Do you want me to read them to you?"

"No. I'm tired. Why can't they wait until morning?"

"You go to sleep. I'm going to enjoy my letters." Curt groaned. He wished he had the same control over Jeane that his father had over his mother. Jeane sat down in the easy chair and read every

Jeane

letter; there were six in all. Curt tossed and turned and groaned again. Jeane did not rush. She was stubborn, too. Jeane chose to read Faith's letter first.

July 15, 1957
Dear Jeane,
I am still in La Jolla in my apartment. I am happy and I feel this is where I belong. Basil isn't at either Illinois or Yale. He is now at Brown University. Dr. Handel has a grant for him to work with her in psychiatrist exploration. Since Basil's grant at Yale was limited, Dr. Handel was able to find the opening at Brown. She wrote and told me Basil worries about me. She said he felt guilty because he didn't consult me about these moves.

Dr. Handel said he still dreamed of working at Los Alamos in defense research again. I'm not sure he knows what he wants, but I don't think it will ever happen. He told me he had turned down good offers, but he needed more time to make an important decision. She told him he felt guilty about leaving me in La Jolla, but she believed he was happy at Brown even though he felt temporary.

She telephoned me and asked me if I would see him and I said I would. "As a doctor I feel the two of you must talk about this and make a permanent decision. If I can get him to come to La Jolla, will you be willing to meet with him and try to plan your future."

I told her I would see him if that was what he wanted. I said if he was coming soon he should tell me because I will be in Illinois during August.

You know I haven't ever made friends easily. My mother keeps urging me to come and rest for a long time at the farm. Since my father died, mother has done well, but I think I am better here. I want to stand alone.

I know that if you are reading this letter you must be in Auburn, Washington with Curt's parents. You never spoke much about them except that his father was very opposed to your marriage.

I wish I could have seen you before you left your mother's home and started west to Japan, but to tell the truth I still feel so

Jeane

tired I sleep most of the time. If I feel better maybe I will visit you in Japan, Sayonara! Do enjoy yourself and write often.
Love,
Faith

    Jeane was worried. It seemed to her Faith was doing well yet she kept saying she was tired. Jeane wondered why Dr. Handel was pushing so hard to force a decision. She had suspected Dr. Handel was in love with Basil for several years. Jeane thought Basil was afraid of change.. He married Faith for better or for worse and now he wanted someone to help him. Jeane wondered what was really going on. She was sure Faith would not have told any other person about Basil's attitude. Jeane put away her other mail and wrote Faith. She wanted her to know how much she missed her and how much her letters meant to her. Jeane could not understand what had happened. She decided to write Father Glasson while they were at sea. She knew Father Glasson had helped Faith before.
    By the time Jeane finished her letter to Faith, she thought Basil needed more help than Faith did. He had always been a strange man but now he seemed more confused and depressed than Faith. Jeane wondered if he cared about anyone. She hoped Faith would go home for awhile. She had always thought of Basil as a strong man but now he seemed to suffer more than anyone.
    Jeane wrote Faith a short note and reminded her all mail had to be sent with Curt's name on it. She folded her letter and put it in an envelope and sealed the letter. She turned the envelope over and put the new return address in the upper left corner, then she wrote Faith's address and put on a stamp.
    She looked at the address:

        Lt. Curt McLyrre
        U.S. Navy
        C/O San Francisco, California

    It was late when Jeane climbed into bed, but her head was still spinning. She wished she could talk to Faith, but it was too late. She felt Basil was suffering, too. He seemed to be a man who could not accept failure.

Jeane

The next day they turned in their car at Bremerton and had a quick physical. The doctor found April needed more typhoid serum and Danny needed more cholera serum. The children would get their shots during the time the adults listened to their final lecture. No one had found their express shipment. They all shopped at the ship store at Bremerton and bought a special kind of candy the children liked and notebooks for them to draw or write in about the trip. Curt's parents wanted to show them all the important sights around Auburn in the next few days. Sunday, after church, Dad McLyrre drove 150 miles to show them Mount Rainier National Park. He wanted them to see 14,445 foot Mount Rainier that was snow capped all year. Unfortunately the park was foggy and the peak was hidden. They had their picnic in Paradise Park wearing heavy jackets. Before they finished lunch it was snowing. It had been a dry pleasant day even with the snow. The children slept the 150 miles back to Auburn.

It was finally the fourteenth of August and Curt's father was anxious to get his son and his family to Fort Lawton where the McLyrre family had to report for orientation. On this last night in the United States they were required to stay in certain hotels where their bags would be picked up the following morning at six o'clock and delivered to the O'Hara. They chose the New Richmond Hotel. It looked terrible, the lobby was strewn with old newspapers, candy wrappers, and beer bottles. Jeane called it a flea trap. She wondered if it had ever looked nice. Curt checked once more on their express luggage. He finally learned the express had been in San Francisco but no one knew where it was now.

Jeane was miserable; she could picture her mother crying as they pulled out of the driveway in Norton. Now she felt a coldness in Curt's parents, especially from his father. Jeane wished they were not going to Japan, but *they had no choice*. She had very little experience with the Navy but she had to keep quiet and smile. She looked around the lobby filled with crying babies and dirty children racing in circles around each other while their parents sat and drank beer with their friends. No one there was in control of their own children.

Curt's parents stayed with them until eleven that evening as though it would be forever before they saw them again. They were

Jeane

leaving for Missouri the next morning and would not be on the wharf to wave good-bye. Jeane's mother called during the evening and wished them a safe trip. Jeane knew how hard it was for her to call, but she hadn't cried.

After a short night their sailing day, the fifteenth of August had arrived. Curt got up before six to be sure all of their luggage was in the lobby before six, to see it loaded. Only twenty families from the New Richmond Hotel were going on the O'Hara.

The McLyrre children were so excited they ate very little breakfast. It was nine o'clock when a bus picked them up and took them to the pier. Jeane tried not to think about the crossing and all that could happen. She had always been afraid of the water. She wondered if she would be seasick or would have trouble standing up on the ship. She smiled a lot but she didn't feel happy.

Time to Go

When they arrived at the port, they stood in a long line to pick up their passports. After they were checked and rechecked to be sure they had all their necessities, they boarded the MSTS O'Hara. They were handed their stateroom key, 0112, and their seat assignment in the dining room for first seating. Their stateroom was on O deck right under the boat deck at midship. They were told it was the best place in the ship in case of rough water. When they saw their state room, they were pleased. There was a crib for Patrick, plus two bunks on each side of the room. The top two bunks folded against the wall during the day and the lower two became couches. Instructions were taped to the back of the door. There were so many Jeane was sure she would do everything wrong. The times for meals was on the list. First seating: breakfast 0700 to 0730, lunch 1130 to 1215, and dinner 1730 to 1900. In the morning they had to stay out of their stateroom after breakfast until 1030 for the cabin to be cleaned. The type of time used by the Navy was the 2400 system.

The ship sailed at exactly 1100. Everyone stood on deck,

Jeane

watching as they pulled in the gangplank and cast off the lines that held the ship to the pier. Jeane had a funny feeling when she knew the last rope was pulled onto the ship. She had never been on an ocean going liner and she was afraid of what lay ahead. Now her only contact with the ground was gone. She was careful not to show her feelings. The children were excited about sailing on a big ship like they had seen on television or at the movies, but their exploring had to wait because their first meal on the ship was at 1130. Everyone was impressed with the white linen table clothes and napkins. The waiters all wore white jackets and black pants. The food was wonderful and with a wide number of choices. Their food cost was $1.44 for each person nine years or older and $0.77 for under nine.

After lunch Jeane met the people in the stateroom next to theirs they were Capt. and Mrs. Peter Sika. They had no children but they had a black French Poodle named Smokey. Animals had to be caged on the upper outside deck unless they were being exercised on their leash. Danny and Patrick learned very quickly to save bits of meat for Smokey every day.

Jeane relaxed after she found a note on their door that said their express shipment had arrived and was on board. It was cool on deck, and a sweater felt good. The sky was clear except for a few cumulous white clouds. Most of the people aboard stayed on deck all afternoon just to enjoy the landscape. Before dinner the ship passed Victoria Island on the left and the Canadian shoreline on the right. This was the inside passage that she had heard so much about. The water was calm and the stars were shining brightly.

This ship was prepared for both families and servicemen. On the top deck there was a security net ten feet high around the playground with a sand box, a badminton net and other play equipment. Movies were shown every morning, afternoon, and evening. Many of the children spent most of the day in the theater for several days. They had to be in their stateroom by 2000 in the evening. Jeane had trouble learning to use the twenty-four hour clock.

The McLyrre children preferred to spend most of their time in their stateroom. They hated the rough older boys on deck. Patrick liked his crib where he felt secure. Jeane spent most of her time

Jeane

with them playing games or reading.

On the fourth day at sea an announcement came over the public address system that the next day the ship would reach Adak in the Aleutian Islands. It was announced there would be a film about Adak shown at 1800. Everyone was anxious to see the film. No one knew what to expect. The film was especially for the people who would be stationed there for the next two years, but anyone was welcome to watch. The film showed the mountainous, barren, windswept, islands with nothing but strange grasses and tundra. It was made up of one hundred fifty small islands that separated the Pacific Ocean from the Bering Sea.

The film showed how difficult life was in the winter in Adak. For five months there was very little natural light and the people were forbidden to go outdoors. They were told to use only the tunnels that connected everything on the base.

Before the ship docked, an announcement was made over the loudspeaker that everyone could go ashore from 1200 until 1800. When the ship docked the land looked worse than it had in the movie. Adak was rocky and mountainous. The only vegetation was the tundra and a mossy type grass. Jeane stood still and looked around. The only people she saw had come out of one of the tunnels to see the ship. Tunnels honeycombed the entire island and a brisk wind was blowing so hard it was hard to stand up.

Jeane decided to look in the ship store and shop, and then she was ready to get her family back on the ship. As she looked through the wire fence that surrounded the port she saw great breaks in the tundra. She couldn't see how deep the cracks were, but some looked to be three to four feet across. From the film she learned that in the winter it was so cold in Adak that people would freeze if they went outdoors at all. She saw the one tree that lived outdoors during the summer, but now it was wrapped and ready to be brought into the Adak Officers' Club for the winter. Jeane was surprised when she was told it was almost dark at 1800.

Everyone had been out on deck when the O'Hara docked at 1030 that morning. Now the pier was busy with a barge and an oiler waiting for space at the pier. Jeane didn't know any of the people who disembarked to stay for the next two years. There wasn't much variety in the landscape except the mountains that

Jeane

surrounded them.

Most of the passengers went ashore down into the big tunnel and the ship store. They didn't stay long and they wouldn't take a chance on being left there. Most of the passengers were on deck to watch the ship sail. Jeane was surprised to see so many passengers had trouble navigating the gangplank as they came aboard. Curt explained they had probably spent the afternoon in the bar since no alcohol was allowed on board the ship.

The O'Hara left promptly at 1900. Jeane and Curt stood on deck as the ship turned and started toward the open sea. When the ship was out of sight of land, the children were happy in their stateroom with their new comic books and two new games. Jeane could hardly believe the ship could avoid all the rocks that were showing around the ship. She was thankful it was still twilight as she watched the ship maneuver its way into the open sea.

Jeane overheard one woman tell her friend that she had heard drinking was one of the biggest problems on these isolated islands. She said some women almost went crazy when they couldn't get outdoors. The women talking said every winter several wives had to be air evacuated back to the mainland. Jeane never wanted to see Adak again.

As the ship sailed west on what was called the Great Circle route the ocean became rough. An announcement on the ship said this would be a rough night. The O'Hara had caught the tail end of typhoon Agnes. It was reported that Okinawa had severe damage. Some of the waves that crashed against the ship were twenty to thirty feet high. The ship pitched and rolled, and the spray came over the decks. No one could walk without holding on to the lines that were put up in every hallway by the crew.

Many people became seasick during the night and through the next day. After the storm passed, the whole ship relaxed. April and Danny had both been sick, but now they were fine. Jeane bundled them up and took them up to the sundeck where it was safe. The children played tetherball, and volleyball when they could stand up. Patrick dug in the sandpile and built forts to knock down. The fresh air kept him from nausea.

One evening when Jeane was dressing for dinner, Curt asked her what she thought of Heidi Jones.

Jeane

Jeane stopped and turned toward Curt. "Not Much! Heidi dresses like she was going to a cocktail party every evening in her tight silk pants and low cut silk blouses. Every morning she has on short shorts and a tight knit shirt. She smiles at any man who looks at her. Capt. Jones is old enough to be her father, but he seems to be proud of how she attracts the officers. She looks at a man as though she wants to pull him into her arms and more. Curt, I think she's a tramp."

To the contrary Curt thought she was cute. "You better be nice to Heidi; Captain Jones will be in command of Atsugi Naval Air Station and my boss; that means Heidi can control all of the station wives." Jeane would never like Heidi. She wasn't sure how she would like the next three years. She thought it might be best that they had to live in a private rental.

One morning soon after the typhoon Jeane saw a wife watching her five children on the sundeck. Jeane had Patrick up there and he joined the other children. Jeane walked over and sat down beside their mother who looked up. "I see your children seem to be healthy. We were lucky too."

"We are all fine, but the hallways smell pretty bad today. I thought it would be better up here. I saw you with your little boy up here before we docked at Adak, but there was no time then to get acquainted. My name is Pat West and we are going to Atsugi, Japan. My husband, Donald, will be the supply officer at Atsugi. Where will your new station be?"

"We are going to Atsugi also. We hoped for base housing but we have to go into private rental. I have never been overseas, and I have to confess I am a little frightened." Jeane felt she had found a new friend.

"My name is Jeane McLyrre and my husband will be with the GCA Unit. I hope we will see you again up here where it is so easy to watch the children."

Pat said, "We were stationed in Germany from 1950 to 1953. I felt we learned so much since we lived off base. We hope to find a big old Japanese farmhouse with off base Western plumbing and heating near Atsugi."

Jeane had no idea why she would want an old farmhouse, but she didn't ask. Jeane had traveled very little before she was married.

Jeane

Before now she had only seen Tijuana, Mexico. Jeane wondered if Japan would look like Tijuana with shacks everywhere. She had searched the library in Norton, but she found very little information about Japan. She visualized something like she had seen in the movie *Sayonora*.

The typhoon passed and the people aboard ship relaxed. Nearly every morning Jeane and Pat sat on the top deck. Pat told Jeane she and Don had been high school sweethearts and when Don graduated from the Naval Academy they were married in the chapel. Pat said they went to very few parties. They preferred to be home with their children. Jeane was impressed with Pat and her real values.

Everyone counted the days until the twenty fifth of August. This was the last day aboard and there was a party on the ship the last night. Curt and Jeane paid their respects to Captain Marsh for the safe crossing. Jeane told him she felt pampered and would find it hard to cook three meals a day and clean house. The captain reassured her she would not have to do that for the next three years. In Japan, everyone has help.

Book Three
Welcome to Japan

1957-1960

Welcome to Japan

The *O'Hara* came into Yokohama Harbor in a heavy fog making it impossible to see anything beyond the wharf. When the fog began to lift, the McLyrres went up to the top deck and watched the sky clear and the fog disappear. From the top deck they saw beyond the port and across the city where the sky was clear blue.

It was noon before the ship's public address system announced the *O'Hara* had docked and the passengers should listen for further instructions. The McLyrres were going into the dining room when they heard the news. Curt insisted they have lunch. He realized there would be no way to find snacks after they left the ship until they reached Atsugi.

It had been a long morning for the families who would leave the ship and start to make a new home for the next three years. The children kept asking their parents when they could debark the ship. Since they sailed from Seattle, the children thought it had been ten days in jail.

The McLyrres had finished lunch when the next announcement came over the public address system. The families were advised to listen carefully; they would be the first passengers to leave the ship. Almost immediately the dining room was empty. Most of the families gathered as near the gangplank as possible. It wasn't long before the McLyrres heard their name called.

Suddenly Jeane stopped; she caught her breath before she could go on. She looked at Curt. "What will happen if we get separated?"

"We won't get separated. You remember I told you Ed Hill, my sponsor, would meet us at the ship. He will be anxious to get us to Atsugi. I'm sure I told you we exchanged pictures so we would recognize each other when we were allowed to leave the ship. I

Jeane

just saw him near the foot of the gangplank. We will be fine, this is just another new experience. When I saw him again he hadn't moved."

The McLyrres stepped off the gangplank and Ed Hill stepped in front of Jeane and handed her a bouquet of flowers. "Welcome to Japan! Follow me and let's get out of here!"

Ed looked at Curt and smiled. "You look like your picture! Your shipboard luggage maybe in Atsugi before we are. Your first stop is the immigration office." As they walked along Ed told Jeane what a wonderful experience this would be for their whole family. He said his wife had enjoyed their tour, but now she was ready to go home. He admitted after three years she still hated the one out of three nights when he had to sleep in the GCA Shack. He told Jeane before they got quarters his wife threatened to go home. Jeane listened to every word he said.

Curt had never mentioned there was an unusual kind of duty like Ed described. No one said a word until they reached the immigration desk where their passports were examined and returned. Next was the customs desk where they were waved through.

Ed smiled as he turned toward Jeane and saw she was holding a handkerchief over her nose. "Mrs. McLyrre I see you have now experienced the one thing you will never forget."

"What is it?" Jeane asked.

"Mrs. McLyrre, I'm not sure, but it will be with you until you go home after three years. When you open your suitcases in your new duty station the smell will be there, but it won't be there after your clothes are aired out."

He was quiet as he led them to his car. Curt sat in front with Ed who had been with the GCA (Ground Control Activity) for three years. He told Curt he was tired of overnight duty and the enlisted men who brought prostitutes to the GCA Shack nearly every night. Those women were anxious to make money so as soon as it was dark they started digging under the fence from the outside until they could crawl under the fence and run for the Shack. Often the sailors worked from inside the fence so the girls could wiggle through sooner. The men were eager for company and when the women left all the dirt had to be replaced. Jeane was shocked; she knew Curt had decided not to tell her anything in advance because she

Jeane

might have stayed in Norton.

Ed was the McLyrres' sponsor and he knew he was responsible for the them until they were settled. Jeane kept looking back toward the port, but all she saw were people milling around as though they didn't know what to do next. The women were dressed in many different costumes, but Jeane never saw anyone wearing a kimono.

"Atsugi will be about an hour drive." Ed said. "On the way I will show you things you never expected to see. It is a real introduction to Japan!"

Jeane looked around and saw no tall buildings, yet she had been told Yokohama was a big city. She looked outside the fence and was surprised there were people standing in the middle of the narrow street, and there were shops on both sides of the street. The streets were filled with bicycles and strange three wheeled trucks that looked like toys. Men on bicycles carried huge bundles on their back wrapped in big squares of tough fabric.

Jeane was curious, "Ed, why do these people wrap their packages in fabric?"

Ed answered. "Its a cheap way to protect the furniture or whatever they are delivering. If its big furniture the material is like heavy canvas. All the fabric can be used again and again and washed when it gets dirty. To carry small packages, they use a square of material called a furoshiki. When a woman goes shopping, she always has one or two furoshikis folded and tucked into her obi (belt) or basket."

Ed continued to talk as he drove down the narrow street, again he turned to Jeane. "Have you noticed all the shop fronts are open to the street and each shop sells only one kind of thing. In other areas there are different small shops where they sell food that includes noodles, rice, soy sauce, and fish. If you haven't noticed, it seems none of the shops have ever been painted.

In one small shop Jeane saw a special flag and ask Ed what it was. He quickly answered it was a shop for men only. Jeane didn't understand what Ed meant, but she decided to wait and ask Curt later. Ed told the McLyrres most of the shopkeepers lived with their family in the back of their shop.

As they passed a pagoda where paper lanterns surrounded the grounds and bits of paper hung from the trees. According to Ed the

Jeane

bits of paper were prayers. He told them most Japanese people were Shinto, the religion that believed their Emperor was God. Jeane had read the Japanese could have several Gods. Most Japanese were both Shinto and Buddhists because every day the Buddhists prayed for their dead ancestors and put fruit in front on the shrine in their home. They couldn't understand why Christians could have only one religion.

Ed told the McLyrres many Japanese wanted to accept Christianity, but they could never reject the religion of their forefathers. Jeane began to see how complicated the Japanese really were. She remembered during WW II the Kamikazi Pilots who would crash into an American warship and destroy the ship and themselves to honor their Emperor.

During all this time April had sat quietly looking from side to side. She was fascinated with everything she saw. Danny watched the bicycles and all of the different kind of trucks, wagons, and buses. The most interesting vehicle was the three wheeled truck. Everything was different from home and Jeane was confused. She wished they were all back in Kansas.

Curt had been quiet until he saw a banner beside the road that said, "Send the Americans home! Communism best for Japan!" He turned to Ed, "Does that banner mean the Japanese are turning to Communism? I thought my family would be safe here."

"Curt, you will see many of those banners, but it only means some poor guy put it up and made a few yen. Some Japanese think waving a banner is better than working. I don't even notice them anymore."

Ed entered a wider road as he drove away from the port. He moved quickly to the left side of the road and suddenly Jeane remembered she had been told in Japan everyone drove on the left side of the road. The article said everyone would be comfortable on the left side of the road in only a few days. The letter advised them to just follow the traffic.

In the street there were hundreds of bicycles. Many of the riders carried their load tied on their back or on their bicycles back fender. Sometimes the load was bigger than the bicycle. She even saw one bicycle pulling a trailer. Most of the men wore short kimonos with strange writing on their back. Ed explained the writing was

Jeane

Kanjii, the written language of Japan.

There were women as well as men working on the streets. They wore white aprons that covered most of their clothes. Ed called them mama-sans. He told Jeane the aprons were worn by working women to protect their clothes and some women had their hair covered with a white cotton scarf.

The whole McLyrre family was fascinated with how the mothers carried their babies and young children tied on their back with a big piece of fabric knotted in front just under the mother's arms and breasts.

It seemed they had been driving at least an hour when the shops begin to disappear and there were fewer bicycles. Jeane was confused; she was sure she would never understand Japanese ways. When they got into the country, Ed slowed down as they approached a high unpainted wooden fence. The gate was open and he urged the McLyrres to look quick. When they looked they could see an unpainted farmhouse with a narrow porch along the front of the building. Behind the porch they could see sliding screens covered with oiled paper. Ed said there was a second set of sliding doors that would admit light and cut out the cold winds. In front of the porch there was not a blade of grass. Instead of grass there was sand that had been raked into a pattern around a big rock. Near their gate there was one lonely pine tree.

Ed looked back. "Jeane, that is one of the most beautiful farm houses you will ever see in Japan." She couldn't answer, but she smiled and nodded and told herself it was one of the ugliest houses she had ever seen. Soon after they passed the house Jeane saw an old man looking at her. He slipped his hand into his pants and pulled out his penis. Then he started to urinate as he stared at Jeane. She was in a state of shock.

April looked at her mother, "What is that man doing?"

"April, I guess he had to go to the bathroom and couldn't wait. I don't know why he didn't turn away from the traffic on the road."

Ed was ready to answer. "Mrs. McLyrre the Japanese are different than Americans. "Some men step down off the road, but if it is an old man who had seen an American woman coming they want to shock them. You will get used to it."

Jeane

The road was narrow and crowded with dump trucks full of material for road repairs. All the way to Atsugi she saw buses loaded with people and one farmer who pulled his stubborn cow along the side of the road.

Jeane noticed another man who had a yoke across his shoulders with a bucket attached by rope on each end of the yoke to keep them balanced. Jeane asked what was in the buckets.

"Mrs. McLyrre, I am not sure you want to know. The buckets are called honey buckets. Do you know what a honey bucket is?"

Jeane looked at him. "I know very little about Japan. Maybe you will explain it to me."

"This is common in Japan. Most homes have no sewers and the people don't want them. They save what the body has eliminated into a toilet connected to a tank outside their house. That man you saw with the buckets empties the tanks every day and sells it to a farmer. When the collection is made it smells terrible! When the farmer puts it on his field it smells worse. They claim it is the best fertilizer in the world. We are advised not to use any fresh vegetables or fruits grown here unless the shop advertises their food is hydroponic grown. We never took chances. We bought all our fresh fruits and vegetables in the commissary, but the Japanese fruits and vegetables look beautiful in the markets and it was hard not to buy them ."

April sat still and looked out the window. She didn't say a word but she saw everything. She was confused when she saw the rice paddies. She had studied how important rice was to the Japanese and it looked different to her here. Ed explained in the spring the farmer planted the seed in the drained paddies and they kept the ground wet until the plants were strong and then they transplanted all the small plants and drained away the standing water in their paddies. She asked Ed why there was no water now.

He answered. "April, since this is fall the paddies have been drained so the plants can mature and be harvested. Next spring this will all be repeated.

After an hour, they left heavy traffic and arrived in the little village outside the gate of Atsugi Naval Air Station. Jeane was surprised when she saw the base. She expected something dismal

Jeane

and bare, but this was well landscaped with flowers and green grass. She saw tall pine trees on each side of the Atsugi gate. The buildings were all painted and the streets were paved. Since they had just arrived Curt had to present his orders at the gate house. The quarters Ed had reserved for them was a Quonset near the Officers' Club and swimming pool. The unit consisted of three bedrooms, a small kitchen, dining and, living room plus a screened porch. Jeane thought it would be a perfect place to live, but she knew that after one week they would have to have permanent housing.

Ed had picked up their mail and it was on the dining room table. Jeane was anxious to look at it. They walked over to the Officers' Club and sat down in the dining room. A Japanese waitress handed each of them a small basket that held a warm damp cloth. Jeane looked around and saw people were wiping their hands.

After dinner they walked through the club which was air conditioned, then they went back to their hot humid quonset. Jeane knew she couldn't sleep until she had read all of their letters. The first letter was from her mother.

August 16, 1957
Dear family,
I miss you already. It was wonderful having you with me for these last six months. I wish you were now in California instead of Japan. I could visit you there, but when I look at a map it looks like Japan is on the other side of the world. I could never come that far.

Don't worry about me. I have always adjusted to whatever happens. This afternoon three of my friends will be here to play pinochle. I baked cookies for them this morning. Remember how I cleaned house after your dad died? I did the same thing after all of you were gone.

I will be busy tomorrow. I want to wash some windows in the morning and in the afternoon I will work at the Norton Sale Barn. I have to be sure all the books are in perfect order. The owner of the Sale Barn is Frank Sellers. I have known the Sellers ever since we moved to Norton. Frank's father farmed the land behind the motel and always gave us roasting ears.

Jeane

Do you remember? He farmed with a team of horses and a wagon. Frank knew my dad and he knows Gilbert.

I like being there; I see farmers I knew years ago. They all seem glad to see me working for Frank. He is alone. He told me he and his wife were never interested in the same things and finally they were divorced two years ago.

I enjoy the sale days. Every week after the sale everyone who works there meet in the cafe for pie and coffee. Winifred Root runs the cafe; she is a good cook and fun to be around. I have known her all my life. She was our neighbor and friend when I lived out south of Almena. Frank insists I join him in the cafe every week. I think he's lonesome. He says I am fun to be around.

Tomorrow I will go to Almena and see Mother Brown and Faye. Just remember, I am fine. My neighbors know I am lonesome so they come over every time they see me outdoors.

Write often!!

Love,
your Mother

Jeane was tired but she felt much better after she read her mother's letter. The Quonset remained hot all night and Jeane was exhausted. In the morning Ed was waiting for them when they got back from breakfast. He was anxious for them to find a house. He suggested the children stay in the Quonset and go to the Officers' Club pool when it opened at ten and they could have a hamburger and coke for lunch. April said she would watch Patrick all the time. They thought it was fun to have a swimming pool so close.

Ed looked at Jeane. "Mrs. McLyrre remember, you may not be invited to see any of the houses where we are going. In Japan most men believe a woman's place is at home. I'm sure you will understand." Jeane didn't comment; she had been in a bad mood since Curt told her she should stay in the hot car. Again she wished they were back in Norton.

Ed had arranged to meet a Japanese contractor at his new house. The house was less than a mile from Miramar. After they left the base Jeane watched the people who repaired the roads. She asked Ed why the men wore painted signs on their jackets. He

Jeane

told her they were called happi coats and the design was the name of their employer. On a hot day they wore a white rag tied around their forehead so perspiration would stay out of their eyes.

"Jeane, many of the women have been widows since 1945. They work beside the men and wear long pants of dark material to protect their legs. Some cover their hair with a white cloth. On hot days they wear their mama-san apron without a blouse."

Ed asked Jeane to look at the workmen's feet. "These people don't wear shoes like ours. In summer their shoes are called zoris. If it rains they wear wooden getas that keep their feet out of the mud. Some men cut a flat shoe from a piece of old car tires that can be tied on like sandals. The Japanese are very imaginative; they seldom seem angry with Americans.

Some women work sprinkling the streets to keep the dust down. Where there is heavy traffic, another woman directs traffic during construction. In cold weather some of the men wear long black socks and rubber boots."

The Japanese contractor told Curt he had only one house near Miramar. He was a smart man because he sold his houses only to officers. That made him make a bigger profit. He told Curt this house was one of his best.

He turned and opened the back door of Ed's car and he motioned for Jeane to get out. He put out his hand and kept smiling and bowing until Jeane took his hand. He giggled and kept smiling and bowing as he said, "American way!" over and over like a puppet on a string. He led them to the house he said had just been finished. He held the door for Jeane and Curt to inspect the house.

The house had three bedrooms, a living and dining room combined, a small kitchen and American bathroom. The whole house was about 20x20 feet square.

"Curt, that is smaller than my mother's garage. The floors are so rough the children would get splinters. What do you think of the patio off the living room? The house sits on a corner twenty feet above a busy highway that goes to Atsugi town. Look, see the cloud of dust now."

The contractor kept smiling, "Fine house! American house! You like house?"

Jeane turned to Curt. "I can not live here. I will take the children

Jeane

and go back to Norton! This is awful. I'm sure you can live comfortably in the BOQ."

"Jeane settle down! This house will not do, but other people make a go of it here and we will too! Ed just told me the man does have a two bedroom house very near the base that is for rent. I told him we would look at it."

The Little House in the Woods

Now the Japanese builder became a Japanese landlord. The next house was in a small neighborhood of five or six western style houses with trees! Jeane saw children playing near one of the houses. The Japanese landlord did not have a key for the house, but they looked in all the windows. There was a large screened porch on one end of the house that would give the children a place to play when it rained.

The house was stained dark brown, it was divided into four parts. There were two bedrooms on one side of the house that were connected by a short hall. The house had a tiny foyer that was a step lower than the main level of the house. The living and dining area was about 14 feet long. The kitchen and bath were both off the dining area.

The Japanese landlord explained. "Mrs. Officer, Japan small country, people live in small house. In Japan this is very big house! All people in Japan come inside, remove shoes and put on slippers to wear inside. Jeane could see most of the house when she looked through the windows in the living room and dining room. The landlord told them the house was modern. He reminded Curt it had a gas heater to keep the house warm, a gas refrigerator to keep food cold, and a gas cook stove with an oven. "Very good" he smiled. "Only need three tanks of bottled gas. The landlord put on a big smile that showed three big gold teeth.

He began to smile behind his wire framed glasses. He smiled and rocked back and forth. He looked at Jeane, "You like big house, good! Very, very good!. You must hurry. Me, landlord, have no more big house. You want big house?"

Jeane ignored him. He seemed disappointed as he looked at

Jeane

Curt. "You like big trees? Nice big trees!" He turned to Curt and stuck out his hand.

"Mr. Commander, you important man, now you want nice house near Atsugi?" Finally he walked away. He no longer had a spring in his step.

It was past noon when Ed Hill told the McLyrres his wife expected them for lunch. The Hills had no children, yet they lived on base. Most of the base housing were duplexes with an enclosed utility yard between the units. The Hills' duplex had a bathroom and three bedrooms upstairs. On the main floor there was a large living room, dining room, kitchen, bath, and utility room that doubled for maids' quarters. They had nice furniture throughout the house. The kitchen was long and narrow with a refrigerator, electric stove, and an automatic washer, but there was no dryer. Clothes were dried on clothes lines in the utility yard. Jeane insisted Curt apply for base housing right after lunch. He was told it would be at least six months before anything would come up.

After house hunting all day the McLyrres decided to rent the little brown house in the woods. Jeane thought she must find a night light so no one would fall in the big square sunken tub in the bathroom. The toilet looked like those at home so they decided the house would do.

Ed was delighted when they told him. He called the owner who brought the rental agreement immediately. Curt signed it, and Ed took Curt and Jeane to Camp Zama to get their passes for the Post Exchange and Commissary.

Next, they had to fill out the forms to enroll the children in the Camp Zama Schools. They learned the children would be picked up by an Atsugi bus in front of their house, and taken to Camp Zama for school then returned home at the end of the school day. April was in seventh grade and Danny in third. Patrick had to stay home.

Ed told Jeane everyone had a maid. The going rate was 10,000 yen {$28.00} a month. Jeane had never liked house cleaning so it sounded wonderful. That afternoon Curt had to go to Camp Zama and get the house inspected before the Army would provide the necessary furniture. Jeane learned later the inspectors had to be

Jeane

sure the toilet flushed into a sanitary system and not into a honey bucket.

Curt knew Jeane was having a hard time accepting off base housing. She seemed afraid. "Jeane, let's go to the Officers' Club and call your mother." Curt put in the call at five fifteen in the afternoon in Atsugi. When Ethel answered it was two fifteen in the morning in Norton. Jeane told her they were in Japan safe and sound and had already found a house. Jeane promised to write soon. The call lasted three minutes and cost $12.00.

The next morning Curt checked in to the G.C.A. Unit. He explained to Jeane the initials stood for Ground Control Activity. He told her there were three officers attached to the unit and one had to always be there overnight. There was one officer for each team of twelve enlisted men. Curt didn't say much more except that there were important things happening at night near the flight line. He told her his work in the unit was confidential and she would not know what happened there. She didn't mention that Ed had told her about the 24 hour shifts. He had told her some nights were busy and some nights were quiet and they slept. Jeane had listened carefully because she was sure she would never know anything more from Curt. She hadn't forgotten what Ed said about men who brought Japanese women in for their recreation.

The next morning the children weren't interested in going anywhere. When they got back to the Quonset after breakfast all of the children complained about stomach pains. By noon April and Patrick felt better, but Danny was vomiting. Jeane was frantic when she called Curt. He came quickly with Ed's car and took Danny to the dispensary. The doctor said it was probably the change of water and it would improve quickly. Jeane refused to leave Danny. She had never seen anyone more miserable.

About two o'clock Jeane heard someone at the Quonset door. "Hi, are you Jeane? Doris Martin sends you her best regards from Jacksonville, Florida."

Jeane laughed, "You are Marsha Scott! Doris wrote me you were here; please come in, its been a long time since I saw Doris. Are the Scotts coming out here?"

Jeane

"I know she would like to come, but there are no orders." Marsha answered. "My husband, Jeff, reminded me it is hard to get around here without a car. He suggested you take our second car and use it until yours arrive."

The Scotts had been in Japan since the summer of 1955 and their tour of duty was almost over. When the Scotts came to Japan they had been offered quarters on base. However, they wanted to live off base in a Japanese house. They wanted to learn more about the Japanese people and make friends with them. Marsha made sure it would be an experience their five daughters would never forget. The Scotts had to add an American plumbing system to their Japanese bath room.

Before Marsha left, she handed Jeane a little book. "I know you will learn many things from this book, *Welcome to Japan*. It was written by a military wife who lived in Tokyo and the book is filled with things it would take years to learn."

Curt came back to the Quonset at three. He looked at Jeane. "I heard this morning there will be a Hail and Farewell Cocktail Party at the Officers' Club tonight. Ed told me we will be expected to attend. It is to welcome the new Naval Air Station skipper, Capt. Gerald Jones and his wife, Heidi. You must remember them from the O'Hara. I told you he was my new commanding officer."

Jeane certainly did remember Capt. Jones and his wife, Heidi, who chased every man on the O'Hara.

"Jeane, we have to be at the Hail and Farewell Party tonight. I told you everybody wants to meet us." Jeane didn't answer. She was much more concerned about their children than the party. She hadn't given a thought to the party or what she should wear. At five o'clock, Curt went out and came back with hamburgers and soft drinks for the children. He looked around the Quonset and was shocked to see clothes all over the floor.

"What is the matter with you, Jeane? Don't you understand this is an important occasion. We will be welcomed aboard tonight and people will judge us by how we look."

"I couldn't care less, Curt! We have a sick son, that's what is important to me. You go to the party and tell everybody I'm sick!"

Curt glared as he turned toward Jeane. "Do you have a poor

Jeane

memory? Remember, *we have no choice.* We are a long way from home and its like we are both in the Navy as long as we are here."

Jeane was exhausted and angry, but she had learned how best to handle Curt. She simply turned and went back to the bedroom. She slipped on the wrinkled dress that had been in a trunk for six months and the shoes she had worn on the ship. She couldn't find the ones that matched the dress. Her eyes were tired and her dark hair was stringy so she pulled it back and secured it with a rubber band, then she tied a pink taffeta bow over the rubber band. Her dress had roses around the bottom of her skirt which helped some.

Curt took her by the arm and started out the door. She stopped, "April, come and get me if Danny throws up again."

When they walked into the club, Jeane saw Capt. Jones and Heidi and she was looking for an interesting man. While Jeane watched, she saw Heidi capture a handsome officer. Jeane was shocked and Capt. Jones was smiling.

Jeane couldn't believe her eyes. "Curt, is that Carol Conway? Do I have to associate with her? Why are they here?" Curt didn't answer. Jeane was shocked and instantly decided to avoid Carol whenever possible. She had never forgotten that first 'Courtesy Call' in La Jolla, California, when she talked about information she didn't know was secret. It made her first months in California very difficult.

She whispered to Curt. "Am I having a nightmare? Is it really possible the Conways are here? I wonder how Carol and Heidi will get along."

"Jeane, you know, *there was no choice.* Yes, I did know they were here, but I was afraid if I told you, you would have stayed in Norton. I want my family here with me; that's why I didn't tell you. Just smile and give the ladies a limp handshake. Remember we don't live on base, maybe it is for the best. Carl Conway is the executive officer under Capt. Jones. The Conways have been here for about two years."

At last the introductions were over and Jeane was relieved. She could see Carol Conway was the same as she had been in California, but her eyes were glassier and she seemed less steady

Jeane

on her feet. She swayed back and forth as she waved to every man she passed. Her eyes lit up when she saw Curt and she headed toward him. Curt met her with a big smile. She whispered to him, he took her arm, and they headed for the bar.

Jeane slipped away and went in the ladies lounge. She heard two ladies talking. One said "What do you think of Heidi Jones? I wonder if she's his wife or his daughter? I'll bet she will have trouble with Carol Conway."

Jeane slipped out the door to go and check on Danny. He had not eaten for two days. She opened a warm coke and gave it to him with a cracker. She sat down on the edge of his bed and washed his face with a cool damp wash cloth. She thought he seemed better; she felt his forehead and it was cooler.

April looked up from her reading. "Mother, why don't you go back to the party; you know Daddy will be mad at you."

"I don't care." Jeane answered. April was right but she had been so worried about Danny she just sat on the couch and dozed.

About eight o'clock Curt, stomped in the door. "Jeane, are you trying to ruin this tour of duty for me already. Everyone has asked where you were and I had to admit I didn't know. The Hills are expecting us to sit at their table for dinner. Get up, wash your face, and put on a smile."

"Curt, when did you miss me? I saw you give Carol a hug and lead her into the bar. Is it Carol Conway who is important to you? Is she more important than your family or the Navy?"

"Leave Carol Conway out of this! Jeane, I don't want a fight. You know I love my family, but there are certain things we have to do and going back to that party is one of them." She was tempted to refuse, but she knew Curt could get ugly. She stood up, slipped on her shoes, and followed him out the door.

Home in Asugi Heights A-17

Monday morning the McLyrres moved out of the Quonset and moved into the house. The Navy had already put their express luggage in the house. The furniture from Camp Zama would be delivered afternoon. All the neighbors stopped to welcome the

Jeane

McLyrres to the Yama (mountain in Japanese). The house was less than half mile from the base. After the furniture was delivered Jeane worked hard to get the beds made before bedtime. There were snacks in the refrigerator, but not enough to feed five people. At five o'clock their neighbor, Joy Osborne, brought food enough for two days. The Osbornes had lived on the Yama two years with their three sons. Danny was delighted to have new friends already. Jeane mentioned to Joy that Curt insisted they go to a Sayonara Party for the Hills that evening who were leaving in less than two weeks. The party was given by their friends. Jeane said she would not leave the children the first night in a new house.

Joy interrupted, "I understand Curt's insisting that you go, certainly you can't leave the children alone. Let your children stay with us until you get home. My boys will be delighted. Since you are new, everyone will look you over. People here don't have enough to do!!. Everyone has full time help, some have help in the house day and night. We don't have room and neither do you. Let your children stay here until you get home. We all have to compromise."

Jeane began to realize this life would have its problems and she understood the saying that was so true, *there was no choice*. Curt was pleased they could go to the party.

Curt and Jeane got up the next morning, and found there was no water in the house. Jeane ran over to the Osbornes to find out if there was a reason for the lack of water.

Joy smiled, "You'll get used to it. There isn't enough water pressure for all these houses. We think the Japanese turn off the system until the pressure builds up again. Everyone on the yama experiences it often."

Curt had the Scotts' second car and the first thing he did was go to the base and pick up a ten gallon jug of water so they could flush the toilet at least once.

Joy saw Curt was home, so she offered to take Jeane to the commissary. On the way she told Jeane she knew a good maid who had always worked near them and was now free. Joy knew she needed work.

"Jeane, she lives in the village of Otska Homachi, down over the hill. It's about a quarter of a mile down there. She lives with her

Jeane

brother and his family and she has worked for Atsugi people for ten years. She always wants to work near her home."

"Joy, I want to ask you, why do some Japanese add 'san' after a name?"

Joy smiled. "It is an honor to be called san after your name. Its like we use Mr., Mrs., or Miss. In Japanese they would call you Oku-san {wife} instead of Mrs. McLyrre."

Joy knew where Kimi lived in Otska Homachi so after dinner when her maid was cleaning up the kitchen Joy drove Curt and Jeane to meet her. They rang the bell outside the lumber yard door, where she lived with her brother and his family. Joy heard someone call to them from down the side of the building and they waved and walked down to where a young woman waited. A young woman stepped ahead so they could step in. She opened another paneled screen and bowed to her guests as they slipped off their outside shoes. Joy introduced the McLyrres to Kimi-san. She had explained to the McLyrres they had to take off their shoes and step into slippers before they followed Kimi into the big room.

Jeane was fascinated with the big room they had entered. The floor was covered with tatami matting which was over rice straw pallets four inches thick. The only furniture in the room was a low oblong table with six large floor cushions. Kimi knelt on one of the cushions and invited the others to join her.

She spoke excellent English; she had worked for Americans since 1948. Now she lived with her brother and his family and worked days for Americans. Joy explained to Kimi this new family needed a maid. Kimi smiled, then giggled after she put her hand over her mouth. Joy told her the McLyrres would pay her the fair price of 10,000 yen each month ($28.00 American money). Kimi agreed and was anxious to start.

The next morning, Kimi appeared at A-17 Atsugi Heights at eight o'clock. She was tiny, less than five feet tall, and probably weighed no more than ninety pounds. She appeared to be in her late twenties. With no water to flush the toilet, the house smelled like a barn in Kansas. The dishes couldn't be washed until Curt went to the base for more water. The children stayed on the screened porch or outdoors until there was water. Kimi assured

Jeane

them this happened often and wouldn't last long. Jeane had prepared breakfast and they all ate on the screened porch. Kimi ignored the smell. She took the dirty dishes to the kitchen and washed them with a small amount of the clean water. She used the water again to start cleaning the stove.

Later Curt brought more water from the base and Kimi finished cleaning the stove and started on the refrigerator. The house was small and the children were crowded but each had a chest of drawers. The other bedroom had a double bed, a small closet, two chests of drawers, a desk, and an easy chair.

Later in the morning Marsha Scott stopped by and invited the McLyrres for a sukiyaki dinner Saturday night and they accepted. The McLyrres' car had arrived by then so Curt drove the Scotts' station wagon and Jeane drove their new white Ford station wagon with the children. The Scotts lived near Camp Zana in an old Japanese farmhouse that looked like the house Ed Hill had shown Jeane on the way to Atsugi the first day. The Scotts lived mostly Japanese. Their big room was covered with tatami mats that covered the compressed straw pallets six meters long and three meters wide. The only furniture was a large low table similar to what Jeane had seen in Kimi's home. Marsha admitted the house was very cold in winter.

Curt wasn't eager to remove his shoes, but no one stepped on the tatami wearing western shoes. Jeane felt things were coming too fast and she was sure at the end of their tour she would not have learned half of what she needed to know.

The Scotts' house seemed cold to the McLyrres even though it was just the end of August. The Scotts had only another month to complete their tour of duty and go back to the United States. Jeff Scott had orders to the Bureau of Naval Personnel in Washington, D.C. They had enjoyed their old Japanese farmhouse, but Marsha admitted she was ready to go home to hot running water and the appliances she had left.

Since they were settled Jeane and April went to services in the Atsugi Chapel. From the time April had polio in 1953 Jeane promised herself she would be in church every Sunday. She believed the prayers across the United States helped April recover.

Jeane

After church Curt decided the family should explore in the area where they lived, then he decided to go to Atsugi town five miles west of Atsugi Naval Air Station. They parked the car and started walking through the shops. It seemed strange to see all the stores open and road crews working on Sunday.

Curt had sold the new white Ford station wagon the first day it was advertised. The car had to be in Japan for a year before it could be delivered to the Kyoto Police Force. Curt hated to drive it on the busy roads.

In Atsugi town the children were fascinated with the strange kinds of shoes in the shops. One brave shopkeeper motioned Danny to come in his shop and sit down. Curt gave Danny a little push toward the merchant. Curt smiled at the shopkeeper and pointed to Danny's feet. The merchant was pleased and urged Danny to sit on a low stool. He pulled off Danny's tennis shoes and socks then he pulled out a flat straw sandal. The merchant smiled at Curt. He looked around and shrugged his shoulders and pointed to himself. He said, "Japanese, English dami dami (bad). The merchant pointed at the fitted straw sandal under Danny's foot and said, "zori". He showed Danny how the soft ties held the shoe in place.

They walked along several streets and before they started home April wanted zoris too. They stopped at another shoe store after the owner said "Hello" with a big smile and pointed to Danny's zoris. He explained there were three common types of foot ware. In both winter and summer they usually wore tabis in their zoris. Tabis were like white socks with the big toe separated by a thong between the big toe and the other toes, The storekeeper showed them how to tie on the zoris or getas with torn strips of cloth.

Danny stood up and took a step. He was smiling. "Hey, dad, look at me! I wonder if they wear these to school. I'm surprised, but they are comfortable." The getas were made from a block of soft wood. The shoemakers cut away pieces of wood that allowed the getas to keep their feet dry. Danny walked around smiling until April had to have a pair too. The zoris were flat on the ground and worn most of the summer when it was dry. The road workers wore zoris cut out of old car tires.

The shopkeeper told the McLyrres in the winter the men working on the roads wore tall rubber boots and warm socks.

Jeane

The Camp Zama schools were part of the United States school system. Classes started the day after Labor Day and they had the usual vacations as the children in the United States. There were several families along the yama (mountain) who had school age children. The McLyrre children had never ridden in a school bus. It seemed strange to Jeane not to go to school and meet their teachers. When April and Danny got on the Navy school bus Patrick had a temper tantrum. He wanted to go too. Kimi put him on her back and ran to Otska Homachi and bought him a stick of Japanese candy.

Curt thought Jeane would be lost when the children were in school all day so he often came home and took her to the golf shack for lunch. She felt she lived in luxury to have a maid every day who did all the work including cooking. Curt said things were usually quiet at the G.C.A. Shack during the day.

Curt insisted Jeane go with Joy to the monthly All Officers' wives luncheons. Joy knew everyone there. She introduced Jeane to several women, then she excused herself to talk with her friends. Joy had been in Japan for over two years and had lived only on the yama. She looked forward to the luncheons to see the women she knew. Joy's husband didn't like parties, he liked to stay home evenings and enjoy their boys.

Jeane had met only a few women so far and when Joy walked away she felt lost. She turned around and then she saw Marsha Scott coming toward her to suggest they have lunch together. Jeane wanted to be angry with Joy but she couldn't. Joy's name fit her perfectly; she was happy and friendly with everyone. When Curt came home Jeane told him what had happened.

"Forget it, pretend it didn't happen, we are neighbors and we will be for some time. Joy is so friendly she forgets others."

The next day it was dark and dreary. It rained steadily until everything was dull gray. Jeane tried to distract herself. There was no housework and Curt had the car. It was too cold and nasty to walk anywhere. They had no telephone as there were only a few telephones in all of Japan. If they had a telephone the Scotts were the only people she knew with one. Every day that week was the same. It was depressing at best.

She remembered her little book, *Welcome to Japan*. She read

Jeane

it again and made some notes. She learned please and thank you in Japanese. Dozo was please and arrigato was thank you. She found the word for police which in Japanese is keisatsu. Later she included hospital, in Japanese was byooin. Next she learned, how much, became ikura deska and how many was ikutsu. She repeated her new words every day, but usually she couldn't remember the word when she needed it.

The rain continued and Jeane wrote letters and tore most of them up. She didn't want anyone to know how miserable she was. One day she kept the car, but she didn't know where to go. Day after day the rain continued. Jeane thought this was like Washington State in winter. She missed seeing the sun every day like it was in Kansas. She was lonesome and miserable and she wished their tour was almost over instead of only beginning. She wrote another letter to her mother and tore it up too.

The rain continued and Jeane became even more miserable. Joy came over and explained this was typhoon season, like hurricane season in the eastern United States. Jeane was tired of reading; she wasn't ready to sew and she didn't know where to go. Finally she decided to write her mother again.

September 17, 1957
Dear Mother,
Just think, I don't have to do any housework!!! We hired a Japanese maid whose name is Kimi. Here people put 'san' on the end of some names like we say Mr. or Mrs. Jones. She has worked for various American families for ten years and she speaks English very well. Some words sound strange because the Japanese can't pronounce 'L', they slur over it. Navy families have been here since 1946 so most of the Japanese have learned enough English to get along.

April and Danny started to school last week. Atsugi doesn't have enough students to have a school here so the Navy bus picks up the children on base and in private rental like we are and takes them to Camp Zama, a large Army base. I haven't even seen their school yet. All the enrollment was done by letter. I guess they don't have room mothers here.

One day last week I signed up for my first bus trip to Tokyo,

Jeane

the capitol of Japan. We were told to be at the Officers' Club at 8:30 in the morning. I got there on time along with two other women I had already met. We ordered coffee and watched the others drag in. Finally at 10:00 all fifty eight women were there and we climbed aboard the two buses. The Japanese roads are narrow and full of holes. Road repairs are being made every day. The roads are full of building materials and big gravel trucks. You can imagine what it was like when our buses met the trucks. I have heard the United States offered to build good roads here and Japan refused. They said they needed jobs for lots of people and if we put in good roads there would not be enough jobs for those that needed them.

Soon after we left Atsugi the first bus was hit by a gravel truck on the front left fender and that made all of us have to wait for the police. The bus driver and the truck driver stood in the middle of the road arguing until traffic was tied up in both directions. Each driver signed a piece of paper for the policeman who finally arrived and we were moving again.

We were supposed to have a guide meet us at the Reader's Digest Building in Tokyo at eleven o'clock, but the guide had given us up and gone home. I forgot to mention it was still raining. Part of our tour was a special lunch at Chin-zan-so's. It is famous for its restaurant and gardens. There was a real Chinese Pagoda on the grounds, but with it raining steadily we saw very little.

After lunch we were supposed to visit a famous Shinto Shrine and go somewhere to shop. On the way to the shrine a woman on the other bus had been hurt when their driver had to slam on the brakes to avoid an accident. We all sat for an hour waiting for the Military Police and a Navy Ambulance. Now there was no extra time so the drivers started back to Atsugi.

In crossing the city the bus drove down the Ginza. That is the main street in Tokyo with all the big fancy stores. We could see the windows and they looked just like the ones in Kansas City. The driver knew we were disappointed with how little we had seen so he drove slowly past the Imperial Palace Grounds. There is a moat and a high stone wall all around the grounds. We could not see the palace at all, but we could see trees,

Jeane

grasses, and ugly green water in the moat.

We arrived home just after five tired, but anxious to go to Tokyo again.

One nice thing here is the Special Service Office plans at least one tour a week for us. It is probably wise because none of us have enough to do. There is a bridge game every Monday afternoon at the club and often another game on Friday morning. I played yesterday and had bad cards all afternoon.

I'll close for now! The children are fine. We are terribly crowded in this two bedroom house, but I have seen other houses that were worse.

Love,
Jeane

Curt insisted they invite the Hills for dinner before they left for the United States. Jeane dreaded entertaining in such a small house. She thought it would be impossible. She planned to have a beef pot roast, but she had never cooked on a bottled gas stove. When Kimi volunteered to cook the dinner Jeane accepted at once. Kimi had been taught to cook by several Americans she had worked for. Now Jeane had time to go to Otska Hommachi to buy flowers. She hung her oil paintings of the covered bridge and the cold snowy river on the long wall above the book shelves.

As Jeane sat with her guests and sipped wine she decided living in Japan might turn out very well. Kimi's beef stew was full of beef plus carrots, celery, tomato juice, parsley, and potatoes. Kimi made fruit salad, and heated the rolls. Jeane had bought an apple pie from the commissary at Camp Zama. The Hills came at six and Curt served red wine with cheese, and crackers. Kimi served the children's dinner in their bedroom and they thought it was a new game. After the children finished their dinner Kimi took all of them for a walk. Curt and Jeane never had kept after dinner drinks, but he had brought a bottle of dessert sherry that afternoon and the Hills stayed until eleven as they sipped the wine until it was gone. The party had been a success.

They were hardly settled on September 18th when Jeane looked at the calendar and realized it was fourteen years since she had met Curt at the USO when she was a student at Kansas University.

Jeane

Now that seemed like ancient history! Today they lived in Japan in a two bedroom house in a strange country where toilets wouldn't flush, lights went on and off all the time, and she was afraid to drive on the left side of narrow roads full of gravel trucks.

She hated to drive their shiny new white Ford Station Wagon anywhere. She would be glad when it could be delivered to the police in Kyoto. They had made a big profit, but they couldn't deliver it until next September when it had been in Japan one year.

Jeane didn't tell Curt about their anniversary because he never thought of romantic things so she didn't mention it.

The sun finally came out after eight days and Curt was anxious to get the plumbing improved so he went to Otsaka Homachi for a plumber, but since he spoke no Japanese he found no plumber. When he got back Kimi volunteered to go with him and she found the plumber. Curt was embarrassed that he had to depend on Kimi for a plumber and an electrician to rewire the fuse box.. The McLyrres wondered if they would ever know how to get along alone. Everything they needed had a different name, a mix between English and Japanese!

Curt knew Jeane had trouble reaching the upper cabinets in the kitchen and he decided to lower them. Kimi was shocked, she thought an officer in the United States Navy wouldn't do anything like that. When the cabinets were lowered, Kimi smiled and bowed, then she looked at Jeane, "Lt. Curt, di-jo!!" The McLyrres learned to use that phrase often and knew it was the Japanese substitute for okay, or good job.

Every day was a challenge. Many Japanese had learned some English from the Americans who were stationed in Japan. English had been taught in the Japanese schools since 1946. As the days passed Jeane became curious about the life style of the Japanese. She saw them walking down the road pulling carts filled with green grass. Kimi told her the green grass was to feed the cows that were tied to a tree. They couldn't graze as they did in Kansas. In Japan the farmer brought them their food.

Curt and Jeane enrolled in a Japanese language class less than a month after they got to Japan. The teacher (*sensei* was Japanese)

Jeane

was good, but Jeane had never been able to learn any foreign language. Curt learned much faster but when he tried to help Jeane she became cross. Next she enrolled in a Sogetsu School of Japanese Flower Arranging Class because the class was taught in the teacher's home. This was one of several well known flower arranging schools that had been known for many years. All of the schools agreed that a flower in full bloom had started to die so most arrangements were made with buds, vines, and branches.

The Special Services people were aware that life was difficult for American women in Japan. Whatever Jeane did was with the other wives and Curt didn't object, but as time passed she found her way into all the tiny villages and antique shops near the base.

Curt and Jeane never missed a Hail and Farewell Party or a Sunday Brunch. The Officer's Club was the center of all Atsugi life. Some Sundays it was a small market and tables were set up so the merchants could sell their pearls, fans, knives, and sometimes antiques. The Japanese merchants were eager to please the Americans. Joy told Jeane to enjoy the tours now because during the winter it was cold indoors and wet outdoors. Japanese restaurants and stores had very little heat.

Jeane didn't complain about the constant run of parties and Curt didn't want to miss any. She was never sure she was dressed exactly right and she wasn't sure who were wives of senior officers. Jeane had been taught to treat everyone equally; now Curt insisted she kowtow to someone just because their husband had the power to ruin his career. She avoided Carol Conway and Heidi Jones who were trying to prove which one could get the most attention from the officers on base. Capt. Jones watched Heidi's every move and smiled. He seemed to feel Heidi was his prize, but he was willing to share her.

As soon as the McLyrres arrived at a cocktail party Carol started toward Curt. She looked her best during the first hour of the party. Jeane knew Curt would meet her with a hug every time. Carol knew he would always be ready to take her to the club bar. Before the party was over Carol needed an arm to lean on. Jeane didn't know what to do, but usually there were other women alone who didn't seem to care where their husbands were or what they

Jeane

were doing. Most of the men alone wanted to talk about airplanes or golf.

Jeane never spoke to Carol. If she saw her coming she dashed into the ladies' lounge. She would never forget the Courtesy Call in LaJolla the summer of 1951 when they called on the Conways. Jeane thought Carol had a crush on Curt and she wondered if he might play into her hands.

Jeane watched as Carol smiled and whispered to Curt as she passed by. Jeane was jealous and she realized Curt had a lot of free time during the day. She never asked Curt what he did all day and he never told her. It made him angry and he reminded her of *the need to know*. Jeane couldn't understand the secrecy that Curt honored about everything. She was a small town girl and she hated to pretend.

The evenings were long and boring when Curt was home and their television didn't work. Finally they decided it was best to have an early dinner and take the children to the movies on base at least twice a week. The movies were ten cents for admission.

Jeane was not comfortable sitting at home while Kimi worked. She haunted the PX and the beauty shop. She played bridge, took flower arranging classes, and studied pattern drafting in a class at Camp Zama. The time went slowly and she could hardly believe they had been there only six weeks. To Jeane it seemed like six months or six years.

Some days Curt met Jeane at the golf club for lunch and Curt gave her the mail. She looked at it and noticed a letter from Faith. She was anxious to read it so she stopped at the library.

September 10, 1957
Dear Jeane,
Since I wrote you last, Basil called and asked if he could come to California and talk to me. He told me his old friend, Dr. Margaret Handel, told him it would be good for me to know what was happening. I wondered what she meant, but I didn't ask.

We arranged time for him to come the next week. I thought a lot before that meeting. Somehow, I believe when I was so

Jeane

sick in 1953 Dr. Handel wanted to come, not to help me, but to be near Basil. At that time I didn't care. I know she did help me some, but it was Father Glasson who helped me the most and convinced me God loved me.

I discussed the letter with John and he told me I must pray for the strength to do what was right. He reminded me how nervous I was when I lived with Basil. I thought about what John had said and it convinced me it was time to end that marriage. I have prayed and I feel better. I know I could never live in New York.

Dr. Handel had written and told me how happy Basil was in his new job. She wrote he didn't talk about Los Alamos anymore. It seemed to me she wanted me to think she was the one who made everything happen for Basil

When Basil came I felt I wanted to be alone for awhile. I told Basil I was at peace and I knew I could never live in a big city. Again he offered to come back to LaJolla. I told him it was too late.

Once I loved Basil very much. Now I can see even though he is a brilliant man, he has never known what he wanted other than returning to Los Alamos. Of course being on McCarthy's list ruined his chances of returning to Los Alamos. It will be better if we each go our own way.

I want to tell you about my dream of John and me. The dream was so real I hated to wake up. In my dream my divorce was final and John had proposed to me. I keep thinking maybe that could be true and maybe, just maybe, we might have a baby. Is that selfish of me?

How I wish you were here so we could talk! Do write me as soon as you can. I feel like this could be the beginning of a new life for me.

Love,
Faith

Jeane sat quietly and reread her letter. She felt Faith was strong enough to continue with the divorce even if Basil tried to stop it. She knew even if Faith lived in California and Basil moved back to La Jolla, she would still want a divorce. Jeane wanted to think

Jeane

about what Faith had written.

She opened her mother's letter to see what was new in Norton. She felt good about her mother; she was building a life for herself. She had friends who gathered for Sunday dinner in a restaurant, then they went to one of their homes and played cards until evening. Jeane was proud of her mother because every week she visited her Grandmother Brown. They had never liked each other, but now there were just the two of them. Jeane remembered as a child how her grandmother and her mother avoided each other.

Jeane was in church every Sunday and usually April went with her. This Sunday Chaplain David Matthews, didn't give a regular sermon. He said he wanted to tell the congregation about a small Japanese Christian college and middle school less than an hour from Atsugi named Oberin Gauken. The people who started the school had been educated in the United States. The schools were named for Oberlin College in Ohio where this Japanese couple met and were married. The Japanese can not pronounce "L" so Oberlin became Oberin in Japanese. Gauken is the Japanese word for school or college. Chaplain Matthews met them when be was in college at Oberlin and became friends with them. He heard they stayed at Oberlin until they both had earned their doctorate.

Before the Matthews came to Atsugi he knew about the Chimmizous' Christian schools close to Atsugi. Their dream came true when they came back to Japan and started their Christian schools. Chaplain Matthews urged his congregation to give whatever they could to help.

Jeane and Martha Matthews had become friends. After church Jeane asked Martha to tell her more about Oberin College. Jeane thought her degrees in Home Economics, English, and Education from the University of Kansas might be helpful at Oberin. She told Martha she would be willing to teach a class one day a week. Martha was delighted and she called Dr. Clarissa Chimmizou about Jeane's offer. She thought a cooking class would be a perfect way to help the students learn more about the United States. Dr. Clarissa Chimmizou agreed and named the class American Foods and Etiquette. Jeane was delighted. She told Curt and he didn't comment.

Jeane

Curt paid little attention to Jeane and her interest in the Christian schools. He was annoyed by the signs the Communists pasted on buildings and he hated seeing their flag on every corner. In the fall the Japanese newspapers were full of articles saying how much better the Japanese would be under Communism. Articles were printed day after day and passed out to people in the train station and other public buildings. The claim was the Communists took care of the poor. The poor people believed every word. There were riots, parades, and confrontations near all of the American military bases.

The Americans learned there were men hired just to frighten and cause trouble near most of the bases. It wasn't long before Curt noticed if a riot was planned and it rained nothing ever happened. The demonstrators were paid in American Dollars to demonstrate at the gate, but if it was raining they found shelter and stayed dry. All the Japanese laborers knew it was easy work.

Curt told Jeane they were perfectly safe off base, but she wondered about the night noises she heard, when Curt had overnight duty. She heard how the dogs barked, but she heard no cars on the street. She was shocked when her neighbor, Pat Robbins, came to her door looking haggard.

"Jeane, we were robbed last night. The thief came in through the front window and left the same way." Jeane caught her breath while she listened. Pat continued, "Dave found muddy footprints on the floor close to the window and more footprints outside. When we looked around the house, we found the thief had taken all our cash and cigarettes. Dave is taking the day off and he plans to nail all the windows shut and install double locks on all the doors."

Fear!

When Jeane told Curt about the robbery, he went to the housing office to see if they could move on base, but the answer was no. Curt knew this would be hard on Jeane. When he told her they had to stay in private rental she said she was going to sit up all night when Curt had to stay on base. There was a small table between

Jeane

the living and dining areas. She had unwrapped Curt's shot gun and insisted he show her how to use it.

"Jeane, you never wanted to shoot a gun."

Her eyes flashed, she was furious, "I know, but as you always say, *we have no choice*! I wish we could go home, but we can't. I will shoot anyone who tries to come in this house!! Joy told me if they see someone is awake they will run away. I know, *we have* no choice, so don't lecture me! I didn't want to come here! I don't want to stay here, but I repeat, I will make the best of it. If you won't show me how to shoot that gun one of our neighbors will! I can see all the windows and doors in this house from this table. Curt, it will be like this as long as we live here."

The Conways never missed a party. Cdr. Carl Conway was required to attend since he was the second in command. He was aware Carol had problems with alcohol but she seemed to only get worse a little at a time. Carl didn't worry about her when she played up to Curt. Curt made an appointment with Carl and told him he wasn't interested in Carol, but he felt he could help keep her out of sight at the parties. He told Carl no one would know. He respected Carl and knew he was a wise officer and Carl thanked him. Carl thought Curt's wife would be hurt, but Curt was helping him. He knew Carol's behavior was harmful to his career.

Jeane never enjoyed the parties when people saw her alone and Curt with Carol Conway. The gossip was the McLyrres' didn't get along. Jeane knew it, but there was nothing she could do. She simply went along and said nothing.

One morning late in October when the McLyrres were having breakfast Jeane looked at Curt. "I haven't seen Pat West once since we got here. I wonder if she is well or maybe they found their Japanese farmhouse."

"If you want me to, I'll stop by Cdr. West's office this morning and ask him where they are living."

Curt found Cdr. West in his office and he was happy to know Mrs. McLyrre wanted to visit his wife. He told Curt they were living on base in quarters and he gave Curt their address. He explained they were not party people and seldom attended any of the social gatherings. They preferred to stay home with their five

Jeane

children. When Curt started to leave, Cdr. West said he knew his wife would be delighted to see Jeane anytime. He told Curt it was easy to find Unit- 47 in the housing area.

That evening Curt told Jeane about his call. Since they had no telephone she decided to go and ring the doorbell on Unit- 47. The next day Curt was home so she took the car and found the Wests' quarters. When Pat opened the door; she smiled and hugged Jeane. She apologized for the mess her preschoolers had created as they picked their way through the kitchen and into the dining room.

The wives were delighted to see each other. Pat smiled. "We were disappointed when we learned we had to live on base. We had hoped to live on the economy but after we looked at only one Japanese farmhouse we knew we had to be on base. We quickly learned a farmhouse wasn't big. None of them have big families and only a few have water in the house. With the tatami floors our toddlers would have ruined the floor in less than week. This is much better for us."

"How do you like living on base, Pat?"

"I'm not sure how to answer that. We go to parties only when it is necessary. We love our big family and hope for another baby while we're here. We're living now like we did in the states. We send our maids home before dinner because we want to enjoy our family with no strangers.

"Just the other night Don asked me if I would still like to live in a Japanese house on the economy. I had to admit there was so much to do even in this house, I would have to say no. The one old farmhouse we looked at belonged to Don's secretary's grandfather. It was very different, I knew we couldn't live there. The kitchen was so small two people couldn't pass each other. Little Japanese girls cooked like their mothers and grandmothers, from the time they are six years old. "The first thing the farmer's wife does each morning is make a charcoal fire in the bottom of the hibachi and start cooking enough rice for all day. It cooks slowly for several hours. They have a bottled gas ring that is used to heat water for soup or tea. The Japanese breakfast consists of rice from yesterday and miso (fish) soup."

Pat continued. "The Japanese have their green tea very hot and almost everything else is room temperature. The miso soup

Jeane

cooks slowly over the gas ring in a big kettle with lots of chopped vegetables and fish. Any vegetable in season can be included and water is added if it is needed.

"I was told their cooking has not changed for many years. The soup is healthy and the rice satisfies them. They always eat their rice at the end of the meal. The Japanese don't have ovens and bread is almost an unknown. Rice is their staple whether it is boiled, made into cakes or a wonderful snack called o-sembei. Those who can afford the finer things buy their sweets from a bakery.

"Jeane, what we have learned was amazing! They have no bathrooms as we know them. The honey bucket is emptied into a bucket outside the house and that bucket is taken away every day. It sounds primitive to me, but it has worked for them for hundreds of years."

Both Pat and Jeane were anxious to continue their friendship. Jeane was restless and she wanted to learn as much about Japan as she could while they lived there, but she always stopped for coffee at least once a week with Pat.

The days and weeks were much the same, church and brunch every Sunday, a cocktail party every Friday night, Monday and Thursday afternoon ladies' bridge games, and Wednesday a trip to the commissary since the maids could not go in there. Jeane soon found there was no place she could be alone. She liked to read and she liked peace and quiet, but with a two year old son at home there was no quiet time except during his nap.

Curt had more free time than ever before. He worked around the house and read the Stars and Stripes every day. He found articles about interesting places to see in a one day trip. With Kimi in the house, it was easy for Curt and Jeane to have their day free. They took day trips once a week. On one trip they bought a hibachi and charcoal to heat it.

Jeane was excited, all the McLyrres loved terriyaki since the first time they ate it in La Jolla, California. Jeane tried to create a recipe, but it was never the same when it was broiled in the oven. Now they had a hibachi! Maybe they could have good terriyaki now. Jeane knew thin slices of lean beef was mariinated in soy sauce, fresh ginger, brown sugar, garlic, and bourbon.

Jeane

In November the new legal officer, Cdr. William Savage arrived alone. News travels fast with the Navy wives. There was a rumor Cdr. Savage had left his wife and five children in San Francisco and was bringing the wife of another Naval Officer. The woman he was bringing had been his wife's best friend. Cdr. Savage found it was not easy to find passage for his new love, but he asked Capt. Jones for help and within a week Cdr. Savage had his roommate. There were rumors Capt. Jones might have a short tour at Atsugi.

Cdr. Dan Kline was a legal officer temporarily assigned to Commander Fleet Air Japan and Fleet Air Western Pacific for temporary duty with quarters assigned at Atsugi. He knew later he would be part of NAS Atsugi. Martha Matthews had known Dan's wife, Dottie, before she married Dan..

Dottie was anxious to get involved. She was a perfect example of a southern lady. She loved to meet new people and she was never too busy to help with any project.

Martha Matthews called on Dottie as soon as they were in quarters. She wanted to tell Dottie about Oberin Gauken. Dottie immediately agreed to write to her church in Virginia and ask her minister to put an article in all of the church papers up and down the coast with the article Dottie sent him. The article told of the Christian College, Oberin Gauken, that needed help badly. She added a special paragraph about a Naval Officer's wife with three children who taught at the college one day every week. Dottie hoped the article would stir up some donations. Dottie gave generously and thought all the Christians should so that too. She had been impressed when she learned Jeane had volunteered to teach American Foods and Etiquette at Oberin.

Special Services gave out a list of interesting places that were planned for the fall. Curt wanted the children to see everything, on sunny weekends The McLyrres followed instructions from Special Services. On rainy Sundays they had brunch at the Officers' Club and spent the afternoon reading various newspapers from the United States.

Curt was anxious to see Mt. Fuji, so on a pretty fall day he insisted the family should all go up to Lake Hakone. When they

Jeane

saw Mt. Fuji it was across the lake. There were Japanese tourists standing beside them by the lake and they were as excited to see Mt. Fuji as the McLyrres. The Japanese like to travel, there houses are small and cramped.

The next morning at breakfast, Curt looked at Jeane. "Are you as bored as I am? All this free time is hard to take. Have you ever played golf? It is kind of expensive, but its a great way to get exercise and find some peace and quiet."

Jeane smiled. "Yes, I played golf when I was thirteen and we lived in Almena. The business men wanted to learn to play golf so a farmer they all knew told them they could lay out a course in one of his pastures. The men called it 'Pasture Pool'. My dad tried it once and refused to try again. The men had collected used golf clubs and in less than a month we teenagers took over the course. By fall everyone was bored and the farmer had his pasture back. Why do you ask?"

"I don't know, but I thought maybe I would like to try it. I've been told they have clubs at the ships' store in Yokouska. Would you like to go down there and see?"

"Yes, if we can go the first day you are off. I told Marsha Scott we would meet them today at the club after church. When we were talking Marsha mentioned they had known the Klines when they all had duty in Pensacola, Florida and Dan and Dottie were newlyweds. Dan is divorced from his first wife. She is a doctor and she didn't want to move around with their two sons. Dan met Dottie less than a year after her husband had been killed in a flight training accident. A student pilot lost control and both instructor and student were killed."

The next day Curt was off. "Jeane, let's take that furniture back to Yokohama; we don't need it. Everyone I meet talks about Motomachi Street in Yokohama and I want to explore there. I understand all the merchants speak good English."

"Marsha told me the fabric stores display their fabrics like they were works of art. I think I am about ready to sew, Let's go! I'm glad I brought my Singer Sewing Machine."

After Curt returned the furniture they found Motomachi Street.

Jeane

Curt admitted what he wanted was a red plastic saki lamp to hang outside their front door like all the other Americans who lived off base. They were all the same. It was a red plastic cylinder thirty inches long and twelve inches across and had an electric light bulb inside. That lit the Kanjii writing on the cylinder. Someone told Curt the red cylinder announced the house was a saki bar. Every American family who left Japan had one or more in their household shipment.

After Curt put the saki lamp in the car he suggested they eat lunch on Motomachi Street.

Jeane looked up. "Yes, let's do! I've been told every restaurant puts plates of plastic food that look real in their front window with the price beside it. You simply point to the plate you want and since the yen is weak everything seems cheap."

"We should do this more often, Jeane. I'm convinced we are going to have a wonderful three years here. Each of us can do the things we like to do." Jeane was fascinated with many different things. She learned to make the most of all the experiences, but she still knew if she could go home she would go, but as time passed she began to feel pampered. She had never had so much time for herself. She took classes in flower arranging, pattern drafting, and Japanese language. She never became fluent in the Japanese language, but she learned enough to shop!!

Dottie Kline was what the base needed. She was friendly and nice to everyone. She was happy and she wanted everyone else to be happy too. If she saw one of the officer's wives standing alone she immediately excused herself and introduced herself to the woman. She knew how to make everyone comfortable. After Martha Matthews met Dottie she was anxious to tell her about Oberin Gauken. Martha was anxious to have Dottie meet the Chimmizous. Dottie was impressed at how much the Chimmizous had accomplished in the last ten years.

Oberin Gauken

After Jeane's interview at Oberin, the Chimmizous were

Jeane

anxious to have her begin teaching American Cooking and Etiquette every Tuesday afternoon. Jeane offered to bring the ingredients she needed for the classes and she agreed to start teaching the first Tuesday in December. After she thought about it she decided her first class would be spaghetti with red sauce since it was so popular in the United States. Jeane was a dedicated teacher and for awhile she haunted the Japanese shops for the ingredients she needed, but finally she gave up and took her own spices and herbs to class.

She took ground beef and spaghetti she bought in the commissary. She spent hours making the tomato sauce. She followed a recipe she had used at home. She took the same ingredients and showed the girls how they could make sauce. While the sauce cooked slowly on a hibachi and Jeane heated water on the gas ring and boiled the spaghetti.

Dr. Chimmizou explained to Jeane she wanted all her classes taught in English. Jeane urged the students to gather close and watch her demonstration. This was a new experience for Jeane and her students. Jeane had never taught Home Economics over half a school year.

Dr. Chimmizou assigned Michiko Nasi, an older student who spoke English well and was Jeane's interpreter. The first day of classes all the girls came to class dressed in their clean white mama-san aprons and their hair covered with white scarves. It was cold in December, and all the girls wore several layers of sweaters under their white apron. When Jeane had the sauce hot and the pasta cooked she asked Michiko and a student to take the first serving to Dr. Clarisse Chimmizu.

The girls waited patiently for Michiko and the student to return. When Michiko and the student were back in the classroom the student told the other students Dr. Chimmizou had eaten every bite of the spaghetti. Before class was over each girl had a serving of spaghetti and red sauce for herself.

After the first class Jeane realized most of the girls had never eaten with silverware. It didn't work well to eat spaghetti with chop sticks! Everyone laughed when the spaghetti slipped off the chop sticks again and again.

After class and the girls were gone, Michiko helped Jeane clean up. She told Jeane Dr. Chimmizou had looked at her plate of spaghetti

Jeane

and asked for the soy sauce. She ate it all and insisted it was delicious.

Jeane drove home while her head was spinning. She wanted to know more about Oberin and the Chimmizous. She was amazed that Oberin was both a preparatory school and a junior college. The buildings were built of rough wood and each building looked the same with entrances at both ends of each building. When you stepped inside, you walked on a raised wooden walkway above any mud. If it rained it helped the students keep their feet dry. The class rooms had windows opened on to the covered walkway, however there was no heat in any of the rooms and as the weather got colder Michiko told Jeane she should wear more layers of clothes under her mama-san apron. In each classroom the students wore soft slippers. Their shoes were outside the door on the edge of the walkway.

In Jeane's classroom there was a long thin table with benches on one side of the room so everyone could see the demonstration. Jeane had a small table in front of the class to demonstrate the lesson. All she had to work with was a bottle gas ring for coking, mixing bowls, chopping knives, and big spoons.

All the girls were anxious to learn more about cooking and the United States. Most of the girls had never talked to an American. The first thing the girls asked to make was a sweet. Jeane thought about it and tested several cookie recipes. The most successful cookies were thin and crispy. Finally she was sure she could make cookies in her electric skillet. For the next class she brought her electric skillet to class and explained the skillet was like an oven. The cookies were baked in the skillet with a tight lid. The girls could hardly wait to taste them. They worked in teams of six and each team made two batches. Every girl had several cookies to take home.

The girls wanted to learn how people in the United States set their table. Jeane went to the Officers' Club and ask if she could borrow a white table cloth long enough to cover the table in her classroom and she borrowed twenty sets of silverware, twenty plates, and twenty large napkins. Most of the girls had never used a knife or fork. Most of the students were anxious to learn the American

Jeane

way. Jeane taught all her classes in English and Michiko helped the girls learn the new words.

Jeane felt it was necessary to teach the girls how to use a knife. There was no budget for food, but with help from Dottie and the Matthews Jeane was able to take three dozen eggs and she made omelets. She explained the proper way to cut meat was to cut one bite and eat it before cutting another. The girls were used to cutting eggs with their chop sticks. Everyone giggled, but they learned the basics about cutting food.

Curt was worried. He knew there was a new GCA Officer senior to him and they would have base housing. He knew Jeane would be disappointed. Curt came home nervous. "Jeane, the Warriors are here; we have to go to their Hail and Farewell Party and we have to smile a lot! They arrived this afternoon and will be at the party. I haven't met him yet."

"Curt, do you remember how you forced me to go to that party? I hope the Warriors don't have sick children." Curt didn't answer; he knew Jeane was still angry about that night. This time Jeane chose a becoming dress and matching shoes. She had already learned it wasn't what or who you are, it is how you look. She hated to be judged that way.

When they reached the Officers' Club, Curt looked for the Warriors. Jeane stood behind him as she put on her best smile. Curt saw the Warriors' sponsor so he knew the Warriors had arrived. He squeezed Jeane's arm and pulled her along so they would be the first to welcome them to Atsugi.

Curt saw them near the bar. He said, "I'm Curt McLyrre and this is my wife, Jeane. I'm glad you are here. We need you. The Shack is small and I'm sure we will be seeing a lot of each other. Jeane glared at him and smiled at the Warriors. She put her arm around Mrs. Warrior who looked a little frightened.

Mrs. Warrior asked Jeane if she would show her the ladies lounge. Jeane smiled and led the way. "I'm glad you are here. The GCA is a small group, but important to the base. I don't know why, but as Curt says *I have no need to know*."

Mrs. Warrior looked at Jeane. "My name is Sarah and this is my first time out of the United States. Sam is a pilot and he has had

Jeane

seven years of sea duty off the west coast. I hope he won't fly here. He told me he had to stay close to the GCA unit."

"Sarah, it's hard to be new here. We have been here three months. The GCA Officer in charge had an emergency at home and he left last week. Sarah don't worry, you will get acquainted since you are on base in quarters. I remember my first night and it was awful! I hope I never have to do it again." Sarah smiled as she looked at Jeane.

The Warriors' sponsor rushed up and insisted they go and meet Capt. Jones and his wife, Heidi. After the introductions Heidi walked away without saying a word. Heidi did what she wanted to do and no more.

Curt watched for the Conways. When Curt saw Carol he smiled and she started toward him. Sam looked at Curt. "Who is that woman coming toward you?" Curt introduced Carol to Sam as Carol pulled Curt toward the bar. She smiled and waved at Sam and glared at Jeane. "Curt and I will be around. Do you know if there is a combo tonight? I know you remember how great Curt and I looked on the dance floor at Miramar.

Jeane was embarrassed. Sarah looked surprised. "What was that all about?"

"Don't worry. If you watch you will soon know Carol is an alcoholic. Before the children and I joined Curt at Miramar in 1951 her husband was the skipper of our squadron. He didn't pay much attention to her so as a new Naval Officer Curt thought he should not leave Carol alone at the bar. He said it was obvious she was lonesome and since we got here she seems to think Curt will entertain her again."

"Jeane that is terrible! Don't you hate it?"

Jeane smiled. "It never lasts long. Carol still thinks she can have any man she wants, but she is usually so drunk her husband has to take her home early, and he comes back. It's a bad scene that no one can fix. By the way, what did you think of Heidi?"

"That's what I want to know. What is that blonde bomb shell? Surely she isn't married to Capt. Jones?"

"Sarah, we all wonder where she came from. She flirts with any man who looks at her and Capt. Jones just sits and smiles. I've heard she particularly wants the young married men just to prove

Jeane

she can get them. I have seen how she walks up to Curt and pats his arm, then rubs against him. He doesn't respond, but he doesn't move away either."

Curt came back alone and suggested the Warriors sit with them for dinner. Sarah was relieved; she told Jeane she hoped there were not many evenings like this.

Mr. Ashii

After church on Sunday, the McLyrres went to Camp Zama to talk to an artist they wanted to paint the children's portraits. The artist expected them and he asked Curt if he would drive him home to get his sketching material and his camera. He wanted to see the children when they were relaxed.

Mr. Achii said he lived nearby. The McLyrres were surprised when he pointed to a big Japanese house and smiled. Curt could see he had two big gold teeth. He bowed, "Thank you sir, or Go-men-ia-si in my language is excuse me. Would you honor me by stopping at my humble home? My wife would be much honored." Curt shook his head, but Jeane immediately accepted the invitation and got out of the car. They looked around and Mr. Achii bowed again. "Achii explain, once house of big Japanese General before World War II. During World War II, Achii lived in Australia, where he taught art in a Christian College!

"After the war was over, Achii come home to Japan and saw house ruined and General gone. He learn United States Army leased huge property that included this house. Camp Zama had been built on part of the land. I finally approached important man for permission to rebuild house and later they allowed me to live in it. Now I must talk no longer, excuse me, please. Now house belongs to Japanese government and I am privileged to live here."

Mr. Achii saw Curt was anxious to leave so he picked up his camera and pad of paper and walked toward the car. Jeane thanked him and said she had never seen such a big Japanese house. Later in the afternoon after Curt took Mr. Achii home Jeane wrote her mother a letter.

Jeane

October 30, 1957
Dear Mother,

This has been a very interesting day. After church we went to Camp Zama PX to hire the artist, Mr. Achii, who works from there. He specializes in children's portraits and he invited us to visit his typical Japanese home. Curt wasn't pleased but we didn't know how to refuse.

I was excited! The house was behind a board fence like all houses here. The streets in Japan are so narrow no one could pass until we drove on. We have seen several Japanese houses and most of them have one large room and several large closets which included the kitchen. Mr. Achii's big room was huge.

Their kitchens are tiny but they do have a wood floor. I think I told you all the houses had a kind of woven grass mats called tatami laid over a straw base that was about four inches thick. That is the reason we have to take off our shoes and leave them inside the front door.

Mr. Achii has a big house built on only one level. He was very pleased that we visited his 'humble' home. Believe me, it was not humble! A Japanese General lived there during World War II. I hope you keep my letters. I don't keep a diary anymore and I will forget many things I have seen here.

I'm so glad you like keeping the books for the Norton Sale Barn and enjoy talking to all those people you used to know. Just think, the woman who runs the cafe lived close to you when you were growing up. It is nice everyone who works there goes in after the sale to eat and visit.

I have to close now; Curt had to go to the base to spend the night. I hate that! This country is so different I will never feel absolutely safe here even though everyone tells me the people here don't hurt you. However they will steal from us, because they need money to pay their bills before the New Year. If their bills aren't paid by the New Year they are disgraced.

Mr. Ashii told us neither of his two sons had ever been in a Western Style house so we plan to invite them to come with

Jeane

their father when he comes to sketch the children's' portraits next week. It will be interesting to have the boys in our house for awhile.

Love,
All of us

When the next Sunday arrived Mr. Achii was delighted his boys were invited to come. The boys were fascinated with the bathroom. The younger boy was eager to light the cigarette lighter and had to be watched constantly. Jeane was amused how hard the boys worked to be sure there was no dirt on their shoes. It was like they couldn't accept the fact all Americans wore their shoes all day. Mr. Achii sketched a rough picture of each of the children.

Jeane signed up early for every Special Services day trip. Usually there was one every week with a typical Japanese lunch. Everything served for lunch was room temperature except the green tea that was very hot. During the morning, the food had been beautifully arranged in red or black lacquer boxes. It all looked like a picture out of *Gourmet Magazine*. There were carrots cut like flowers with a sprig of parsley for leaves. Of course we had a warm damp towel first, then cold soup served in rice bowls.

All of the guests sat at low chow tables on cushions. The dessert was served on special plates and was usually a bright pink cake with flowers made out of thin edible paper and was eaten with chopsticks.

Jeane continued her Japanese language classes and started another flower arranging class. She tried a koto class, a type of harp that lay on the floor to be played. After her first lesson she quit. The koto had a sharp twang the Japanese called music.

Curt insisted his work was very important. He admitted to himself this was his most interesting duty yet. Even if he was home he was always alert in the night when planes were leaving or returning. When he had duty sometimes he went over to the flight deck and talked with his friend, Jim Lake.

No one mentioned what was going on at Atsugi. Curt never told Jeane why this assignment was important. She remembered how he acted in California so she never mentioned his work. There

Jeane

were many rumors going around at Atsugi. Some said there were very important airplanes at Atsugi that were always under cover. There were whispers about the planes that were called U-2s and flew over special targets in Russia to take pictures, and fly back to Atsugi while it was still dark. It made no sense to Jeane, but she had learned to listen and never asked questions. No one talked about planes in the night. Those who knew never said a thing.

One day, Martha Matthews, the Chaplain's wife, asked Jeane to go with her to J-Tag. The houses in J-Tag were all new and in an area that was hidden from the rest of the base. The houses were all on one level. Jeane was shocked when she saw the big rooms with beautiful furniture and all the appliances they would have had at home. She sat quietly when Martha told how she offered to teach American Foods and Etiquette at Oberin Gauken. No one mentioned anything they could do for Oberin. The Chaplain worked hard to help the Chimmizous keep their schools running. Martha was proud of what Jeane had done in her American Foods and Etiquette Class.

After Jeane and Martha left they discussed how they could get more help for Dr. Chimmizu. The students who attended the school were all Christians and the Americans wanted to help them.

November 10, 1957
Dear Jeane and family,
I miss all of you! How are the children doing in school? My only wish is you have a wonderful Christmas. I tell myself it is just another day. If the weather on Christmas is good I will be with the Grahams.

Most people here are excited about the new National Guard Armory. It is a big building that will be used by the men who joined the National Guard and are trained to be soldiers if there is another emergency. Some evenings the building will be available for dances, meetings, and roller skating. The Sunflower Times said the building would be dedicated this month and it should be finished next spring. The people in Norton hope the Armory will bring more people to live in Norton.

Oh yes, J.C. Penneys moved from the corner by the court house to the Muir Building because they needed more space.

Jeane

Now it is next to the First State Bank on State Street. We are all anxious to see the new store. The Masonic Temple will have an Open House November 10th.

                Love,
                     Mother

Robbed!!

    Jeane awakened at seven on the morning of November 15th. When she went into the living room she felt a blast of cold air coming from an open window. She walked over to close the window and instantly she saw their television on the window sill. Suddenly she knew what had happened. She looked out the window and saw muddy footprints leaving their house. She was stunned; she stood there for a minute before she stepped back and ran into the children's bedroom. She found they were all sleeping soundly.

    She knew they had been robbed! She looked for her billfold and found it was gone. She thought she had misplaced it until she saw the yen box was gone too. She sat on the bed and stared at the chair near the window. Suddenly she realized there were footprints in the seat of that chair and she knew how the thief had come in the house. She felt dirty and she shivered as she pulled on her warmest sweater. The children had awakened and didn't understand why their mother was upset. To them it was just another adventure. Jeane looked through her desk. The thief had tried to steal their television but had left it. They had taken all the McLyrres' cash and their Argus 35 camera. Later she found the robber had taken every cigarette in the house. She felt sick although she realized everything could be replaced.

    To Jeane it was a terrible shock. She was sure she could never relax in that house again. She wondered why he left the television. Kimi arrived, and she was less upset than Jeane. She said it happened often to Americans in private rental. She went back to Otska Homachi and alerted the police. She called the GCA unit and told Curt what had happened. She said the robber must have been inexperienced because she noticed there were books everywhere and things had been thrown out of all the drawers in the house.

Jeane

They had even moved the dishes in every cabinet.

Ken Robbins came over when he noticed the activity at the McLyrres. He told Jeane he had heard dogs barking most of the night, but it happened so often he just went back to sleep. When the police came they took pictures and dusted for fingerprints. They didn't move fast since Kimi kept the coffee pot full and all the Japanese enjoyed American coffee.

All the neighbors told Jeane the dogs were nosier than usual that night. Curt came home and was shocked by the news. He saw Jeane huddled in the corner of the couch. She had been afraid before, but never like this. The children were only curious.

Dan looked up at his dad, "Maybe the robber ran away when he saw my dog. Maybe he thought it was real since it was so big." He repeated his story often for a few days and insisted he had scared the robbers away.

All day Jeane shivered in bed under two blankets. Curt reported the theft to the local police. They came again, looked around, shrugged their shoulders, and left. Jeane urged Curt to go to the housing office again just to please her. The policeman came once more; he looked around again, shrugged his shoulders again, and had a cup of coffee before he left.

While Jeane was in bed that day, she decided they had to have a dog. Joy had told her if they had a dog they wouldn't have been robbed, but Jeane thought the house was too small for a dog. Now she knew Joy was right. They had to have a dog. When Curt came home she told him they must have a dog. Now she was afraid, she sat up every night alone with the shot gun across the table.

Curt saw Jeane looked haggard and he knew he would have to find a good dog. The next day he went to the Navy Animal Shelter in Yokohama. He explained to the man in charge they had been robbed and his wife insisted they had to have a good dog. The man in charge was delighted. He said, "I have the perfect dog for you! The family who owned him were heart broken at the thought of leaving him here, but they knew they couldn't take him home unless he stayed in quarantine for six months."

Curt had never had a dog. The man in charge brought out a medium sized dog on a leash. The dog looked up at Curt and started

Jeane

wagging his tail. He tried to rub his head against Curt's leg. Curt smiled and he knew this was the dog for them. The man in charge told Curt he would call the dog's family and let them know their dog had a good new home where there were three children.

The dog was a mixed breed and as happy as he was gentle like Curt had been told. The dogs name was Red. The McLyrre children wanted to give him a new name and settled for Fred. At night Fred sat up with Jeane and watched the windows. Any time he heard a noise he stood on his hind legs, looked out, and growled. No one attempted another robbery.

One morning when Curt came home from the base Jeane met him with a smile. "Curt, now I feel safe! Last night Fred watched the windows and growled if he heard a strange noise. I chill when I think about it. I know everyone told me we wouldn't be robbed since we have Fred. Every night he stays beside me. When the children are in bed and asleep I get out your shot gun and lay it across the table. Sometimes I still pick it up and aim out the front window. Now I am sure I can stay awake for days!

"Curt looked at her and shook his head. He could never change Jeane. She kept her word, she sat at the table and watched the windows, always with Fred. She played solitaire and some nights she read and wrote letters. If she got sleepy she walked around the living room. One night about a month after their theft Ken Robbins came and told Jeane he had heard noises at their kitchen door. Jeane grabbed her gun and followed Ken around the neighborhood threatening any robbers.

In late November 1957 Curt brought home several letters for Jeane. She went through them and saw one was from Faith mailed October 10th. She could hardly wait to read it.

October 10th, 1957
Dear Jeane,
I am so happy I don't know where to start. I talked to John and asked him to help me find my answer. I spent hours praying about it, but I could always see Dr. Handel talking to me and smiling at Basil. He followed her with his eyes. I feel now like I could never forget what I went through.

Jeane

Really it was you and John who helped me. I know Basil went to St. James and asked Fathr John to come to our home and he came and he helped me. I believe if he had not come to me I would not be alive now.

I wrote Basil and told him I would be glad to talk to him here. As soon as he received the letter he called me and said he would come the first week of October which was acceptable with me. I knew I wanted a divorce, I wanted our marriage to be over. Basil is brilliant, but he has never been satisfied with anything less than perfect. No one is perfect, but Basil could never accept that.

Yesterday he called me. He said he was in La Jolla and asked when we could meet. I told him to come to my apartment at one o'clock. When the doorbell rang my heart skipped a beat. I opened the door and stood there in shock.

When I saw him I hardly knew him! He had lost weight and his clothes hung on him; they were clean, but rumpled like he didn't care. His hair had started to gray and it needed to be cut. I invited him in. He smiled as he walked through the door.

He was nervous. I had made coffee and when I sat his cup on the table I noticed his hand was shaking when he started to pick it up. Then he took both hands and lifted his coffee cup to his mouth. He sipped the coffee and sat it down. He looked around the room and complimented me on my decorating. I knew I didn't want this meeting to last long.

I said, "Basil, why are you here? We both want to go on with our lives. Are you happy in New York? Do you like your work at Brown University? Does Dr. Handel enjoy her work there?"

Basil interrupted me. "This is between us, it has nothing to do with Margaret Handel. I want you to come east and be my wife. I know you will have a hard time. Will you come?"

I sat a little straighter on my chair and sipped my coffee, then I answered. "No, Basil, I will not come and live in any eastern city. Even if you left the east coast, the answer would still be no."

Basil looked up before he answered me. "We have had a hard time during our marriage, but I am sure our place is in a

Jeane

great University on the east coast where I can continue with my research.

He looked at me with tears in his eyes. He said, "Faith, won't you consider it?"

I can still remember how he looked at me. I answered, "I have been praying and searching for several months and I know I could never live in New York. Where I am now will always be my home. I have made real friends and I am happy. Father Glasson and the ladies in the Altar Guild have made a place for me. I have many friends in La Jolla and I feel needed here."

I told Basil, our needs and wants were different so let us go on from where we are now. I told him I couldn't live like we did with him locked in his laboratory all day and half the night, when I needed him. I looked straight at him and said, "I need people!"

Basil didn't answer, but as he stood up he brushed away a tear. He said he was sorry we needed different things, but he admitted his research was necessary for him. He told me to hire a lawyer here. He assured me our divorce would be fair.

I told him I wanted the divorce to be final and I wanted to belong only to myself. John is proud of how I know myself. Now I feel strong and ready for a wonderful new life.

Love,
Faith

Jeane was glad Faith felt strong. Days passed when she didn't think of her. Now she knew Faith would have a good life. She wondered if Faith had ever understood Basil.

Communism and Japan

Communism was on Jeane's mind. When they were in California she remembered Basil was on Senator Joseph McCarthy's list and how it hurt him. Faith was sure Basil would never become a Communist. In all Jeane's years in Kansas she never heard anyone talk about Communism. When they lived in Ohio she read the Dayton

Jeane

paper every day there and seldom was there any mention of Communism, except paid advertisements that told how Communism would save the world.

The English newspapers printed in Japan urged the Japanese to reject Communism and continue their lifestyle that had helped them for many years. Around Atsugi there was more activity. There were demonstrations around all of the US bases in Japan and since the McLyrres arrived the riots had gotten worse. Around the train stations there were men in work clothes yelling, Yankee go home! Japan hates Americans! Then they began hurling all kinds of filth that included food, trash, rotten eggs, vegetables, and fruit. With so many people around the train it was hard to get on or off. The riots continued around the main gate at Atsugi unless it rained. If it rained the rioters stood under umbrellas next to the shops and screamed at anyone who entered the gate or left.

Jeane realized she was different from most of the Navy wives. She didn't want to run around all day taking tennis and golf lessons. Most of them had their hair styled every time there was an Officers' wives club function and at least one facial a week. Everyone who lived in private rental lived in small houses and they had to leave home to find any privacy. Some of them even took their morning coffee into the library where they chatted with friends. Jeane needed space and she needed friends. She still wanted to know more about Japan.

At an All Officers' Wives luncheon in conversation she mentioned she read Kamakura was one of the oldest cities in Japan. A lady across the table looked up. "Haven't you been to Kamakura yet? We live there and it is wonderful. I wish all of you could see it. Its only an hour drive from here. If some of you want to see it, let me know and I will show you lots of its history."

She looked at Jeane, "Have I met you before? My name is Ginny Lake and my husband is on the Admirals staff. We have been here since August and this is the first time I have heard anyone mention Kamakura."

"I'm interested in Kamakura," Jeane answered. "I'm almost sure we haven't met since we have been here less than four months. My name is Jeane McLyrre, my husband, Curt, is with the GCA unit."

Jeane

Ginny smiled. "This is the first luncheon I've come to here. We came to Atsugi last August and had to rent a small house near here until we could find something bigger. My husband heard there was a big house in Kamakura that would be available in October. We rented it! It is huge and impressive, but in terrible condition. We moved in and have worked on it whenever we have time. We have four children; three are going to school on base in Yokosuka and our youngest goes to a Japanese kindergarten in Kamakura. I hope all of us want to learn as much as we can while we live here. For us living in Kamakura makes this tour worth while. We are able to learn so much more about the Japanese than we could ever know if we lived on base."

Jeane was impressed and she hoped they would meet again. She wanted to learn more about the history of Kamakura. She had heard about the Great Buddha (Daibutsu) and the Red Torri Gate at Hachiman Shrine that was built 1063 in honor of Emperor Ojin who reigned from 250 to 310. She wanted to see all of them and more.

Jeane enjoyed her Tuesday afternoons teaching at Oberin. The students were using a few English words now and they could understand the names of what they were cooking and eating. There was never anyone absent from her class.

Only a few people in Japan had ovens. Those who could afford an oven bought their sweets from a bakery. Jeane had no oven in her class room. The girls in the class were anxious to learn to make American cookies and cakes so Jeane brought her electric skillet to class and baked a cake, it came out well and the girls were delighted.

At home Jeane still sat at the table all night when Curt was on base. She laid the shot gun across the table, but she had begun to look tired and had dark circles under both eyes.

One morning in mid November, Curt came home smiling. "Jeane, how would you like to move?"

"On base?"

"No, but something much nicer than this. I had a call from the housing office this morning and they told me a house on the Yama would be available November 30th. The owner lives in Tokyo and

Jeane

is a correspondent for several newspapers. The rent is $75.00. Do you want to look at it?"

"Of course, I want to look at it!"

Curt smiled; he had already arranged for them to see the house. The maid let them in and went back to her ironing. Jeane was excited, the house had two bedrooms and another room created on half of the glassed in front porch. There were heavy curtains on the porch windows that made another bedroom and April wanted it for her own room. There was a large living room with a fireplace that burned bottle gas and it heated the room. The living room was open to the porch where there had been windows. Now they were gone There were windows all around the porch.

The tiled bathroom looked like home. A combination dining room and kitchen could be used like a family room. There was a small detached room off the kitchen and laundry room in a small cottage, for the maid's room and Jeane was delighted. She could find privacy in that house.

When they told Kimi they were moving closer to the base, she tucked her head and looked down at her feet.

She looked up, "I must tell you! My brother arrange for me to marry!" Kimi looked down, she put her hand over her face and giggled before she continued. "My brother smart man. My man owns plumbing store close to Otska Homachi. His old mother lives with him and she is not well. I marry him and care for her as long as she lives. I hate to leave you, but I must do what my brother says."

Jeane was shocked "Kimi-San, have you met that man?"

"Oh no, but my brother knows what is best for me. I have friend whose American family goes back to United States any day. I bring her to see you tonight."

Kimi brought her friend, Yukiko, and introduced her to the McLyrres. She had worked for Americans for ten years. Her last family was gone and she was anxious to find a family who had just arrived. She had been hired so she helped with the move from Atsugi Heights to the larger house closer to the base.

Near their new house there were several western style houses including theirs. The McLyrres learned the houses were all built for Americans who worked in Yokohama or Tokyo. Most of the people kept the houses and rented them to Naval Officers at Atsugi.

Jeane

The day they moved and before the Camp Zama truck filled with furniture was unloaded, a man knocked on the back door of the new house. He told Curt he was part of the Night Patrol that everyone hired to protect their home. He assured Curt there had been no robberies in this area in the last three years. He assured the McLyrres the Patrol walked around each of the houses every night. They charged $12.00 a month for their work.

Yukiko took over; she was a strong willed woman! The first night she cooked a good dinner and set the table for the five McLyrres and herself. Jeane explained she would be eating with the children only. She explained she always ate with her families. Jeane repeated, it will be different this time.

Jeane knew she would be busy with the move and she wanted Christmas to be as much like home as possible. She had mailed her gifts before November 15th to be sure they would arrive before Christmas. She had sent her mother a set of Noritake China and lots of little things for her other relatives. She found a picture in the PX of a typical Japanese scene with a lake and Mt. Fuji in the background.

The Officers' Club was decorated the first week in December. The Special Services offered a Tokyo Shopping Tour in the wholesale district of Tokyo on the first day of December. Jeane signed up immediately. When they arrived in the area it looked like Santa had been there already. There were shinny glass balls, some small and some the size of balloons. She saw Santa riding in his sleigh on wheels and waved to all the people who watched. It was a true fantasy land.

Christmas in Japan was a little like home. Santa visited the Officers' Club with gifts for the officers' children, then he went to the enlisted mens' club to meet their children. In Norton, Kansas, and most places in the United States all the children in a town would greet Santa together, but not here.

The McLyrres always celebrated Christmas with the three little celluloid birds that had been on Jeane's first Christmas tree. Now those birds were in storage in the United States. Jeane found the toys at the ship's store in Yokosuka were so cheap she had to be careful not to buy too many. The McLyrres, like most of the officers

Jeane

and there families ate Christmas dinner at the Officers' Club, but after the McLyrres finished they decided next year they would stay at home.

The New Year 1958 brought the McLyrres a surprise. Jeane was pregnant! She felt fine, but she knew she had to be careful. After two miscarriages Jeane and Curt were anxious for another baby and they hoped for a little girl. Jeane continued her teaching at Oberin and she played bridge at the Officers' Club. She wondered how pregnant women dressed in Japan. She never saw a Japanese woman who looked pregnant. She asked Yukiko and was told Japanese babies were small. She said Japanese women who married Americans suffered terribly in child birth. Yukiko said pregnant Japanese women usually wore mama-san aprons all the time.

Jeane hated the way most of the clothes made by Japanese seamstresses for American women fit like the skin. Jeane was glad she had brought her sewing machine. She knew she could create garments that were becoming to her. She knew she could make beautiful clothes from the heavy silks at bargain prices. The style this year was the tent dress and Jeane was delighted. The first thing she made was a beautiful brocade coat dress with long fitted sleeves and covered buttons.

Curt played golf twice a week and was improving all the time; Sam Warrior played too. Curt and Jeane enjoyed the Warriors and worried with them since their white Chrysler hadn't sold. They had heard the Japanese loved big cars, but now they found it was big black cars. They finally sold it with a small profit and put it in storage on the base. They bought a tiny Italian Iseta for Sarah. Sam rode a bicycle all over the base. The Iseta looked like a toy it was so small. The trunk was in front where the passengers got in the car.

For awhile Jeane and Sarah drove the back roads between Otska Homachi, Tsuruma, and even the town of Atsugi. Jeane's pregnancy was normal and she took good care of herself. As time passed she cut back on activities. She still taught at Oberin and walked along the road on the yama. There were few cars on their road, but many three wheeled trucks. Across the road from the McLyrres was a farm owned by a former Japanese admiral who was now a farmer. He was a gentleman who accepted life as it

Jeane

was.

Usually Jeane was home when the children got there after school; she knew when the new baby came there would be many changes. One afternoon Jeane decided it was time to write Faith a long letter. She had cut back on tours and trips and she told Faith she was more content in their big house. She took good care of herself and their baby.

Jeane continued to hope her baby was a girl. She had learned a lot in eight months. When she got to Japan she had never heard of anything with strange names like a honey bucket. She had never heard of Ikabana or Oragami. She had never seen demonstrators who yelled and threw trash at the cars. Curt still took care of Carol Conway at the parties. He would dance with her if there was a band. Curt and Carl Conway had become good friends.

April 16, 1958
Dear Jeane,

I enjoyed your short letter that came Monday. Write me more about what Japan is really like. I am fine but it hasn't been easy, Basil has done everything possible to make me stop the divorce proceedings, but he hasn't called lately because every time he spoke to me he started to cry. He was determined we could have a wonderful life if we adopted a baby. The last time I heard from him was a letter where he promised to resign his research and come back to California and me.

I wrote him immediately and told him not to even consider such a thing. I told him I wanted to run my own life and make my own decisions. I suggested he marry Dr. Handel since they had so much in common.

My divorce will be final April 30, 1958. I can hardly wait. The big house has been sold and settled. I guess I will be a wealthy woman, but it doesn't mean anything to me.

John and I are together nearly every day. He has told me how much I mean to him. He said nothing more.

I am so excited about your pregnancy. TAKE CARE OF YOURSELF!!!

Love,
Faith

Jeane

On sunny days in May Jeane often sat on the tatami floor in the sunny Japanese room surrounded by big pillows like the ones she had seen in Japanese homes. She napped and dreamed of their new baby.

Jeane was easily bored and uncomfortable and she was delighted when Sarah came by in the Iseta and suggested they go for a drive through the countryside. They always drove through places they had never seen before. Jeane was fascinated with cows tethered beside the road eating the freshly pulled grasses. She wondered why there were tombstones with the cows.

"Sarah, do you think they bury the dead standing up to make space for more bodies? For awhile I didn't notice the small shrines right on the corner; now I wish I knew more about them. Look, there is a bigger shrine; lets stop and get a good look inside."

Sarah pulled to the side of the road near the shrine. The women got out and crossed the ditch so they could look inside. They saw an altar with fresh flowers and fruit. Jeane looked around and saw a farmer's wife watching them.

She bowed to Jeane and held her hands in front of her. She smiled, "Oku-san no bow! Oku-san make big baby-san." She looked at Sarah and smiled, then she pointed at the Iseta and shook her head. She smiled and waved as she disappeared into the trees.

The little car was a novelty when they drove through the rice paddies. None of the farmers had ever seen a car like it. The farmers waved and pointed at the car. As the Iseta passed they laughed and went back to work. Jeane and Sarah found tiny villages and watched the people. The Japanese loved fresh flowers and bought some every day. The farmers helped each other like the midwest farmers in Kansas.

The Scooter and the Tank

In May Curt told Jeane he was going to buy a motor scooter so she could have the car all the time. Danny couldn't wait until he was old enough to drive the scooter. When Curt left the house on the scooter, he looked like a spoiled little boy. He always wore his helmet and a rain coat if it was raining. He was careful when he

Jeane

rode on the highway, but he sped up when he entered the base or the narrow road to get home. Jeane appreciated the motor scooter.

It was rumored that Capt. Jones had received orders to be back in Washington, DC June first. His wife's behavior had been deplorable and he refused to stop her. Cdr. Conway was now Capt. Conway and would be temporary skipper. Once Carol would have been proud, but now she didn't care. When she went to the commissary her hair had not been brushed and her feet and legs were dirty. It was rumored Carl had a nurse watch her during the day.

Capt. Jones seemed only interested in his wife and her antics. It was reported she had been seen with different Marine Officers every day and Capt. Jones just smiled.

Sarah told Jeane the third officer at the G.C.A. Unit was going home. The GCA enlisted men knew why he was going home. He was lonely and he had found a special prostitute who came under the fence every night just for him. Curt never mentioned anything about the third officer leaving Atsugi, even after he was gone.

Jeane worried when she drove the station wagon. She felt like it wasn't their car and that was true, now it belonged to the Kyoto Police Force. Curt knew how Jeane felt and when he saw an advertisement for a 1938 Chrysler for $75.00, he called and found the Marine who owned it had orders home this week. Curt bought it and drove it home. It was a steel gray sedan built like a tank. The Chrysler had been in Japan since 1946 and it still ran fine. Curt secured a place on base where he stored the station wagon for $15.00 a month.

Now Jean wouldn't be afraid to take the Chrysler on the busy roads after their baby was born. The month of July went quickly. Jeane wrote her mother and reminded her the baby was not due until early September. Jeane knew she would worry if she thought the baby was due in early August.

June 1st, 1958
Dear Jeane,
I am walking on air. The divorce is final! John proposed in

Jeane

May and now we are engaged and eager to be married. We will be married in St. James-by-the-Sea after the morning service on the first Sunday in July. Our reception will be catered and served in our new church home where we will live. John has been living there since before I knew him. We will move when we get home from our honeymoon in Hawaii. This is like a wonderful dream! Jeane, I have never been happier! I only wish you could be here for our wedding!

I'm sure you are miserable since your baby is due in the next few weeks. I know you want a little girl and maybe you will get one. You never told me if the 'kin-yo-be' (the fish seller) has taken your picture yet. Did the picture you took of him come out well?

I'm so glad you have a bigger house nearer the base and a security guard to watch the house. It is wonderful you don't have to do any house work while you are there.

I will be busy this next month. I must get some new clothes and I want a special dress for the wedding. I must decide what I want to have moved to our new house. The house is so big I can take everything.

Love,
Faith

Jeane was miserable when her due date was close. Her feet and legs were swollen until she could hardly walk and she prayed for a baby girl. She was determined to have this baby soon. She went out and walked down every narrow lane and up and down the road in front of their house.

Finally, about four o'clock in the morning August 4th Jeane knew they should get to the hospital quickly. Curt drove the old Chrysler as fast as he could to the hospital at Camp Zama. She was welcomed with a wheel chair and didn't remember anything until eight o'clock when she awakened in a bed. She was still foggy from her anesthesia, but she reached down and patted her stomach. It was flat!

Just that minute the doctor came in, "Mrs. McLyrre you have a beautiful baby girl; she weighs eight pounds fourteen ounces and she is perfect!"

Jeane

Curt came in the room just as the nurse brought the baby for them to admire. First Jeane counted her fingers and toes. She unwrapped her daughter and looked her over, then she saw the bright red birth mark on her back. Curt insisted it was nothing to worry about.

Four days later Curt took Jeane and their baby girl home, "Jeane, did you bring your passport?"

"No, but we can still stop at the photo shop near the base and have her picture taken. I'm very nervous since there is a rumor that says the dependents may be evacuated any day."

"Jeane, remember China has tried to get Taiwan to come back, but Taiwan knows the United States will help them stay independent and yes, the base has started putting sand bags just inside the fence. Atsugi is important and it has to be protected."

On the way home they had the baby's picture taken to be added to Jeane's passport. They had hurried home because the children were anxious to see their baby sister. Camp Zama Hospital registered the baby's birth the day she was born, but Jeane couldn't relax until she had received the amended passport in her hands.

Curt and Jeane named their daughter Misa, it was short for her great grandmother Melissa Stewart. Before she was born April and Dan both wanted to name the new baby. After several discussions it was decided if it was a girl April could give her a second name and she chose Debra. If it had been a boy Dan would have chosen Henry.

On the fourth day Jeane and Misa were home, all of their Japanese neighbors came to see her. Most of them said, "Isn't it a shame she isn't a boy." Everyone in Japan wanted sons, but they spoiled their daughters. They wanted sons because they would take care of them when they were old and sick. Even the kin-yo-be came with his camera to take Jeane's picture with the baby.

Yukiko enjoyed the new baby girl. She called her Misa-chan and Jeane called her Melissa. The others called her Debi. For a long time Jeane called her Melissa but finally she gave up.

August 10th, 1958
Dear Mother,
I hope you got our telegram; Melissa is beautiful! She has

Jeane

dark hair and big dark blue eyes. She weighed eight pounds fourteen ounces. She was born with a big red birthmark on her back. I remember Grandma Graham had a small dark red birthmark above her upper lip and when April was born you noticed a similar mark on her left thigh. Do you remember anyone else in the family who had birthmarks? We are delighted to have two boys and two girls and now our family is complete.

I feel fine, I only gained four pounds during the pregnancy, and I am determined to keep the weight off.

Were you surprised when you got our telegram? I didn't want you to worry so I told you our baby would be born in September.

Ever since we got the bigger house Curt rides his new motor scooter to the base. Now the old 1938 Chrysler is mine. We call it a tank! I always feel safe in that car!

Soon I will be back teaching at Oberin Gauken once a week!

Love from all of us,
Jean

By September she had read everything worth reading in the Atsugi Library. She was restless and she wouldn't leave Melissa for more than half a day. By October her friends Dottie, Sarah, and Martha agreed there was nothing in the library. Jeane went to the library with Dottie and asked the librarian why the library had murder mysteries and trash. The librarian answered that was what the sailors read. Dottie asked if there was any place to buy better books.

The librarian told her there was an excellent English Book Store on the Ginza in Tokyo. She told them to take the train into Central Station in Tokyo, then go by taxi to the English Book Store. The librarian told them they could make a round trip in about three hours. The four friends agreed they would go together that very afternoon. When they reached the store they found almost every new book they wanted to read.

With so many books it was hard for them to decide. Dottie suggested each of them buy one and read it then trade for one of the others until all four had read each one. Their four choices on the first trip Martha bought *Dr. Zhivago* by Boris Pasternak, Dottie

Jeane

bought *Lolita* by Vladimir Nabokov, Sarah bought *Around the World with Auntie Mame* by Patrick Dennis, and Jeane chose *Ice Palace* by Edna Ferber. It was exciting to know they could sample different books that were read at home. Jeane remembered reading Edna Ferber in college. Sarah asked Jeane how she remembered what she read in college. She admitted Edna Ferber was one of her favorite writers. When the four friends were together they talked about books instead of people.

In the fall, Jeane was ready to continue teaching at Oberin Gauken. Just before classes began; Dr. Clarissa Chimmizou invited Martha Matthews and Jeane to meet with her and a wealthy American business man in Tokyo. Martha arranged for them to have a car and driver to take them to the luncheon at the home of Mr. and Mrs. William Kane.

Jeane was afraid she wouldn't know what to say or do during lunch, but when they reached the Kanes' home she saw Dr. Chimmizou getting out of a long black limousine. They all entered the large entry hall that led into the living room. Jeane was surprised to find the inside of the house was western. George Kane was a tall thin white haired gentleman with a friendly smile. Catherine Kane was a good friend of Clarissa Chimmizou while they were both students at Oberlin College. Mrs. Kane suggested they sit down in the living room and have a glass of sherry before lunch. She asked Dr. Chimmizou if everything was in place for fall classes.

After they finished their sherry Mrs. Kane smiled. "Clarissa, its so good to see you. We have followed your progress at Oberin, but I believe lunch is ready so let's go into the dining room. We want to hear all about Oberin. Please sit by me, we don't see you often enough." When they were all seated the maid served the shell fish bisque.

Mrs. Kane turned to Clarissa and smiled. "You have written me how successful Mrs. McLyrre's classes were this past year. It was rewarding to hear the good news."

When the bisque was finished Mr. Kane looked at Jeane. "Mrs. McLyrre, how were you able to interest your students in American Foods and Etiquette?"

"I think Dr. Chiummizou was the one who created the interest.

Jeane

Our family arrived in Japan last August and I heard about Oberin from Chaplain Matthews during Sunday Services. Dr. Chimmizou interviewed me and felt we should try a class. I found all the girls were interested in how things were done in the United States. The girls spoke no more than a few words of English but Dr. Chimmizou came in and explained what I was doing. She assigned Michiko who spoke English, and she translated for the students.

"I must admit they all wanted to know more about America than cooking. I answered all the questions I could." She looked at Mr. Kane. "I think there are many other students who would like to learn about life in America. I know English has been taught in all Japanese Schools since 1946, but they need Americans to lead them in conversation."

It was a pleasant afternoon. After they left the Kanes, Martha turned to Jeane. "You should be very proud to have suggested more classes in English for the college level students at Oberin. I'm sure with the Kanes' help we will find teachers soon. Dr. Chimmizou has always dreamed of classes in conversation. It will not be easy but I think it is possible."

The Matthews met with other chaplains every two months and tried to stir interest for more classes at Oberin. People were hesitant about committing themselves to a certain day or time, but they were willing to teach occasionally. That was not what the Chimmizous wanted. Most of the military people wanted their families to see everything they could in Japan. Very few people put teaching ahead of their own plans, but the chaplains kept trying.

In late September Jeane was eager to meet her new class and she was anxious to see how much they remembered from last spring. When she walked into her class room she was delighted to see them smiling.

She looked around and suddenly she saw a portable oven on a new butane burner. Now she had two burners she could use in her demonstrations. She was more surprised when she saw stainless steel pots, pans, rolling pins, and measuring cups, plus a long white table cloth, silverware, plates, glasses, cups, and saucers for sampling the food they cooked. Michiko told Jeane Mr. and Mrs. Kane were so impressed with what she had accomplished in such a short time they wanted to help.

A few days later one of the students came to her after class. She tucked her head then she looked up at Jeane and whispered, "Mrs. McLyrre, my father is going to buy us an oven and another propane burner so I can bake cookies at home." Jeane hugged her and smiled; she knew she was accomplishing something that could help these girls enjoy cooking the rest of their lives.

Tunnels and Typhoons

Atsugi was preparing for possible serious problems with China and Taiwan. The gossips on base were having a great time telling stories about how awful it was down in the tunnels under the Atsugi Naval Air Station. They claimed it was impossible to walk anywhere without hitting spider webs. Every person in the tunnels carried a strong flashlight. Big spiders seemed to freeze when the light hit them. Bugs crawled out of all the cracks in the walls. Under foot every where the tunnel was muddy and slippery where they walked. Very few people had ever ventured into the tunnels until now, but everyone had heard about them. The claim was that the whole system of tunnels had not been examined or repaired since the Americans took over the base in 1946. Now there was an order that all people assigned to NAS Atsugi would report to the base any time a siren went off three times.

Everyone was nervous. There were more Communists around the gate every day. Curt did not tell Jeane the sand bags had been increased around the flight lines and still growing higher every day. Most of the pilots were sending their families to Hong Kong and some even sent them back to the United States until this situation cooled off.

Jeane was worried; she slept with her amended passport beside the bed. It was a tense time and worse when they read the Japanese English Newspaper. Everyone was nervous, but especially those in private rental. The McLyrres' new baby was seven weeks old when the siren blew three times. Curt was on base and he hurried home to help Jeane get ready to move on base and into the tunnels.

Jeane

When he got home, she was rocking Melissa.

"Jeane, haven't you done anything to prepare to go into the tunnels on the base?"

"I am not going anywhere. This house is built with solid concrete blocks close to the ground; we are better off here than in the tunnels. I will not take Melissa down there. We have plenty of food and the house is tight. If you feel you should be on base go back there. The children and I will be fine. I have seen tornados and never been hurt. I will stay here."

Curt was furious. "The siren that goes off again twice means the typhoon is turning our direction and we will start to feel the wind in a very few minutes. Are you ready to get to the base?"

"Curt, I told you I am not leaving this house. Go if you must, we will wait for you here."

"All right! Why don't I give up? I know I can't change you! We will wait out the typhoon here. Do you understand a typhoon? It is a violent tropical wind that forms in the western Pacific or the South China Sea. I agree this is the best place for us if it is just a typhoon. It would be different if the Chinese were going to bomb us. A typhoon is the same as a hurricane, but the hurricane forms in the Caribbean."

It wasn't long before the big palm tree outside the McLyrres living room window was bending almost to the ground and the fronds were pushed by the wind against the windows until it was dark in the room. When the wind stopped, the tree leaned, but it was never torn out by the roots. Everyone watched until the wind lessened. It turned ninety degrees and went back toward the Pacific. Melissa slept through the whole show.

It was over a year since the McLyrres arrived in Japan. Curt lived for his work. He had made friends around the flight line and spent extra time in the GCA Shack, as it was called. Curt didn't make friends easily; he was a man of few words. He felt the work he was doing was necessary. He never mentioned U2s to anyone, but he always followed their night flights when he was on duty.

Curt's new friend was a pilot he admired. He was a blunt westerner like Curt. After they became friends it was apparent they had both done intelligence work although neither of them ever

Jeane

mentioned it. Curt learned his friend was on the Admiral's Staff and often away.

His name was Jim Lake and he had been a fighter pilot during WWII. Later he volunteered for active duty in Korea. Jim was dedicated to his work and he never mentioned anything he was doing. One day early in October when the two men met to smoke a cigarette Jim invited Curt to bring his wife and come to a weekend party in their home on Kamakura yama. The party would begin Friday evening and end Sunday evening.

He handed Curt a piece of paper with directions to his home. He told Curt they had lived in the house since March, but it was just now ready for company. He told Curt the house was a mansion with twenty six rooms that still needed work. Before March a group of American Naval Officers had lived there and it was easy to guess the rest. The Japanese owner was happy to rent it to an American family for $110.00 a month.

When Curt told Jeane about their invitation she wondered if she might have met his wife at an Atsugi wives' luncheon in the spring. She remembered the friendly woman who sat across the table and introduced herself as Ginny from Kamakura yama.

"Do you want to go to the party? It seems there will be lots of people and Jim is so relaxed I'm sure everybody will have fun."

"Yes, I want to go! I'm curious about people who want to live so far from the base. I heard Ginny say they had four children, all school age. This party will be different. I guess it will be casual. I have wanted to go to Kamakura since I heard there was a huge Buddha on the edge of a hill and red Torii gates that lead to an ancient Shinto Shrine."

The McLyrres went to Kamakura about noon on Saturday. They drove around the city and saw the big Buddha, some of the ancient Shinto Shrines, and smaller Buddhist temples. They followed Jim's directions until they saw the huge house on top of the hill. It was impressive. There were cars parked along the streets and people coming and going in all directions. When Curt and Jeane got up to the door they took off their shoes and went in. There was no one to tell them which direction to go. They walked along the hall until they saw an open door. Curt looked in and saw Jim was sitting on

Jeane

the floor under the shower completely dressed with the water pouring over him. He was smiling and happy He waved at Curt, "Hi! Welcome! What happened? Who is that with you? What will your wife think?" Curt was speechless and Jeane was annoyed.

They waved and walked on. They saw people they had never seen before. Finally the lady Jeane had met at Atsugi saw them. She stopped. "Welcome, did you have any trouble finding us? Our parties are pretty relaxed so make yourself at home. There is a bar set up in the western living room. Introduce yourself and have fun. Thank you for coming."

She looked at Jeane, "By the way, didn't I meet you at a luncheon at Atsugi? My name is Ginny. I hope we can get acquainted soon, but not today."

Curt had a wonderful time but Jeane was ill at ease. She didn't know anyone and as usual she tried to stay out of sight.

Fall was a busy time for Jeane, she continued teaching at Oberin and continued with her flower arranging and pattern drafting classes. Most important was lots of time with Melissa. Jeane was excited when the Special Services bus trips offered a series of eight classes with the Benedictine Sisters to learn Chinese Cooking. They had stayed in China and taught school as long as they felt safe and then they came to Tokyo and started their cooking school which was very successful. Their classes were always full even though the room was so cold the cooking ring couldn't keep the food hot. After that they limited their classes to May through October. The classes were on Thursdays and the Special Services quickly had fifty people registered and that filled two buses.

The four friends looked forward to their monthly train ride to Tokyo and the English Book Store. In August Jeane bought *Atlas Shrugged* by Ayn Rand, Dottie took *The Scapegoat* by Daphne du Maurier, Sarah liked *Blue Camellia* by Frances Parkington Keyes, and her friends teased when she bought *Peyton Place by* Grace Metalious. All four of the friends decided each would read their own book first. When they had read all four books it was time to go to Tokyo again.

There had been several changes of staff during the summer.

Jeane

Capt. Gerald Jones and Heidi had left for Washington, DC in August. Everyone was glad they were gone. Carl Conway had made Captain last spring. He was assigned temporary skipper of the station and Carol was in no condition to lead the women. Cdr. Savage become second in command and Iris, his friend, was taking art classes in Tokyo three times a week. She wasn't pleased to have to show interest in any activities in Atsugi. The sand bags around the base had grown higher yet, but NAS Atsugi had only minor problems with the Japanese rioting around the front gate.

Someone remembered how much the Japanese loved ice cream so on a warm day in late September the base rolled gallons of ice cream out through the gate and invited the Japanese to a party. The skipper authorized filling the long table with gallons of ice cream, cakes, and cookies. The rioters ate until the ice cream was gone and no eggs hit the gate. They took their riot pay and left happy.

For over a year the NAS wives had had no leader in Heidi and they continued meeting, but she was not a leader. The group elected Jeane president of the NAS wives in September.

Conditions between China and Taiwan were worse and the sand bags still grew higher inside the fence around Atsugi. NAS Atsugi had only minor problems with the Japanese rioting, yelling and throwing trash at the front gate.

Since Capt. Conway was skipper, NAS Atsugi was under control. Carol Conway came to the first meeting of NAS Atsugi after her husband became skipper. She tried to look good. She wore a red wool suit with a white blouse with red earrings and red shoes. Her hair was curled and her eyes were clearer than usual. There was only one thing wrong. Her white slip showed two inches below her skirt.

She didn't know. She sat quietly and drank coffee while the ladies talked. Carol had only one Scotch before lunch. She recognized Jeane and she remembered Jeane in California and what a shy little peasant she was then. Carol wasn't herself, but she was not going to show it.

Iris

At the meeting in October Carol brought Cdr. Savage's friend,

Jeane

Iris, to the meeting. Iris was not interested in what was going on, she announced it was all a waste of time. Jeane suffered, but she knew she had to sit with them She had talked to Martha Matthews and asked her to sit with them at lunch. When Carol saw Martha at their table she immediately called a waitress and ordered a double Scotch. Iris ordered one too as she glared at Jeane. Fortunately Martha knew how to lead the conversation. "Iris, I hear you are studying art in Tokyo. I hope you will hang one of your pictures here in the club and let us auction it off to benefit Oberin College."

"Mrs. Matthews I am a student, I never heard of Oberin. What's the racket? What do these people want? I want nothing to do with them." Even Carol was speechless and Martha was angry, but she smiled and changed the subject.

The next luncheon Iris was back again. Jeane thanked her for coming. Everyone looked at her as she sat with her legs crossed and her short skirt left very little to the imagination. Her fingernails were long and painted the brightest red available. She wore red shoes with three inch heels and she was a chain smoker. No one in the room said a word.

Jeane stood up, "Many of us wonder what we should do for Christmas. There are many Marines here without their families. It is November and this is a good time to begin. I want everyone to think about this and let's meet again in two weeks here at ten in the morning."

The special meeting of the NAS Atsugi wives' club to plan for the holidays was well attended. Jeane was surprised when Carol was there and Iris wasn't. Jeane ask each person there to suggest something. It was a difficult time for everybody to be away from their family and friends. There were many single men since none of the Marines were allowed to bring their families. Jeane suggested they have an old fashioned Christmas with Christmas trees in every room in the Officers' Club. She wanted old fashioned decorations with strings of cranberries and popcorn and colored lights for all the trees. The Ships' Store had lots of decorations that included all sizes of colored glass balls and tinsel for the trees.

When Jeane sat down, Carol stood up. "I think what Mrs. McLyrre wants is ridiculous. That's done every year. Let's have

Jeane

something different! How about a Damon Runyan celebration of satire. The single men like the ridiculous. They don't want Santa and his elves. They want drinks, snacks, and spiked punch bowls in every room; believe me, I know. I want these men to know Santa Claus is over the hill. Let's have some different music with jazz from the twenties and jive from the forties plus that newcomer Elvis Presley. Some of this new stuff is great!! They will be glad to forget Santa Claus and his elves. We will have 'The Music Man', 'Come Fly With Me and Jump Out', 'South Pacific', and 'Prostitutes on every island'. Let's be different. Get more records from the PX and keep the music going from morning until morning."

Jeane said "Let's all go home and think over the two plans we have been offered for the holidays. We will meet again, one week from today at ten o'clock. Everyone will vote on paper for their choice for the holidays."

The next week when Carol counted the paper votes and read the results. "Ladies, most of you voted for a traditional Christmas. Jeane will you take over. You need people to head the different committees." Carol ordered another Scotch.

December arrived and the ladies decorated the club with red and green and almost everyone was pleased. Neither Carol or Iris came near the club while the decorating was being done.

There was gossip everywhere about Bill and Iris. One story was that Iris had been a neighbor of Bill and his family. Her husband was a banker and Iris was bored. She wanted some excitement in her life so she walked away from her five children and her husband, then she flew to Japan. Another story said was she left her three children with her husband and a note that said "Sayonara, I'm off to see the World."

The McLyrres wanted to celebrate their Christmas season at home with family and friends. Jeane hung all sizes of glass Christmas balls on threads from the porch ceiling and they had a small party Christmas Eve. They ate Christmas dinner at home. The children enjoyed their gifts and Jeane felt all was right with their world.

New Year's Eve was always party time at the Officers' Club. Jeane was shocked when they saw every reminder of Christmas was gone and everything Carol and Iris proposed earlier in the fall

Jeane

was in place. There was no sign of Christmas anywhere. Iris smiled, but she didn't look friendly. Early in the evening she kept close to Bill, but when she saw Jeane, she turned and rotated her hips with the music.

As the evening progressed people were filled with free booze from the punch bowls that were in every room. The drunks stayed on the dance floor and created their own dances. The rooms were filled with noise and drunk people and the band played on.

Iris kept dragging Bill out on the dance floor so she could show off her Flapper costume. Both Bill and Iris appeared to have drank too much, but Iris would get on the floor and do the shimmy alone or with any man she could attract. She danced with one sleek stranger who was very interested in caressing her breasts after he had pulled her to him and rubbed her back and bottom.

She put on a much better show than what had been done in the twenties. When she was tired of one man she spun away from him and grabbed someone else. She clapped her hands and twisted her whole body until every glass bead was in motion. The Warriors and the McLyrre's were anxious to leave as soon as the chapel bell rang out the old year. All four of them were ready to go home, but they sang one number with the band and danced one dance before they left.

On New Year's Day during breakfast, Jeane looked at Curt. "What will 1959 bring us? I have adjusted to this life, but I know it won't be forever and I'm glad. Sometimes I wonder how I can take care of four children, clean house, and cook when we get home. I wonder where the Navy will send us."

"Jeane, you have adjusted and you are doing good work at Oberin. You make me proud of you. I have asked for orders to Washington, DC, but don't forget our tour is only half over. Have you made any New Year's resolutions? What would you like to do?"

"I don't know Curt, but I still wish we could have quarters on base. Life would be so much easier. April could go to all her activities on base in a Atsugi bus. Danny wants to play Little League on base and he could go to practice alone. I wouldn't have to worry about Patrick running off to Otska Homachi. I like it here but life would

Jeane

be easier there."

The Japanese celebrated the first four days in January after they had paid all of their debts and made calls on their family and friends and gave them small gifts. Curt had promised the children they would go to Atsugi and watch the festivities. Every evening there were fireworks over the river.

After breakfast Curt took Danny and went down to the GCA Shack. Everything was quiet so he picked up their mail and came home. Yukiko had asked for two days off to visit her family. Jeane worried about taking Melissa into the crowds so they drove through several small towns and let the children buy the New Year's treats.

Curt had brought their mail and Jeane waited until the children were all in bed to read them. Faith's letter was on top and she opened it.

December 3, 1958
Dear Jeane,
This fall I was surprised when I didn't see or hear from Basil again. It wasn't like him to give up, but he had looked discouraged and sick when he came to see me. In early November, I wrote and thanked him for being so fair about our divorce.

He didn't call or answer, but just before Thanksgiving I got a special delivery letter from New York. I looked at the name on the envelope again and knew it was Basil's lawyer. When I opened the letter, there was a short letter from the lawyer. He wrote Basil had given him a sealed envelope to be opened only after he was dead. I took the letter and put it in my safe. He refused to answer any questions, but he had prepared the letter for me. I will never know what happened to him, but now he is at peace. You have read my letter so now you must read Basil's letter.

October 15, 1958
Dear Faith,
When I saw you early in October, I gave up. I realized you were right when you wanted our marriage to end. I couldn't

Jeane

understand why you said you could never live in New York and I could never live anywhere else. When I realized that was true, I considered marrying Dr. Handel and when I got home after I saw you in October, she was waiting for me in my apartment. She could see I was unhappy so she held me in her arms. I could tell she was tense, but I didn't know why.

When I sat up, she looked at me. She said, "You are a Communist aren't you?" I was shocked and then angry. She said if I hadn't admitted I was a Communist I should join the cause for her. When I didn't answer she cuddled closer to me, then she told me she had been a card carrying Communist since long before she left France in the late 1940s and she was proud of it. I told her I would never have anything to do with a Communist. I stood up and asked her to leave.

It was then she told me she was the one who had reported me to Senator McCarthy. She told me since I was a Russian she believed I had always been a Communist even though I claimed to hate them. I couldn't believe what she was saying. I ordered her out of my apartment and told her I would never see her again.

She sneered and said she didn't believe what I had said. She said I was wrong to reject Communism. She had planned since we were both Communists we would go to Russia and help with further development of a world under the Communists. As she walked to the door she turned and glared at me again. She said she would give me one more chance. She seemed determined I would become a Communist, marry her, and go to Russia with her.

Faith, a long time ago I met Dr. Handel while I was a student at Columbia University. She followed me everywhere and tried to interest me in Communism. I was young, she was brilliant, and she told a great story. One Sunday I took her home to visit my parents; they were polite, nothing more. That night she came to my apartment and told me how much she admired my family. I was confused, it was obvious to me my parents didn't trust her. I was young and not ready for marriage. After I got my Ph.D. she was still around. I didn't want to see her then so I took the fellowship at the University of Illinois where I met

Jeane

you.

After we were married and you were so sick, I found she was still at Columbia. I called her and explained your problems. She volunteered to come and help you. Soon after she came I realized it was me she wanted to help not you. That was when I went to Father Glasson and asked him to come to you and he did help you.

Faith, I still remember how happy we were at Los Alamos, but neither of us were happy in La Jolla. I believe Dr. Handel helped you, but it was me she came to see and by that time I needed her help.

When you were better and wanted a divorce, I told Dr. Handel. She told me if I didn't marry her when the divorce was final, she would turn me in to the FBI.

I have evaluated my life since I came to the United States with my parents. I had a great education and when I fell in love with you and we were married, I thought my life was perfect. I always wanted anything I did to be perfect so when Brian was born imperfect I fell apart. Maybe I was wrong when I refused to let you take him home with us.

After I had to leave Los Alamos, my parents gave me the money to build the house in La Jolla. They recognized I was depressed and thought the laboratory would help me create miracles. It didn't do a thing. I wanted to go back to Los Alamos, but that would never happen..

I wanted you to come to New York but I understand now you could never survive my parents and their friends.

You were stronger than I was. You saw me early in October when I was trying to find myself, but when I saw you so radiant I knew we could never live together again. You want to help people, I want to design a bomb that could stop the hydrogen bomb and save the world, but that would never happen.

I am taking this letter to my lawyer tomorrow. I will ask him to keep it until I am dead. I want to die, but I hope it will be an accident. I did help perfect the Atom Bomb, but now my head is confused.

Remember me like I was when we were first married and

Jeane

the time we had in Los Alamos.

When you read this I will be dead. I hope you have many happy years ahead. You seemed so content when I last saw you.

Basil Marko

Jeane was shocked; she simply sat and stared at the wall. She had always felt afraid of Basil, although she only heard about him and saw his picture. She was at a loss to know what to say to Faith. Finally she sat down and wrote a short letter.

January 1, 1959
Dear Faith,
How I wish I could be with you now. Thank you for sharing the letter Basil prepared for you. After I read it, I realized his life was not what he had hoped for. He trusted Dr. Handel for too long. I know how you have suffered too, but you have found peace and comfort through your belief in God and with the help of Father John. Basil did what he needed for himself. You could never have helped him. You have told me he was never happy unless what he had done was perfect. I will pray for him to be at peace now.

This is a season for celebration. Enjoy the happiness with everyone around you.

Our Christmas was as nice as I could make it. We wanted it to be like it was when we were in the United States! We stayed at home with our children on Christmas Eve and Christmas Day. This is a season for families to be together.

Peace be with you,
Love,
Jeane

Over the holiday season there had been parties every night, but Jeane wanted to be home with her children and do things they enjoyed. She never told Curt about Faith's last letter.

On January 1, 1959 Curt, was asleep at noon. Yukiko had the day off to be with her family and friends. The Japanese closed their shops only once in the year and that was on the New Year. It was

Jeane

important for them to have their debts paid; visit relatives and friends during the holiday. Jeane was glad for a day at home and when Curt got up he suggested they all go to lunch at the Officers' Club.

The dining room was full. Apparently most parents had forgotten how to cook and entertain their own children. The club had put out noise makers, balloons, candy and cookies for the children.

When Jeane went to Oberin after Christmas her classes were larger every time she saw them. She went to Dr. Chimmizou and explained if the classes were over fifteen students they could hardly get close enough to see a demonstration, and Dr. Chimmizou agreed to smaller classes in the future. She smiled at Jeane and asked her to sit down for a minute. She handed her the new Oberin promotion booklet. Jeane was surprised when she looked at the cover and saw her own picture with several students watching one of her demonstrations. Dr. Chimmizou told Jeane the American Foods and Etiquette was one of her most popular classes.

The winter passed smoothly. During the cold winter months Jeane tried to keep busy. She wrote her mother how fast Misa was developing. She had sat up alone in February and started to crawl. She knew her mother was proud of the successful classes she taught at Oberin College.

Late in February Jeane had a letter from her mother.

February 20, 1959
Dear Jeane,
I have to write you some sad news. Your Uncle Gilbert is dead. You know he went to livestock sales all around Almena and Norton and two weeks ago he was coming home from a sale in Holdrege, Nebraska late in the afternoon. He was driving fast, when he saw a big county road grader setting on top of the hill. He swerved to avoid the grader and when he topped the hill there was another grader facing him.

He swerved and hit the rocky bank on the side of the road. The accident was near Alma, Nebraska. The workmen stopped all traffic and sent one car back to call an ambulance. Gilbert was unconscious. The ambulance brought him to Norton Hospital where he lay unconscious for three days before he

Jeane

died.

Everyone who knew him was at the funeral. I sat with Opal and the children.

I'm angry! Those road men should be in prison! Opal didn't say much, she was very strong. She never knew anything about Gilbert's business, but I'm sure she can learn fast.

I'm afraid we will have to sell the Graham cattle soon. Now there is no one to see they are taken care of. That will be a sad day. There have been Graham cattle on the Graham homestead since before 1900.

I hated to tell you but I knew you had to know.

My love,
Mother

Happy Day!

Curt came home with a big smile early in March. Jeane thought how handsome he was when he wasn't glaring at her. She wondered if they had orders this early. "Jeane, what do you want more than anything here in Japan?"

She looked puzzled. "Is this a guessing game? Is it orders home? I would like that the most! I guess my next choice would be quarters on base."

Curt was still smiling. "I grant you your wish! We have quarters available March 15th!"

Jeane couldn't believe it. "I've dreamed about quarters for so long! I will soon know all the news like Sarah. She always told me the important things. I like this house, but if we are on base it will be much better for all of us. Are you sure we will get it? I have wanted it for so long and we still have almost a year before we go home!"

The move in March was easy. Melissa was eight months old and sitting alone. She was a friendly baby and trying to talk. April and Dan were delighted with life on the base. Patrick was four years old and anxious to explore around the quarters.

Jeane felt this was like home. They had three bedrooms and two bathrooms. The living and dining room had attractive furniture with space for six guests. The kitchen was well equipped and now

Jeane

Jeane could entertain. The kitchen was connected to the maid's quarters and the laundry room.

Misa never crawled because she was always in someone's arms. She learned to talk very young and her first word was "U" for Yukiko. Jeane was hurt, but very soon Melissa had a name for everyone in the family. Some Japanese and some English.

Everyone in the McLyrre family were happy on base. April had always been a quiet girl and never volunteered anywhere. Now she had a smile for everyone. She chose her school clothes carefully and she put on a little lipstick and curled her hair every morning. Jeane noticed April always wore a ribbon in her hair when she ran out to catch the school bus. Jeane was puzzled, but she didn't ask questions. April was still quiet at home.

Jeane was happy to see her friends and meet her neighbors. Her evenings were lonesome when Curt had GCA duty so she offered to chaperon the teenagers anytime she was alone. After the first night she saw April watching a blonde haired boy who seemed to be friends with everyone. When the club closed at nine she saw April follow the blonde boy to the bus. Jeane turned off the lights and locked the door. She smiled as she drove home. She saw several of the teenagers still talking under the street light. Very soon April came in, said goodnight, and ran upstairs. Jeane watched her, but never asked questions.

Curt played more golf and Jeane decided she wanted to take oil painting lessons again. First she went to Camp Zama and asked Mr. Ashii if he would paint Melissa's portrait to match the other three children and he was delighted. He didn't know she planned to watch him. One day she asked him if he ever gave painting classes. He said yes and told her his price for a class. Jeane was shocked with the price, but she found three other women to share the expenses. Mr. Ashii came to Atsugi every Wednesday morning and Jeane picked him up at the gate and took him to their quarters for their three hour class.

One morning she mentioned to Dottie they had too much free time. Dottie agreed. She suggested they plan to go somewhere one day each week. The four friends enjoyed many of the same things. On there next trip to Tokyo and the English Book Store they

Jeane

talked about where they could go to a different place each week. Dottie was the only one with money and time to plan their day. She wanted to buy Japanese antiques.

A friend of Dottie's had written her about an antique shop in Kamakura. In the letter she said the owner had closed his shop during WWII and opened it again as Americans started arriving. Dottie and her friends wanted to find that shop. Jeane asked Ginny Lake if she knew the shop, and she took them there. Dottie was delighted, the owner of the store soon knew she was a good customer for antique jewelry.

After their first visit to the shop all four women knew his antiques were reasonably priced. The owner was Chinese and he sat in the middle of the shop in a huge Chinese chair. He was so fat Jeane wondered if he could get up without help.

Ginny always took time to join her friends when they were in Kamakura. She always knew special places for them to have lunch. Ginny knew and loved Kamakura. Jeane wished she knew Ginny better, but her husband, Jim, was on Admiral Shaws staff and Ginny was busy with the staff wives.

In late April, Jeane had begun to worry about Faith. Her baby should have been born by now. She wished she could talk to her. She thought of her often and prayed every day that her baby had arrived and was healthy.

May 15, 30,1959
Dear Jeane,
Our daughter is here. I wanted to name her Angel, but John thought Angie was a better name. She weighed six pounds and she is a doll.

Forgive me, I crowd so many things into each day. I neglect the people I love most. John and I will soon celebrate our first anniversay. Sometimes I think this must be a dream and if it is I don't want to wake up. I still work with the Altar Guild whenever they need me.

Last summer John and I were afraid I would never become pregnant, but by September we were both excited. My gynecologist told me I was healthy and there would be no

Jeane

problems. My prayers were answered and all is well. I was thrilled when your last letter came with the wonderful news you have a baby girl.

Love,
Faith

Jeane was happy. She enjoyed not having to do any housework or cooking. All she had to do was go to the commissary and buy all of the food and household supplies. She kept busy and she still enjoyed driving the 1938 Chrysler that she called a tank.

Her favorite antique shop was the one in Kamakura where the four friends knew the owner was dependable. The shop was full of treasures even though Jeane could not afford them. From the first time she went there she told the owner, she had very little extra money and she wanted to buy a big old chow table. Each time she went there she repeated her request.

Dottie was friendly with the store owner. She thought he looked like Tiger Joe in the comics and he seemed pleased. Other people in the shop thought he looked like Buddha as he sat in the huge Chinese chair he never left. Jeane wondered if he could get out of the chair alone. She thought he must weigh three hundred pounds.

On a cold cloudy day in May Jeane and her friends went shopping in Kamakura. When they got there Tiger Joe was smiling, He motioned to Jeane's salesman and the young man nodded and asked Jeane to follow him. Finally she let him lead her to the back room of the shop, where he showed her a handsome chow table. It was diffcrent from what she thought she wanted, but the salesman kept repeating, presento, presento. Tiger Joe called his salesman and in Japanese talked to him.

When the salesman returned he explained, "Tiger Joe insist you have table, no money. Tiger Joe say you nice lady, he give you nice table. You bring other nice ladies to Tiger Joe store. Now nice lady must take old table. Now she have nice old table for good luck in nice new home."

Jeane asked Tiger Joe the price and he refused. He told her the salesman would wrap the old table and put it in the trunk of her big car. Jeane smiled, she loved the table and knew she could never have bought it, but now she would never let it go.

Jeane

Dottie and Tiger Joe understood each other. He always kept a treasure, just for her. Her first choice was old Japanese jewelry and Tiger Joe always had something for her to see.

It was late when the four friends realized it was almost dark. Jeane wanted to take the shortest way back to Atsugi. Usually she enjoyed the drive through the little villages between Atsugi and Kamakura, but she had never driven through the villages in the dark. That evening the village streets were filled with people. Children and dogs dashed back and forth through the village. All the dogs chased the Chrysler and barked at the tires.

When Jeane drove into the next village, there were even more shoppers than usual; she saw a policeman half a block away waving his arms. She was confused and slowed down. Suddenly the back door of her car opened and a man tried to jump in. Dottie had been asleep on the back seat, but when she heard the back door open she screamed. Jeane could still see the policeman waving her on, urging her to go faster. She sped up, slammed on the brakes and the man was hit with the back door and fell to the ground.

The policeman was running toward Jeane and urging her to drive on. She passed the policeman and he motioned her to speed up even more.

Jeane was afraid she might have killed the man, but she knew she couldn't stop. She had been told early in their tour if you killed someone you would be required to take care of his or her family for the rest of your life. Jeane lay awake many nights and worried. She was afraid she might see him again. She remained worried, but she never told Curt about the man in the street.

May 1, 1959
Dear Jeane,
I hope this won't be a surprise to you. I vowed I wouldn't marry again, but Frank Sellers has been so nice to me since I started working at the sale barn in the fall of 1955. I felt so alone since your dad died and you were ordered to Japan in 1957, then your Uncle Gilbert was killed in February 1959.

Frank seemed to know how much I needed him. He had proposed to me several times, but this time I said yes! We were

Jeane

married on Easter Sunday.

I am happier now than any time since your dad died. Remember, I am only fifty seven years old and I would have had a long time to be alone.

Be happy for us!!

Your mother

When Jeane showed Curt the letter he insisted they send Ethel and Frank a telegram wishing them many, many, happy years together!

Late in May it was finally warm. Jeane was delighted with life on the base. All her friends were near enough to see them often. Pat West looked for Jeane to stop for coffee at least once a week. She was always busy and happy with her children.

Jeane continued her art classes and was pleased with her progress. She had painted a small picture of a typical Japanese garden for Faith. She hoped to send her mother a large oil painting of April for Christmas. Mr. Ashii was a fine teacher and all the students wished they had known him sooner. Jeane loved the picture he had painted of Misa. The four portraits had to be seen together.

It was hard for Jeane to remember how unhappy she had been when they arrived at Atsugi. Curt told her nothing. Everyone on base were aware there were more pilots and more U-2 flights every night. No one mentioned anything. It was like having a silent squadron. The J-Tag wives joined in the Special Service trips, but they were seldom seen around the base. Jeane had visited the J-Tag women to try and get help for Oberin Gauken. She never thought about the planes that took off after dark and came back while it was still dark. Curt knew Jeane couldn't keep secrets.

Both Curt and Jeane realized they had less than a year more in Japan. Curt never mentioned what he did at the GCA Shack. No one mentioned night flights. Every person on the base seemed to understand the need for secrecy and the importance to the United States. Curt never said anything about planes flying during the night, but people who lived on base could always hear them take off after dark. No officer talked about what they heard. One story claimed a plane limped back damaged, but the plane had a good pilot and no more was heard.

Jeane

Misa celebrated her first birthday. She talked constantly, but Jeane only recognized what she was saying. There were no classes at Oberin during the summer and with two maids in the house Jeane had to get away. She decided to try golf and she bought a set of used golf clubs at the golf shack. She took lessons for two months with no improvement. The pro suggested maybe she should try tennis.

Jeane was ready to go back to her classroom. She remembered how excited the class was when she baked cookies in her electric skillet. The students were always interested in knowing what people ate in the United States. Some asked her how the students felt about the Japanese. Usually the questions and answers took place at the end of the class time.

On Monday afternoon Dr. Clarissa Chimmizou asked her to come to her office and she went there after class. Dr. Chimmizou welcomed her. "Mrs. McLyrre you know Michiko will graduate from our college next June. I appreciate how much you have done for us here. I know your husband will soon have orders back to the United States.

"We want Michico to go to college there. We can arrange for her tickets to the United States and your chapel is working to arrange tuition in a college there.

"Would you talk with your husband and see if she could live with you and your family there? You have helped her develop skills she can use here and in the United States."

When Jeane told Curt about Michico he asked her if she thought it was a good idea. She knew Michico would help her in the house and watch the children. "Curt, I know it would be nice to have good help when we get home. As Jeane thought about it she knew it would help Oberin too.

Curt said, "If you are sure, tell Dr. Chimmizou she can live with us where ever we are assigned. We won't know where we will be assigned until about the first of January."

Ethel's letters told Jeane how glad she was that she had married Frank. He was happy and anxious for the McLyrres to come home so he could buy a pony for the boys. The Graham cattle had been

Jeane

sold in March. There was no one to take care of the cattle now. She decided she would rent the pastures. It seemed wrong, but now there was nothing else she could do.

Jeane relaxed when her mother wrote and told her Frank was anxious to know her children. His grandchildren lived in California.

> September 20, 1959
> Dear Mother,
> I was so pleased when I got your letter that told me Frank wants to know our children. Patrick never knew his grandfather so Frank will be his grandfather now. I am anxious for you to see Debi. She talks all of the time and is running everywhere now. She speaks a combination of English and Japanese.
> We will be back in the United States next summer, but it is too soon to have orders yet.
> I have started teaching at Oberin Gauken again. I enjoy teaching the girls Western Foods and Etiquette and answering all their questions. There first question is usually, do the Americans hate us? I reassure them that is not true. It is hard to teach them to cook like we do. None of their parents have an oven. They grill vegetables on a hibachi, sometimes with a little meat. This week I taught them to make custard; next week I will teach them to make a good healthy soup. None of the girls have an oven in their home.
> I am much happier since we live in quarters. The children have more freedom and April is growing up. I think she has a crush on a popular boy who lives near us.
> Be happy!
> Love,
> Your daughter

The McLyrres enjoyed their quarters. April and the blond boy were together a lot after school. Jeane continued her art classes. She was busy and content with her painting and her little daughter. The four friends continued their monthly train trip to Tokyo and the English Book Store. All of them looked forward to the best antique store in Kamakura where Ginny Lake always met them. All of the four friends knew they would be back in the United States in a

Jeane

year.

In early February, the McLyrres had orders to NAS Coronado. They were scheduled to sail at noon June 10, 1960 on the *USS Barrett* to San Francisco.

Jeane sat down and wrote Faith the good news even before she wrote her mother.

It was spring and the McLyrres would leave Japan in July. Jeane didn't ever expect to see Japan after they sailed away in less than six months. She had hoped she could see Kyoto and Nara. They seemed to be even more interesting than Kamakura. Curt urged her to go, but he was needed at the GCA Shack and at home.

"Jeane, can't you understand. I can't expect anyone to take my responsibility. You know that. Frankly, I don't think both of us should be away from the children. This is something you wanted to see more than anything else in Japan. Why don't you find someone else to go with you.

Jeane thought about it, then she walked out her front door and up to the Klines.

When Dottie opened the door, Jeane was all smiles. "Dottie, I have an idea! You like antiques and the best ones can be found in Kyoto and Nara. I want to see everything before we go home. Would you go with me?"

Dottie looked up. "I have wondered why so few people go there. It is less than a day on the super fast Bullet Train from Tokyo. Yes Jeane, yes, I will go! This morning I was bored. It seems like I have done everything, and now we will go to Kyoto and Nara.

Dottie smiled, "Yes! I remember when the Lakes went down there; Ginny couldn't stop talking about it. We should go soon. I will arrange for us to stay in a nice Japanese Ryokan. My husband will be delighted that he doesn't have to go.

In less than a week, the two friends took the Bullet Train to Kyoto. The Ryokan was an experience of its own. When Dottie unpacked she decided they should have a bath in the hot tub called an O-Furo. Dottie made a reservation for a massage after they had the bath.

Jeane

"Jeane have you ever gone into one of the Japanese baths. I have wanted to try one for a long time, Jeane I wouldn't be here except for you. Dan doesn't appreciate what is off the base. Jeane, I want you to remember this trip as long as we live. I would never have seen Kyoto if it wasn't for you. I want to pay all the Ryokan expenses, don't argue it's my treat.

At four o'clock Jeane and Dottie put on their cotton kimonos and zoris. Dottie looked at Jeane. "In a Japanese Ryokan no one wears their own clothes after they check in. Let's get down to the baths." When they entered a small room the attendant took their kiminos. Another attendant poured warm water over them, and then someone soaped them. In a few minutes they poured more water over their whole bodies. Next they took their towels and walked into a room with a pool so big it looked like a small lake. They both knew the baths were for nude men and women. After the first shock, they enjoyed the bath and the massage.

This was the time everyone wanted to come to Kyoto. There were flowers blooming everywhere. The trees were trimmed and not a leaf on any of the paths. There were older women with a short handled brush and a small basket. Every place they walked a guide was with them. He spoke excellent English and knew his history. Dottie had arranged for him to guide them for three days.

They saw the Pavilion of Gold and the tall Torrii Gates of a Shinto Temple. Everywhere it was crowded. On the streets they saw many different flowering trees and bushes. The second day the guide took them to Nara on the train. It was the first capitol of Japan. The largest bronze Buddha in the world was inside the biggest wooden building in the world. The guide wanted to tell them more than they were able to remember. Around the Buddha temple, the deer wandered free over the grounds. People were feeding and petting them.

The third day Jeane wanted to explore alone so they separated. The next morning they took the fast train to Tokyo and then home to Atsugi.

Time passed quickly until July. Jeane kept her painting class through June. It was over! She wished she had written a diary. She

Jeane

still remembered the rainy, dismal days in September and their robbery while they lived in the tiny house. Their special treasure was their year old daughter.

Now it was a peaceful time for Jeane until on June 6th, 1960 Nikita Khrushchev announced a United States U-2 Air Force plane employed for photographic reconnaissance was shot down inside Soviet territory. Most of the people at NAS Atsugi were shocked and within three days there was no one in J-Tag. Everyone she knew felt the loss. The pilot, Gary Powers, was alive in a Russian prison. Jeane was ready to go home. A few days after the Soviet Union shot down the U-2 the United States admitted conducting reconnaissance missions over Soviet territory for the last four years.

When Jeane and Curt went to their Hail and Farewell Party the end of June, she knew most of the people there. She thought she had learned to be a Navy Wife. Now she talked less. It had been a privilege to teach Oberin Gauken students something about the United States. Their household was packed and taken away by a moving van. Jeane would remember the last three years for a long time.

The *USS Barrett* sailed late in July, and Jeane could hardly believe she felt a little sad. She knew Japan would always stay in her memory. Some of the Oberin students came to the port to wave and wish them well. Sayanora came from everywhere.

After the coast of Japan was out of sight. Jeane went up to the top deck holding her little daughter. She looked toward the east. She felt good about her three years in Japan and the teaching she did at Oberin Gauken. Some day she hoped to come back to Japan some time as a tourist. The crossing was easy. No one was sea sick. Jeane wondered if she would be able to do her housework and cooking.

After a ten day crossing, the *Barrett* had been cleared for landing. Everyone stood on deck to watch the ship approach the Golden Gate bridge in front of them. There were big trees on the left and houses close on the right with green grass around them. It

Jeane

was cold on deck so she put a coat on Misa and herself.

The ship moved into place, and the gang plank was lowered. Jeane felt a tear run down her cheek.

They were home!

Jeane was anxious to get to Kansas and see her mother, who had arranged for plane tickets to Denver for Jeane, April, Dan, and Patrick. Debi was too young for a ticket.

Jeane's mother and Frank would meet the plane in Denver that afternoon at four o'clock, and they would turn around and drive back to Norton, Kansas.

Curt took a taxi to the San Francisco airport and checked the luggage to Denver. He waved to his family as they boarded the plane. He sat down and waited for his plane to San Diego. He was anxious to get settled in Coronado soon. He knew his family would come soon. Curt's friends had written they had rented a house for the McLyrres. He thought it was good to be home. Curt was anxious to move in. He was happy to be home!!!

Jeane